## *And then he kissed her.*

Knightly. Kissing. Her.

Annabelle felt the heat first, of his lips upon hers. Of him being near.

She felt sparks, she felt fireworks. Her first kiss. A once in a lifetime kiss. With the man she loved.

She had waited for this. She had *fought* for this. She *earned* this. She was going to enjoy every exquisite second of it.

And then it became something else entirely.

*Romances by* Maya Rodale

# MAYA RODALE

# Seducing Mr. Knightly

**AVON**

*An Imprint of HarperCollins Publishers*

AVON BOOKS
*An Imprint of* HarperCollins*Publishers*
195 Broadway
New York, NY 10007

Copyright © 2012 by Maya Rodale
ISBN 978-0-06-208894-9
www.avonromance.com

First Avon Books mass market printing: November 2012

Avon Trademark Reg. U.S. Pat. Off. and in Other Countries, Marca Registrada, Hecho en U.S.A.
HarperCollins® is a registered trademark of HarperCollins Publishers.

Printed in the U.S.A.

10 9 8 7 6 5 4 3 2

*For my sister Eve*
*May you always have the gumption*
*to go after what you want.*

*For my readers*
*Thank you for making this romance-*
*writing dream job possible.*

*For Tony*
*For always noticing me even though I*
*stand below your line of vision.*

# Seducing
# Mr. Knightly

# Prologue

### Young Rogue Crashes Earl's Funeral

#### OBITUARY

*Today England mourns the loss of Lord Charles Peregrine Fincher, sixth Earl of Harrowby and one of its finest citizens.*

The Morning Post

*St. George's Church
London, 1808*

**D**EREK Knightly had not been invited to his father's funeral. Nevertheless, he rode hell for leather from his first term at Cambridge to be there. The service had already commenced when he stalked across the threshold dressed in unrelenting black, still dusty from the road. To remove him would cause a scene.

If there was anything his father's family had loathed—other than him—it was a scene.

The late Earl of Harrowby had expired unexpectedly of an apoplexy, leaving behind his countess, his heir, and one daughter. He was also succeeded by his beloved mistress of over twenty years, and their son.

Delilah Knightly hadn't wanted to attend; her son tried to persuade her.

"We have every right to be there," he said forcefully. He might not be the heir or even have his father's name, but Derek Knightly was the earl's firstborn and beloved son.

"My grief will not be fodder for gossips, Derek, and if we attend it shall cause a massive scene. Besides, the Harrowby family will be upset. We shall mark his passing privately, just the two of us," she said, patting his hand in a weak consolation. Delilah Knightly, exuberant darling of the London stage, had become a forlorn shell of her former self.

In grief, Knightly couldn't find the words to explain his desperate need to hear the hymns sung in low mournful tones by the congregation, or to throw a handful of cool dirt on the coffin as they lowered it into the earth. The rituals would make it real, otherwise he'd always live with the faint expectation that his father might come 'round again.

He needed to say goodbye.

Most of all, Derek desperately wanted a bond to his father's other life—including the haute ton where the earl had spent his days and some nights, the younger brother Derek never had adventures with and a younger sister he never teased—so it might not seem like the man was gone entirely and forever.

Whenever young Knightly had asked questions about the other family, the earl would offer sparse details: another son who dutifully learned his lessons and not much else, a sister fond of tea parties with her vast collection of dolls. There was the country estate in Kent that Knightly felt he knew if only by all the vivid stories told to him at night before bed. His father described the inner workings of Parliament over the breakfast table. But mostly the earl wanted to step aside from his proper role and public life to enjoy the woman he loved and his favored child—and forget the rest.

Knightly went to the funeral. Alone.

The doors had been closed. He opened them.

The service had begun. Knightly disrupted it. Hundreds of sadly bowed heads turned back to look at this intruder. He straightened his spine and dared them to oppose his presence with a fierce look from his piercing blue eyes.

He had every right to be here. He belonged here.

Derek caught the eye of the New Earl, held it, and grew hot with fury. Daniel Peregrine Fincher, now Lord Harrowby, just sixteen years of age, was a mere two years younger than his bastard half brother who had dared to intrude in polite company. He stood, drawing himself up to his full height, a full six inches less than Derek, and declared in a loud, reedy voice:

"Throw the bastard out. He doesn't belong here."

# Chapter 1

## A Writing Girl in Distress

> Dear Annabelle,
>> I desperately need your advice . . .
>>> Sincerely,
>>> Lonely in London
>>> The London Weekly

*Miss Annabelle Swift's attic bedroom*
*London, 1825*

SOME things are simply true: the earth rotates around the sun, Monday follows Sunday, and Miss Annabelle Swift loves Mr. Derek Knightly with a passion and purity that would be breathtaking were it not for one other simple truth—Mr. Derek Knightly pays no attention to Miss Annabelle Swift.

It was love at first sight exactly three years, six months, three weeks, and two days ago, upon Annabelle's first foray into the offices of *The London Weekly*. She was the new advice columnist—the lucky girl who had won a contest and the position of Writing Girl number four. She was a shy, unassuming miss—still was, truth be told.

He was the dashing and wickedly handsome editor and owner of the paper. Absolutely still was, truth be told.

In those three years, six months, three weeks, and two days, Knightly seemed utterly unaware of Annabelle's undying affection. She sighed every time he entered the room. Gazed longingly. Blushed furiously should he happen to speak to her. She displayed all the signs of love, and by all accounts, these did not register for him.

By all accounts, it seemed an unwritten law of nature that Mr. Derek Knightly didn't spare a thought for Miss Annabelle Swift. At all. Ever.

And yet, she hoped.

*Why* did she love him?

To be fair, she did ask herself this from time to time.

Knightly was handsome, of course, breathtakingly and heart-stoppingly so. His hair was dark, like midnight, and he was in the habit of rakishly running his fingers through it, which made him seem faintly disreputable. His eyes were a piercing blue, and looked at the world with an intelligent, brutally honest gaze. His high, slanting cheekbones were like cliffs a girl might throw herself off in a fit of despair.

The man himself was single-minded, ruthless, and obsessed when it came to his newspaper business. He could turn on the charm, if he decided it was worth the bother. He was wealthy beyond imagination.

As an avid reader of romantic novels, Annabelle knew a hero when she saw one. The dark good looks. The power. The wealth. The intensity with which he might love a woman—her—if only he *would*.

But the real reason for her deep and abiding love had nothing to do with his wealth, power, appearance, or even the way he leaned against a table or the way he swaggered into a room. Though who knew the way a man leaned or swaggered could be so . . . *inspiring*?

Derek Knightly was a man who gave a young woman of no consequence a chance to be *something*. Something great. Something special. Something *more*. It went without saying that opportunities for women were not numerous, especially for ones with no connections, like Annabelle. If it weren't for Knightly, she'd be a plain old Spinster Auntie or maybe married to Mr. Nathan Smythe who owned the bakery up the road.

Knightly gave her a chance when no one ever did. He believed in her when she didn't even believe in herself. That was why she loved him.

So the years and weeks and days passed by and Annabelle waited for him to really notice her, even as the facts added up to the heartbreaking truth that he had a blind spot where she was concerned.

Or worse: perhaps he did notice and did not return her affection in the slightest.

A lesser girl might have given up long ago and married the first sensible person who asked. In all honesty, Annabelle had considered encouraging young Mr. Nathan Smythe of the bakery up the road. She at least could have enjoyed a lifetime supply of freshly baked pastries and warm bread.

But she had made her choice to wait for true love. And so she couldn't marry Mr. Smythe and his baked goods as long as she stayed up late reading novels of grand passions, great adventures, and true love, above all. She could not settle for less. She could not marry Mr. Nathan Smythe or anyone else, other than Derek Knightly, because she had given her heart to Knightly three years, six months, three weeks, and two days ago.

And now she lay dying. Unloved. A spinster. A *virgin*.

Her cheeks burned. Was it mortification? Remorse? Or the fever?

She was laying ill in her brother's home in Bloomsbury, London. Downstairs, her brother Thomas meekly hid in his library (it was a sad fact that Swifts were not known for backbone) while his wife, Blanche, shrieked at their children: Watson, Mason, and Fleur. None of them had come to inquire after her health, however. Watson had come to request her help with his sums, Mason asked where she had misplaced his Latin primer, and Fleur had woken Annabelle from a nap to borrow a hair ribbon.

Annabelle lay in her bed, dying, another victim of unrequited love. It was tragic, tragic! In her slim fingers she held a letter from Knightly, blotted with her tears.

Very well, she was not at death's door, merely suffering a wretched head cold. She did have a letter from Knightly but it was hardly the stuff of a young woman's dreams. It read:

*Miss Swift—*

Annabelle stopped there to scowl. *Everyone* addressed their letters to her as "Dear Annabelle," which was the name of her advice column. Thus, she was the recipient of dozens—hundreds—of letters each week that all began with "Dear Annabelle." To be cheeky and amusing, everyone else in the world had adopted this salutation. Tradesmen sent their bills to her addressed as such.

But not Mr. Knightly! Miss Swift indeed. The rest—the scant rest of it—was worse.

*Miss Swift—*
  *Your column is late. Please remedy this with all due haste.*
  *D.K.*

Annabelle possessed the gift of a prodigious imagination. (Or curse. Sometimes it felt like a curse.) But even she could not spin magic from this letter.

She was never late with her column either, because she knew all the people it would inconvenience: Knightly and the other editors, the printers, the deliverymen, the news agents, all the loyal readers of *The London Weekly.*

She loathed bothering people—ever since she'd been a mere thirteen years old and Blanche decreed to Thomas on their wedding day that "they could keep his orphaned sister so long as she wasn't a nuisance." Stricken with terror at the prospect of being left to the workhouse or the streets, Annabelle bent over backward to be helpful. She acted as governess to her brother's children, assisted Cook with the meal preparation, could be counted on for a favor when anyone asked.

But she was ill! For the first time, she simply didn't have the strength to be concerned with the trials and vexations of others. The exhaustion went bone deep. Perhaps deeper. Perhaps it had reached her soul.

There was a stack of letters on her writing desk across the room, all requesting her help.

Belinda from High Holburn wanted to know how one addressed a duke, should she ever be so lucky to meet one. Marcus wished to know how fast it took to travel from London to Gretna Green "for reasons he couldn't specify." Susie requested a complexion remedy, Nigel asked for advice on how to propose to one sister when he had already been courting the other for six months.

"Annabelle!" Blanche shrieked from the bottom of the stairs leading to her attic bedroom.

She shrunk down and pulled the covers over her head.

"Annabelle, Mason broke a glass, Watson pierced himself and requires a remedy, and Fleur needs her hair curled. Do come at once instead of lazing abed all day!"

"Yes, Blanche," she said faintly.

Annabelle sneezed, and then tears stung at her eyes and she was in quite the mood for a good, well-deserved cry. But then there was that letter from Knightly. Miss Swift, indeed! And the problems of Belinda, Marcus, Susie and Nigel. And Mason, Watson and Fleur. All of which required her help.

What about me?

The selfish question occurred to her, unbidden. Given her bedridden status, she could not escape it either. She could not dust, or sweep or rearrange her hair ribbons, or read a novel or any other such task she engaged in when she wished to avoid thinking about something unpleasant.

Stubbornly, the nagging question wouldn't leave until it had an answer.

She mulled it over. *What about me?*

"What about me?" She tested the thought with a hoarse whisper.

She was a good person. A kind person. A generous, thoughtful, and helpful person. But here she was, ill and alone, forgotten by the world, dying of unrequited love, a virgin . . . .

Well, maybe it was time for others to help Dear Annabelle with her problems!

"Hmmph," she said to no one in particular.

The Swifts were not known for the force of their will, or their gumption. So when the feeling struck, she ran with it before the second-guessing could begin. Metaphorically, of course, given that she was bedridden with illness.

Annabelle dashed off the following column, for print in the most popular newspaper in town:

*To the readers of* The London Weekly,

*For nearly four years now I have faithfully answered your inquiries on matters great and small. I have advised to the best of my abilities and with goodness in my heart.*

*Now I find myself in need of your help. For the past few years I have loved a man from afar, and I fear he has taken no notice of me at all. I know not how to attract his attention and affection. Dear readers, please advise!*

*Your humble servant,*

*Dear Annabelle*

Before she could think twice about it, she sealed the letter and addressed it to:

Mr. Derek Knightly
c/o *The London Weekly*
57 Fleet Street
London, England

# Chapter 2

### Lovelorn Female Vows to Catch a Rogue

*Offices of* The London Weekly
*57 Fleet Street, London*

**D**EREK KNIGHTLY swore by three truths. The first: *Scandal equals sales.*

Guided by this principle, he used his inheritance to acquire a second-rate news rag, which he transformed into the most popular, influential newspaper in London, avidly read by both high and lowborn alike.

The second: *Drama was for the page.* Specifically the printed, stamp-taxed pages of *The London Weekly*, which were filled to the brim with salacious gossip from the ton, theater reviews, domestic and foreign intelligence, and the usual assortment of articles and advertisements. He himself did not partake in the aforementioned scandal or drama. There were days were he hardly existed beyond the pages he edited and published.

The third: *Be beholden to no one.* Whether business or pleasure, Knightly owned—he was not owned. Unlike other newspapers, *The London Weekly* was not paid for by Parliament or political parties. Nor did theaters pay for favorable reviews. He wasn't above taking suppression fees for gossip, depending upon the rumors. He'd fought duels in defense of *The Weekly*'s contents. He'd already taken one bullet for his beloved newspaper and would do so again unblinkingly.

When it came to women—well, suffice it to say his heart belonged to the newspaper and he was intent that no woman should capture it.

These three truths had taken him from being the scandal-borne son of an earl and his actress-mistress to one of London's most infamous, influential, and wealthiest men.

Half of everything he'd ever wanted.

For an infinitesimal second Knight paused, hand on the polished brass doorknob. On the other side of the wooden door, his writers waited for their weekly meeting in which they compared and discussed the stories for the forthcoming issue. He thought about scandal, and sales, and other people's drama. Because, given the news he'd just heard—a *London Times* reporter caught where he shouldn't be—London was about to face the scandal of the year . . . one that threatened to decimate the entire newspaper industry, including *The London Weekly.*

Where others often saw disaster, Knightly saw opportunity. But the emerging facts made him pause to note a feeling of impending doom. The victims in this case were too important, the deception beyond the pale. Someone would pay for it.

With a short exhalation and a square of his shoulders, Knightly pushed opened the door and stepped before his team of writers.

"Ladies first," he said, grinning, as always.

The Writing Girls. His second greatest creation. It had been an impulsive decision to hire Sophie and Julianna to start, later rounded out by Eliza and Annabelle. But the guiding rational was: *Scandal equals sales.*

Women writing were scandalous.

Therefore . . .

His hunch had been correct. The gamble paid off in spades.

*The London Weekly* was a highbrow meets lowbrow newspaper read by everyone, but the Writing Girls set it apart from all the other news rags by making it especially captivating to the women in London, and particularly attractive to the men.

To his left, Miss Annabelle Swift, advice columnist, sighed. Next to her, Eliza—now the Duchess of Wycliff—gave him a sly glance. Sophie, the Duchess of Brandon—a disgraced country girl when he first met her—propped her chin on her palm and smiled at him. Lady Roxbury brazenly took him on with her clear, focused gaze.

"What's on this week, writers?" he asked.

Lady Julianna Roxbury, known in print as the Lady of Distinction and author of the salacious gossip column "Fashionable Intelligence," clearly had News. "There are rumors," she began excitedly, "of Lady Lydia Marsden's prolonged absence from the ton. Lady Marsden is newly returned to town after she missed what ought to have been her second season. I am investigating."

By investigating, she likely meant all manner of gossip and skulking about, but that was what *Weekly* writers did. Like the writers at *The Times,* but without getting caught.

No one else in the room seemed to care for the significance of a debutante's whereabouts. Knightly barely did, he knew only that it would sell well to the ton. If the news covered one of their own, they talked about it more, which meant that more copies were sold just so people could understand conversations at parties.

To his right, good old Grenville grumbled under his breath. His irritation with the Writing Girls was never far from the surface. If it wasn't the deep, dark inner workings of Parliament, then Grenville wasn't interested.

"Annabelle has quite the update," Sophie interjected excitedly. "Much more interesting than my usual news on weddings."

Knightly turned his attention to Annabelle, the quiet one.

"My column this week has received more letters than any other," she said softly. She held his gaze for a quick second before looking down at the thick stack of correspondence on the table and a sack on the floor at her feet.

He wracked his brain but couldn't remember what she had submitted—oh, it had been late so he quickly reviewed it for errors of grammar and spelling before rushing it straight to the printers. Her work never required much by way of editing. Not like the epics Grenville submitted or the libel Lady Roxbury often handed in.

"Remind me the topic again?" he said. Clearly, it had resonated with the readers, so he ought to be aware of it.

She blinked her big blue eyes a few times. Perplexed.

There was a beat of hard silence in the room. Like he had said something wrong. So he gave the room A Look tinged with impatience to remind them that he was an extremely busy man and couldn't possibly be expected to remember the contents of each article submitted the previous week for a sixteen-page-long newspaper.

But he could feel the gazes of the crew drilling into him—Owens shaking his head, Julianna's eyebrows arched quite high. Even Grenville frowned.

Annabelle fixed her gaze upon him and said, "How to attract a man's attention."

That was just the sort of thing *Weekly* readers would love—and that could lead to a discussion of feelings—so Knightly gave a nod and said, "Good," and inquired about Damien Owens's police reports and other domestic intelligence. The conversation moved on.

"Before we go," Knightly said at the end, "I heard a rumor that a reporter for *The London Times* has been arrested after having been caught impersonating a physician to the aristocracy."

Shocked gasps ricocheted around the room from one writer to another as the implications dawned. The information this rogue reporter must have gathered from the bedrooms of London's most powerful class . . . the fortune in suppression fees he must have raked in . . . If information was power, suddenly this reporter and this newspaper held all the cards.

There was no way the ton would stand for it.

"That could explain so much . . ." Julianna murmured thoughtfully, her brow knit in concentration. "The broken Dawkins betrothal, Miss Bradley's removal to a convent in France . . ."

This only supported Knightly's suspicions that there would soon be hell to pay. Not just by *The London Times* either.

"Why are you all looking at me?" Eliza Fielding, now the Duchess of Wycliff, inquired.

"Because you were just famously disguised as a servant in a duke's household," Alistair Grey, theater reviewer said, with obvious delight. Eliza grinned wickedly.

"I'm married to him now, so that must grant me some immunity. And I am not the only reporter here who has gone undercover for a story. What about Mr. Owens's report on the Bow Street Runners?"

"That was weeks ago," Owens said dismissively.

"You were impersonating an officer," Eliza persisted.

"Well, has anyone asked Grenville how he obtains access to Parliament?" Owens questioned hotly. All heads swiveled in the direction of the grouchy old writer with the hound dog face.

"I don't pretend anything, if that's what you're suggesting," Grenville stiffly protested. "I sit in the gallery, like the other reporters."

"And after that?" Owens questioned. "Getting 'lost' in the halls like a 'senile old man'? Bribes for access to Parliament members?"

"We all do what needs to be done for a story," cut in Lady Roxbury, who had once disguised herself as a boy and snuck into White's, the most exclusive and *male* enclave in the world. "We're all potentially on the line if authorities start looking into the matter. But they cannot possibly because then every newspaper would be out of business and we'd all be locked up."

"Except for Miss Swift. She would be safe, for she never does anything wicked," Owens added. Everyone laughed. Even Knightly. He'd wager that Dear Annabelle was the last woman in the world to cause trouble.

# Chapter 3

### What to Wear When Attracting a Rogue

LETTER TO THE EDITOR

*I deplore today's fashions for women, which play to men's baser instincts. Unfortunately, Gentlemen do not seem to share my dismay. I fear for the civilized world.*

  Signed, A Lady

  *The London Weekly*

**I**F there had been the *slightest* doubt in Annabelle's mind about the dire need to enact her campaign for Knightly's attention, this afternoon's events had dispelled it. Even if she'd been quaking with regrets, consumed by doubts, and feverishly in a panic about her mad scheme, her exchange with Knightly would have cleared her head and confirmed her course of action.

*Mission: Attract Knightly* must now commence, with every weapon at her disposal. It was either that or resolve herself to a lifetime of spinsterhood. The prospect did not enthrall.

The rest of the staff had quit the room; the Writing Girls stayed. Annabelle remained paralyzed in her place.

"He hadn't read my column," she said, shocked. Still.

She needed to say the wretched truth aloud. If she needed any confirmation of what Knightly thought of her—or didn't—this was all the information she needed. Her own editor, *a man paid to look at her work*, didn't even read it. If it weren't for the thick stack of letters from readers, she might have flung herself off the London Bridge, that was how lonely it felt.

Lord above, it was mortifying, too. Everyone else knew why she sighed when Knightly walked in the room. She was sure they all knew about her inner heartache during her brief exchange with him. How could Knightly not see?

*He hadn't read her column, and it had been about him!*

"Annabelle, it wasn't that terrible. I'm sure he doesn't read all of our work either," Sophie said consolingly. "Certainly not my reports on weddings."

"It's not just that," Annabelle said glumly. "No one thinks I am wicked."

Julianna, who was very daring and wicked, grinned broadly. "So they shall be all the more speechless when it turns out you are! I loved your column on Saturday. Knightly may not have read it, but the rest of the town did. Your next course of action is being fiercely debated in drawing rooms all over town."

"Indeed?" It was strange to think of strangers debating her innermost vexations.

"There seems to be two schools of thought," Sophie replied. "One suggests that you simply confess to him your feelings."

"I am terrified at the thought," Annabelle replied.

"Then you may be interested in the other method . . ." Sophie paused dramatically. "Seduction."

"I couldn't possibly," Annabelle scoffed. "That would be wicked, and you heard Owens; I never act thusly."

"He's an ass," Julianna retorted.

Usually Annabelle would have admonished her friend's coarse language. Instead, she said, "No, he's right. I am Good. Therefore, I am not interesting. Why should Knightly take notice of me? There is nothing to notice!"

Wasn't that the plain old truth!

The mirror dared to suggest she was pretty, but all Annabelle saw was a riot of curls that were best restrained in a tight, spinsterish bun atop her head. She did have lovely blue eyes, but more often than not kept her gaze averted lest she draw attention to herself. Furthermore, her wardrobe consisted entirely of brownish-gray dresses made of remnant fabric from her brother's cloth-importing business. To say the cut was flattering or fashionable was to be a liar of the first order.

She might dare think people would see beyond her disastrous hair and hideous dresses. Most of the time she couldn't.

"Oh, Annabelle. You are rather pretty—so pretty that he, like any red-blooded male, should notice you. Unless he's not . . ."

"See, I am blushing at your mere suggestion!" Annabelle squeaked.

"We do have work to do," Julianna murmured.

"What do your letters say?" Sophie asked, picking one up.

Annabelle scowled and grabbed the first one, reading it aloud.

"'Dear Annabelle, in my humble opinion a low bodice never fails to get a man's eye. It plays to their rutting instincts, which we all know they are slaves to . . . Betsy from Bloomsbury.'"

"A trip to the modiste! I love it." Sophie clapped her hands with glee. But Annabelle frowned. Beggars ought not be choosers, yet . . .

"I want him to notice me for *me*; who I am as a person. Not just bits of me."

"You have to start with certain parts. Then he'll attend to the rest," Julianna replied. "Come, let's go get you a new dress."

"You must wear it for my party later this week," Sophie said, then adding the most crucial detail: "Knightly has been invited."

The opportunity dangled before her like the carrot and the horse. Never mind that the analogy made her a horse. The facts were plain:

There was something she might try (thank you, Betsy from Bloomsbury) and an opportunity at which she might do so (thank you, Sophie, hostess extraordinaire).

She had made that promise to her readers, and it would be dreadful to let them down. She did so despise disappointing people.

Annabelle twirled one errant curl around her finger and mulled it over (Swifts were not known for their quick decisions). She supposed there were worse things than a new gown and a fancy ball. For her readers, she would do this.

Not one hour later, Annabelle was standing in the dressing room of Madame Auteuil's shop. A previous customer had returned a lovely pink gown after a change of heart, and Annabelle wore it now as the seamstresses took measurements for a few alterations.

"I don't think it quite fits," she said. It wasn't the size per se, for she knew it would be tailored to her measurements. It was the dress itself.

It was silk. She never wore silk.

It was pink, like a peony or a rosebud or her cheeks when Knightly spoke to her. She never wore pink.

The pink silk was ruched and cinched and draped in a way that seemed to enhance her every curve and transform her from some gangly girl into a luscious woman.

Annabelle wore simply cut dresses made of boring old wool or cotton. Usually in shades of brown or gray or occasionally even taupe.

The Swift family owned a fabric importing business, which dealt exclusively in plain and serviceable cottons and wools guided by the rational that everyone required those, but so few indulged in silks and satins. Blanche generously provided Annabelle with last season's remnants for the construction of her wardrobe.

This silk, though, was lovely. A crimson silk sash cinched around her waist, enhancing what could only be described as an hourglass figure. It was a wicked color, that crimson.

Madame Auteuil stepped back, folded her arms and appraised her subject with a furrow of her brow and a frown on her lips. She had pins in her mouth and Annabelle worried for her.

"She needs a proper corset," the modiste finally

declared. "I cannot work without the lady in the right undergarments."

"A proper corset fixes everything," Sophie concurred.

"And lovely underthings . . ." Julianna smiled with a naughty gleam in her eye.

Annabelle began to do math in her head. Living as glorified household help for her brother and his sister meant that her *Weekly* wages went to her subscription at the circulating library and a few other inconsequential trinkets, and then the rest went into her secret account that Sophie's husband had helped her arrange. It had been her one small act of rebellion.

"I'm not sure that underthings are necessary . . ." Annabelle began to protest. Silk underthings sounded expensive and no one would see them, so how could she justify the expense when she could have a few delicious novels instead?

"Do you have the money?" Eliza asked softly. She was a duchess now, but she'd had anything but an aristocratic upbringing or connections. She understood economies.

"Well, yes. But I feel that I should save," Annabelle said frankly.

"For what?" Eliza asked.

"Something," Annabelle said. Something, someday. She was always waiting and preparing for an event that never came—or had she missed it, given that she didn't know what she was waiting for?

"Annabelle, this is that something," Sophie said grandly. "You want Knightly to notice you, do you not?"

"And you have an occasion to wear it," Eliza said, adding a dose of practicality.

"But he won't see my unmentionables. Those needn't be—"

"Well he might, if you are lucky," Julianna said frankly. And lud, didn't that make her cheeks burn! The thought made her entire body feel feverish, in a not altogether unpleasant way.

"Annabelle," Sophie began, "you must think of fashion as an investment in your future happiness! That is not some silk dress, but a declaration that you are a new woman, a young, beautiful woman interested in life! And love!"

"But the underthings?" Annabelle questioned.

"I promise you will love them," Sophie vowed. "You'll see . . ."

In the end, Annabelle was persuaded to purchase one pink silk dress, one blue day dress, one corset that enhanced her person in ways that seemed to violate natural laws, and some pale pink silk unmentionables that were promptly stashed in the back of her armoire.

# Chapter 4

## Misadventures in the Ballroom

*Ballroom of Hamilton House*

**O**N the terrace, Derek Knightly leaned against the balustrade, gazing at the party raging within. This morning he had been in the warehouse hauling and tossing reams of paper upon which the next issue would be printed until his hands were filthy with dirt, dust, and ink and until his muscles ached from the exertion and his skin was damped by sweat. Damn, it felt good.

This evening he wore a perfectly fitted, exquisitely expensive set of evening clothes, made by Gieves & Hawkes, his tailor on Saville Row. He sipped the fine French brandy—the only thing the

French were good for—and noted that it was a rare and excellent vintage.

His newspaper empire had brought him a fortune, and with it a taste for finer things, as well as the connections he had always aspired to. Here he was, a guest at the home of the Duke and Duchess of Brandon. They were friends.

Not bad for an earl's by-blow who had sullied his hands in trade.

Yet those damning words still taunted him: *Throw the bastard out. He doesn't belong here.*

Knightly lifted his head higher, damned proud of himself. His Writing Girls stood near the French doors leading to the terrace. He watched them chattering animatedly.

Annabelle glanced his way and he caught her eye. She quickly turned away. Shy, that one. He allowed his gaze to linger. Something seemed different about her. She just seemed a bit . . . *more.* It was probably because instead of meeting at the newspaper offices in the afternoon as usual, they were at a ball and midnight was drawing near. And the brandy was taking effect.

His gaze drifted back to Annabelle. More? Yes, definitely *more.*

Knightly took another measured sip of his drink and watched the party progress from his vantage point on the terrace, alone. A guest, yet an outsider all the same.

Tonight they were worse than usual. He was often tolerated, lest one risk insulting the host who had invited him. With those rumors, however . . . he saw the fear in their eyes as he wove his way through the ballroom. They wondered what he knew, what he would extort from them to keep the information private, or what he would print for all their family, friends, businessmen to see.

With just a few lines of movable type, he could reverse fortunes and ruin reputations. Aye, that explained the wary glances and averted gazes.

The New Earl was here tonight. Even after all these years, Knightly still referred to him in his head as the New Earl. *Harrowby* was his father, not this pompous oaf who still refused to acknowledge his half brother. Refused to even meet his eye, the coward. Upon occasions when they both attended the same function, Knightly made a sport of catching his eye, or even nodding, and watching the New Earl redden.

His fortune had not earned the man's notice. Neither did his ever-growing influence over the London ton due to his immensely popular paper. Nor did the New Earl seem to notice that he never printed anything remotely damaging about him in the pages of *The Weekly*. Nor did his friendships with dukes, plural. Which brought Knightly to the last point in his plan:

An aristocratic wife would make it impossible for the New Earl to ignore and snub him without conferring the same disregard upon a member of the haute ton. Which he would not—could not—do to one of his fellow peers.

It was, for reasons Knightly did not deeply examine, imperative that the earl recognize him publicly.

Most of the ton did not want to associate with him, but unlike his brother, so many could not afford to ignore him. That was also part of the plan.

Case in point: Lord Marsden, cigar and brandy in hand, who now ambled over to where he stood. They were of the same age, approximately. In spite of his young age, Marsden was immensely respected in Parliament—in part from the legacy of his late father, and in part because of his own talents, for the man had been born to the role in more ways than one.

Marsden was a charmer who cultivated a vast array of relationships at every opportunity. He flirted with women—young, old, debutante or spinster, married or widowed. One could often find him in the card room, smoking, laughing, and wagering with his fellow peers. He peppered his conversation with stock tips, minor gossip, compliments, and he listened attentively to one's problems. Far too attentively. He was good, Knightly had to give him that.

The marquis was forever seeking *The London Weekly*'s support for his various causes and political initiatives, given that the paper served such a large audience. Yet Knightly knew those readers flocked to his paper because it was beholden to no one, so the marquis was forever disappointed.

Nevertheless, the men were on familiar terms. It served them both well.

"I'm sure you have heard the news," Marsden said, and when Derek deliberately did not reply, he continued, "About *The London Times* reporter. He's in Newgate after impersonating a physician."

"I did hear rumors to that effect," Knightly allowed.

"Revolting, isn't it? The haute ton is terrified. Or they will be," Marsden said with a ruthless smile. Knightly understood how this would work: in his every conversation, the marquis would stir the pot, disseminating carefully selected bits of information designed to enrage and appall until the Upper Orders become a raging mob, hungry for the blood of newspaper magnates like him.

"I am considering how to portray this story in *The Weekly*," Knightly remarked.

Marsden had a wide circle of friends, connections. But Knightly had power of his own: each week thousands of Londoners read his newspaper full of information that he selected, edited, and presented. And then they discussed the contents with family, friends, the news agent, the butcher, their maids . . . Marsden might wish to stir the pot, but Knightly knew he could blow the whole thing up.

"There will likely be an inquiry," Marsden added casually, tipping the ash off his cigar. He spoke casually, but his words were always deliberately chosen and directed. This was a warning.

Translation: *Heads are about to roll.*

"I'd find that very interesting," Knightly remarked.

Meaning: *Tell me everything.*

"Indeed, I shall keep you informed," Marsden said. And then he changed the subject—or seemed to. "I am here with my sister this evening. This marriage mart business . . ." Marsden heaved a weary sigh, as if Lady Lydia was the last in a long line of troublesome sisters to foist off to the parson's mousetrap. In fact, she was his only sister. And she had missed her second season, mysteriously. Knightly declined to mention this. For the moment.

"You must be eager for her to marry," he said, testing Marsden's suggestion. Among bachelors, marriage wasn't a subject to be broached without an ulterior motive.

"As long as it's a match I approve of. A man who is able to provide for her in a manner that she is accustomed to." Marsden punctuated this with a heavy stare. Knightly's fortune was no secret. Reports of Marsden's declining coffers had made their way to Knightly's desk.

"A suitor whose business interests don't take a turn for the worse, perhaps," Knightly suggested, leveling a stare.

Marsden's eyes narrowed. He pulled on the cigar, then tapped it so the ash tumbled to the ground. Knightly did not look away.

"I am glad we understand each other," Marsden said, blowing a curl of blue-gray smoke into the night air.

It was one hell of an offer: *You protect* The London Weekly *and I will marry your sister.*

ANNABELLE was always aware of him, and so she knew that he was just there, on the terrace. It was a useless sixth sense. But how could she not sneak one glance after another as he leaned against the balustrade? For the hundredth time she wondered how the simple act of leaning could be so . . . so . . . arresting. Compelling. He appeared at ease but she knew he wasn't; he was aware of everything and ready for anything.

She, who never felt quite comfortable in her own skin, envied him that.

As she stood in conversation with her fellow Writing Girls, she kept trying to angle herself so that she might display her new gown to its best advantage.

The front. The very low bodice made her feel utterly naked. Perhaps even a bit wicked. Whatever it was, she barely recognized herself in this pink silk gown that slinked against her skin in a soft and sensual way.

It was just a dress, she reprimanded herself. Except that it wasn't—for better or for worse, this gown gave her a confidence she didn't usually possess. Annabelle caught herself standing up straighter, no longer awkward about her height but eager to show off her dress to the best effect. She smiled more because she felt pretty.

It wasn't just a dress; it was courage in the silken form.

She stole another glance. He was conversing with another gentleman, a handsome one.

She wracked her brain for a reason to go out on the terrace alone. A "Wallflower in Mayfair" had written: "Romantic stuff always happens on terraces at balls, everyone knows that."

She just needed an excuse. *I need air. I feel like trouble. Perhaps I'd like to try smoking a cigar. I'd like to be compromised. I can't breathe in this stifling corset that defies laws of gravity.*

"Oh, here comes Knightly," Eliza whispered to Annabelle, who already knew. She stood up straighter. Butterflies took flight. Her heartbeat quickened.

Knightly's gaze locked with hers. His eyes were so blue and contrasted so intensely with his black hair. Tonight he wore a black jacket and a dark blue silk waistcoat.

*Do not blush. Do not blush. Smile, Annabelle. Stand up straight.*

But the commands were lost between her head and her heart and the rest of her. Knightly nodded in greeting, and likely received a startled doe expression from Annabelle. She watched as he strolled purposely through the ballroom until he was lost in the crowds.

"Oh, look, if it isn't Lord Marsden," Sophie said flirtatiously to a handsome man walking by; the very one Knightly had been speaking with on the terrace.

The man in question stopped and gave the duchess a delicious smile. Annabelle recalled a mention of his name from Grenville's parliamentary reports (the man was apparently a born leader) and from Julianna's gossip columns (the man was widely regarded as an eminently eligible bachelor). She knew he worked closely with the Duke of Brandon, Sophie's husband, on parliamentary matters.

"If it isn't the lovely duchess," Marsden replied with an easy smile and kissing Sophie's outstretched hand.

"Don't flirt with me, Marsden," Sophie admonished. "Please meet my friend, Miss Swift. You may know her as Dear Annabelle."

"From the pages of *The Weekly*?" This, Marsden inquired with brow lifted. It was not an unexpected question, given that it was well known that Sophie wrote for the paper and alternately covered society weddings and the latest fashions.

"The very one," she replied.

Annabelle noted that this Lord Marsden was so classically, perfectly handsome that she found herself reluctantly searching for some flaw. His hair was blond, and brushed back from his perfectly chiseled cheekbones. If anything, he wore a dash too much pomade. But his eyes were warm and brown and they focused upon her.

Most importantly, he knew of her writing. She liked him immediately.

"You have a gift, Miss Swift," he said, and she found herself smiling. "I have often remarked at how gently you advise and rebuke people, whereas I would be sorely tempted to write something along the lines of 'You are a nodcock. Cease at once.' Tell me, did you ever consider it?"

"Everybody deserves sensitivity and a genuine—" She stopped when he arranged his handsome features into a look of utter skepticism. "Oh, very well, yes!" she said, laughter escaping her.

"If you do ever call someone a nodcock in print, it would please me immeasurably," Lord Marsden said, grinning.

Annabelle laughed. Then she caught a glimpse of Knightly speaking with a beautiful woman, decked in diamonds.

"I can foresee an instance when I might," Annabelle remarked coyly. When did she ever say anything coyly? Goodness. It must be those silky underthings she dared to wear this evening, making her bold. Or the warmth and encouragement in Marsden's expression.

"Would you like to waltz, Dear Annabelle?" Lord Marsden asked, offering his arm. She linked hers in his and allowed him to lead her to join the other dancers. It was only after the first steps of the waltz that she realized Sophie had quietly slipped away. And that she had lost sight of Knightly because she'd ceased to pay attention to his every movement. And that she didn't know how to waltz. And that she was quite excited to try with Lord Marsden.

She thought the evening couldn't possibly improve, however . . .

# Chapter 5

## The Dangers of Dimly Lit Corridors

DEAR ANNABELLE

*If one wishes for romantic encounters, one ought to
abandon the ballroom and venture to places more secluded and dimly lit, such as the terrace, or corridors
. . . But do so at your own risk!*
    *Yours Fondly,*
    *A Rakish Rogue*
    *The London Weekly*

*A dimly lit corridor*

ANNABELLE swayed on her feet, light-headed and
breathless.

The hour was late and her senses had been
dulled by the pleasant fatigue of waltzing and two
glasses of finely sparkling champagne. Happily, she
hummed a tune under her breath and imagined
Knightly asking her to waltz as she made her way
back to the ballroom through a dimly lit corridor.

And then she walked straight into a gentleman.
Or he barreled right into her. One might say they
collided. The result was, Annabelle swayed on her

feet, and breathlessly uttered a single, unfortunate syllable: "Oof."

Then her senses started to focus and she noticed she had crashed into a very fine wool jacket, a crisp white linen shirt, and a dark silk waistcoat, all of which covered a rather firm and broad male chest.

Had she known it was Knightly, she might have lingered to breathe in the scent of him (a combination of wool, faint cigar smoke, brandy, and *him*) or savor the feel of him under her palms (and not just the quality of his wool jacket either). She certainly wouldn't have said "Oof" like a barnyard animal.

Two warm, bare hands grasped her arms to hold her steady.

"Oh, I beg your pardon," she had said, stepping back and tilting her head up to see who owned this firm chest that positively radiated heat and impelled her to curl up against it. Her eyes adjusted to light and then widened considerably when she saw whom she had collided with: Knightly, the man of her dreams, the King of her heart, the object of her affections . . .

"Miss Swift," Knightly said, with a nod in greeting. "My apologies, I hadn't seen you."

Of course he didn't. He never did. But that was just the way of things. Also the way of things was her unfortunate tendency to either go mute in his presence or ramble excessively. She had yet to manage a normal conversation with the man.

"Mr. Knightly. Good evening. I'm sorry, I was not attending to my surroundings . . ." Annabelle rambled. To her horror, the words kept coming, oblivious to her fervent wishes to stop. "Obviously, I had not seen you. For if I had seen you, I certainly wouldn't have barreled headlong into you."

Surely some reader was bound to suggest the very tactic.

"So I gathered. Are you all right?" He inquired politely.

"Yes, quite. Though your chest is rather hard," Annabelle said. Then she closed her eyes and groaned. Had she *really* just said that? Was it too much to ask that she not make a complete nitwit of herself all the time?

"Thank you," he replied, ever so gentlemanly. But there was enough light to see that he was amused.

"My apologies. A lady ought not attend to such things, or mention them aloud. Rest assured I would never advise a reader to—" She was babbling. She couldn't stop.

And yet, through the mortification a sweet truth dawned. She was alone with Knightly. And she was dressed for the occasion. Even better, she had felt the firm strength of his chest for one extraordinarily exquisite second that she wished to repeat (albeit in a far more seductive manner).

"I'm sure that would be scandalous, if you did tell a reader to compliment a man thusly. However, I can't imagine any man would be bothered by it," Knightly said, a faint grin on his lips, which was his way of saying it was fine. She exhaled in relief.

"But I do apologize that I wasn't attending to my surroundings. I was quite distracted."

"Something on your mind?" Knightly inquired. And then he folded his arms over his very hard chest and leaned against the wall. He gazed down at her.

That was all it took for the world to shift on its axis, right under her feet.

Because Knightly had asked her a question. About herself. About her *mind*.

How to answer *that*?

"Oh, just enjoying the evening. And you?" she replied, hoping to sound as if she chatted with dashing gentleman all the time and wasn't beset with nerves. Even though every nerve in her body with tingling pleasantly. For here she was in a dark, secluded place having *an actual conversation* with Knightly.

More to the point, it was a conversation that was not about the newspaper.

"This evening has been . . . interesting," he replied.

"How so?" Annabelle asked, still breathless, but now for an altogether different reason.

"Life takes a strange turn upon occasion, does it not?" he remarked, and she didn't quite know what he was referring to, only that it fit her moment perfectly.

"Oh, yes," she replied. What gods had conspired to bring about this fortuitous occurrence of circumstances, Annabelle knew not. But she was happy. And hopeful. And proud of herself for trying; this had to be her reward.

Now if only she could prolong the moment . . .

"The duchess has outdone herself this evening," Knightly said. "We'd better return before—"

"Someone notices that we are missing," Annabelle said, perhaps a touch too eagerly. Not that she would mind being caught in a compromising position with him. Not at all.

"Or before someone else with less noble intentions accosts you in the dark hallway. Can't have any danger befall my Writing Girls," he said, gently pressing his palm to her elbow, guiding them both to the ballroom.

Annabelle only smiled faintly and wondered if it was wrong to wish a gentleman's intentions were less than noble.

# Chapter 6

## The London Coffeehouse: Meeting Place of "Gentlemen"

FASHIONABLE INTELLIGENCE BY A LADY OF DISTINCTION
The London Weekly's *own Mr. Knightly was seen waltzing with Lady Lydia Marsden, whose talents and elegance in the waltz surpass all others. We can only wonder what they discussed; perhaps he has uncovered the secret to her missing season?*

The London Weekly, as edited by D. Knightly

GALLOWAY'S coffeehouse was full of men, high- and lowborn alike, sipping coffee and delving into the assortment of periodicals offered. Everything from literary publications to periodicals devoted to sport. The air was full of men's conversations both serious and bawdy, cigar smoke, the heavy fragrance of coffee, and the shuffling of pages.

Knightly was in the habit of meeting at Galloway's every Saturday, joined by Peter Drummond, a playwright and theater owner—who had been his comrade in trouble since Cambridge—and their scoundrel of a friend, Julian Gage, a renowned stage actor who was better known for his disastrous romantic entanglements than the quality of his acting.

After all, it's not like White's would admit the likes of them as members. They hadn't the birth, status, wealth, or connections required for access to that exclusive enclave. Galloway's was their club instead.

"Women never bloody listen to me," Drummond muttered into his newspaper. He grasped a handful of his salt and pepper hair in utter vexation. "I vow, I could tell a lass to get out of a sinking boat and she'd protest."

"Is that in reference to something specific or the general lament that women don't take the advice of a man who makes up stories for a living?" Knightly asked casually. A copy of *Cobott's Weekly Register* lay before him.

"It's playwriting. And your mother would have your head to hear you dismiss the theater like that. If you must know, I am grumbling about your Dear Annabelle," Drummond answered. He punctuated this with a frustrated shake of the newspaper.

Knightly coolly lifted one brow. The conversation had suddenly turned toward the unexpected and possibly unfathomable.

"She took my advice!" Julian grinned triumphantly in spite of Drummond's vicious glare.

Knightly frowned at his friends. Both usually read the theater reviews, gossip column, and naught much else. Julian, in particular, usually read only articles that were about him.

They certainly never read the advice column in the back, next to the advertisements for hats, corsets, and miracle cures of all kinds. It was women's stuff, presided over by the Dear Annabelle column

in which Miss Swift, who was sweetness and innocence personified, doled out advice to the lovelorn,
socially unsure, etc, etc. He tried to recall her last
column and why she would be in search of advice,
especially from these idiots.

"Oi!" Drummond shouted when Knightly
snatched the paper from his hands. He found her
column on page seventeen and began to read with
annoyance (because something in his paper had escaped his notice) and intrigue (because it was Annabelle. What could she be writing about?):

### DEAR ANNABELLE

*This author was humbled and heart-warmed by
the outpouring of advice from her loyal readers in
response to last week's solicitation for desperately
needed advice on how I might attract a particular
man's attention.*

*Never has this author received so many letters! One
reader wrote that I ought to steal into the gentleman's
bed at the midnight hour as a wicked surprise. I fear
that is too bold, but we shall see what desperate acts
I am driven to. Nancy suggested perfume "delicately
applied to my décolletage" and a gentleman named
Peregrine offered to compose love sonnets that I might
dramatically recite, thus captivating the object of my
affections with his verse. Dozens of letters advised me
to lower the bodices on my gowns. My friends greatly
encouraged this endeavor and I found myself at the
modiste before I knew it.*

*Readers, I know not if it was the dress itself, the
ample display of my person, or the confidence I possessed from such fine garments, but I daresay this
worked! While it failed to attract the object of my*

*affections (that nodcock!), I certainly basked in the
attentions of other charming gentlemen. This week I
shall alter the rest of my wardrobe accordingly. But as
I shall settle for nothing less than true love, I suspect I
require more schemes to enact. Your suggestions are
welcome and will be put to the test!*

Miss Swift requesting love advice from all of
London?

This was not the Annabelle he knew. This was not
the work of a shy girl who spoke softly, if at all. The
girl who usually wore her hair in a bun and dresses
in the style best described as Spinster Auntie. The
girl who had rambled quite charmingly when they
bumped into each other the other night and who
hadn't once made him think of her as a Spinster
Auntie during that darkened interlude.

Quite the contrary. It seemed Annabelle possessed the sort of luscious curves best kept for sin.
It wasn't an altogether unpleasant discovery, even
though nothing would come of it.

He had thought there was something different
about her, something *more*. His suspicions were confirmed. It seemed a lot of things were different with
Annabelle all of a sudden.

She usually advised the masses on proper manners, or offered practical household tips, or con-
sulted, gently, on the love lives of readers.

Annabelle did not use words like "nodcock."

Thus it was the damnedest thing to read this
column from a girl, so sweet and fair, publicly pursuing a man with advice from strangers. Annabelle
didn't know any of these people she was courting
information from!

They could be like . . .

Drummond and Gage. Drummond, who had three broken engagements in his past, and Gage, who had a tempestuous relationship with Jocelyn Kemble, the famous actress, and who never refused female company when offered. As a popular actor, it was offered to him. Often.

Heaven help them all, Annabelle especially.

"I thought she ought to send him an anonymous letter. Perfumed. Romantic like," Drummond explained. "There is nothing like the power of the written word to seduce the mind, and the heart will follow."

Knightly snorted. What romantic rubbish.

"That's pathetic. My advice was better, which was why she followed it," Gage replied arrogantly with a smug smile.

"Lower her bodice?" Drummond scoffed. "Like that's original."

"Annabelle doesn't want original, she wants what works," Gage said, and Knightly frowned at this lout referring to one of *his* Writing Girls so intimately. Gage didn't notice and barreled on. "Since time immemorial, women have flaunted their figures and men have been slaves to their baser natures."

Case in point, Knightly thought. Idiots.

And yet . . .

Was that what was different about Annabelle at the ball? He'd seen her chatting with the Writing Girls, and then waltzing with some young buck. He'd connected intimately with her person for just a second, but it had been enough to discover she had a figure for sin.

But he had not really noticed her lowered bodice.

Why? Was he ill? No, there was nothing the matter with him. He just wasn't in the habit of looking at his female employees In That Way. From the start he had treated his female writers the same as the men; it was just easier.

Should he have noticed?

He should have noticed. If it concerned his business then the answer was yes.

This concerned his business. Thus, he would make a point to look when he saw her next. For the sake of his business. No other reason, such as a dawning intrigue.

"We don't even know what Annabelle looks like," Drummond mused, sipping from a steamy mug of coffee. "For some women, amply displaying their bosoms is ill advised."

"That's true. If they're too small. Or too old," Gage concurred, pulling a face.

"One does wonder about Dear Annabelle. We know nothing about her, except that she hasn't been able to get the attentions of some bloke for *years*." Drummond continued his dissection of Annabelle's situation with the same seriousness with which he examined *Hamlet*.

"She could be a grandmother," Gage whispered, aghast. Color drained from his face. "I might have just written a letter to someone's grandmother telling her to show off her you know whats."

"Oh for God's sake," Knightly cut in. "Annabelle is young and pretty."

"Why hasn't this nodcock noticed her, then?" Gage challenged.

"Damned if I know," Knightly said with a shrug. He had no idea who this bloke was and nor did he care, so long as Annabelle's quest sold issues of the paper. It seemed like it was well poised to do so if these corkbrains were so fascinated with it. "She's very quiet."

"Young. Pretty. Quiet. I think I'm in love," Drummond said dreamily.

"You don't even know her," Knightly said, bringing a dose of much-needed logic to the conversation. One did not fall in love with strangers. Although, his father had fallen in love with his mother at first sight. But that was rare. And neither Drummond or Gage had even *seen* Annabelle.

"I've heard enough. My next suggestion to her will be to forget that nodcock and marry me," Drummond said with a grin.

# Chapter 7

## The Dangers of Sultry Gazes

FASHIONABLE INTELLIGENCE BY A LADY OF DISTINCTION
*There are two questions burning on the lips of every Londoner: Who is the Nodcock and what will Dear Annabelle do next?*
*The London Weekly*

*Offices of* The London Weekly

**A**NNABELLE'S heart pounded. Any second now Knightly would stroll through that door and the butterflies in her belly would take flight.

He would flash them all a devilish grin, and she couldn't help but imagine him grinning at her like that, just before he kissed her under a starry, moonlit sky. Without fail, a blush would suffuse her cheeks.

Then Knightly would say "Ladies first" and she would sigh, a world of longing, desire, and frustration contained in that little exhalation.

This routine occurred like clockwork every Wednesday afternoon at precisely two o'clock when Knightly met with the writers of *The London Weekly*.

But this week things would be different. Of that, she was certain. She had a plan.

"Annabelle, I adored your column this week, and it is the topic du jour in all the drawing rooms," Julianna said as she sashayed into the room and took a seat next to Annabelle, who had arrived early.

Previously, her reason for arriving a good quarter of an hour prior to everyone else had to do with a terror of arriving late, interrupting everyone and finding herself the center of unwanted attention. But lately she thought not of that potential embarrassment, but the potential magic that might arise should she find herself with Knightly, alone.

Sophie and Eliza followed right behind Julianna and took their seats. The rest of the writers began to file in, talking amongst themselves.

"Lord Marsden liked it as well," Annabelle said, and could not hide her smile.

"He's such a charming rake," Sophie said, smiling. "Almost *too* charming."

"That charming and attentive rake that actually reads my column," Annabelle corrected gleefully. "He sent flowers on Saturday afternoon because he was so pleased I had obliged him by using the term 'nodcock' in my column. Can you believe I used such a word? I have shocked myself."

"You might be wicked after all," Julianna replied.

"Let's not get ahead of ourselves," Annabelle cautioned.

"And let's not forget that the gentleman sent you flowers!" Eliza said.

"Pink roses. Blanche and her awful friend Mrs. Underwood couldn't let that pass without an array of snide comments. She couldn't fathom they were for me, and then she wondered what sort of shenanigans I had engaged in to oblige a man to send these to me, and then she said they would look very fine in Fleur's bedroom."

"Fleur is such a whimsical name. I'm quite surprised by it . . ." Sophie said.

"Indeed, coming from my brother and his wife," Annabelle said. "They suffer terribly from a lack of imagination. Fleur's fancy name is the one thing that gives me hope. I later stole them out of Fleur's bedroom and put them in mine. I'm certain I'll find them in Blanche's chamber when I return."

"But you have received flowers. From a gentleman. A very eligible and marriageable one," Julianna said, smiling.

Annabelle beamed. She had also spent hours with a needle and thread to lower the bodices on her dreary old gowns. When Blanche saw what she was doing, she asked why Annabelle wished to look like a dockside harpy. *Because a dockside harpy can attract the attentions of men. So I can marry and move out of this suffocating household.*

If only Blanche knew about her silky underthings and her phenomenal corset—which she wore now, of course, for confidence, along with the pretty blue day dress she'd ordered on that wonderful life-altering trip to the modiste. Sophie had been so very right about the dresses and the underthings, although Annabelle knew she was not yet wicked enough to mention her unmentionables in mixed company.

Ever since that fateful day, she had entertained that wicked thought, "Why me," and life in the Swift household had become more stifling. And after she wore that silk dress, waltzed with a marquis, received a bouquet of pink roses from an eligible gentleman, and had an actual conversation with Knightly, she started to think less about Old Annabelle who did Blanche's bidding and more about New Annabelle who might do anything.

"But what does this mean for you know who?" Eliza asked in a conspiratorial whisper.

"Oh, I have more tricks up my sleeve, thanks to my readers," Annabelle replied in a hushed voice. As per the instructions of "A Courtesan in Mayfair," she had spent hours before the looking glass, as she practiced lifting and lowering her lashes and gazing smolderingly.

Today, Annabelle was armed and ready in a fetching new dress with a remarkably low bodice and sultry glances for her beloved Mr. Knightly.

The clock struck two. First the pounding heart. Next, the butterflies. And then, the sigh.

KNIGHTLY strolled into the room and began the meeting as he'd begun every other one, with a grin and a cheeky nod to the Writing Girls.

His gaze was immediately drawn to Annabelle. To be exact, specific parts of Annabelle. The conversation in the coffeehouse came galloping back to mind. Lowered bodices. Advice from idiots. Young. Pretty. Quiet. Significantly lowered bodices that revealed . . . a handful. A mouthful. A woman.

He cleared his throat.

"Ladies first," he said, hoping not to sound . . . distracted.

Julianna launched into the ton's latest scandal and Knightly didn't listen to a word of it. His gaze kept shifting one seat to her left, to Annabelle. When he managed to wrench his focus away from her very low bodice and up, he saw a dreamy expression on her face. Her blue eyes were focused on something far off and far away. Her full pink lips were curved into the slightest trace of a smile. Annabelle was daydreaming.

In a meeting.

Which he was leading. He would not be ignored.

"Miss Swift, you and your column were the topic of conversation in the coffeehouse Saturday last," he said briskly. He fought to keep his expression neutral as he recalled that bedeviling conversation with Drummond and Gage. He'd be damned if his staff saw that he was affected by her. It was bad enough to mention this topic of her bodice in a room of mixed company, in a professional setting, however indirectly.

He wanted to look. He could . . . not . . . look.

"Oh? It was?" Jolted from her reverie, she fixed those big blue eyes upon him, the force of which stunned him for a second. Then she lowered her lids and lifted them again. And pouted her lips, almost as if she were sucking on a lemon. Was she unwell?

"I urge you to take care with the advice you elect to follow. I'm not sure if indelicate or idiotic is the right word for some of these bloke's suggestions," he lectured. In the back of his mind, he wondered when he'd become so stuffy.

Her eyes seemed bluer today. Why was he noticing her eyes? Was it her blue dress? Didn't she always wear brownish-grayish dresses? His gaze dropped to Annabelle's dress, and he did not take note of the color at all. He saw creamy white skin rising in tantalizing swells above an extremely low bodice.

"With all due respect, Mr. Knightly, it seems to be working." She said it softly, with a hint of defiance mingling with deference. Her mouth reminded him of an angel's pout—sulky, sweet, mysterious and mischievous.

The kind of mouth a man thought of kissing.

And thoughts like that were exactly why women were not oft employed with men. Damned distracting.

"Annabelle's column has taken the ton by storm," Sophie said.

To Knightly's surprise, Owens—the most promising young rogue reporter who covered all manner of sordid stories—spoke up. "My mum and sisters keep yammering on about it. Miss Swift, they are of the opinion that you should try a different manner of styling your hair. I told 'em blokes don't notice that sort of thing. Instead what they really notice is—"

"That's enough, Owens," Knightly said sharply. If that cad mentioned anything below Annabelle's neck . . .

Knightly snuck another glance.

*Damn.*

She had caught his eye and then closed her eyes for a second or two, slowly lifting her lashes, fluttering them, and then sort of pouting again. How odd. Truly strange.

"Is this more rubbish about attracting a gentleman's attentions?" Grenville muttered. "Because the word in Parliament is that an inquiry is being formed to examine journalistic practices in light of *The London Times* reporter's arrest and subsequent imprisonment. I for one am concerned about what this means for our own publication."

Knightly offered a prayer of thanks to Grenville for ending the conversation about Annabelle's . . . charms. And for sitting on the far side of the room so that he could focus on Grenville and turn his back to her . . . charms.

"Will that parliamentary inquiry be focused on *The London Times*, specifically, or other publications, generally?" Owens asked. "Rumors are flying. I heard every periodical will have to submit to a government review before publication. A footman was fired from Lord Milford's employ after it was suspected he sold secrets to the press."

"Oh, it's worse than that," Julianna added gravely. "I heard Lord Milford gave the poor footman quite a thrashing before turning him out on the streets. To quote Lord Marsden, 'One is appalled at the peddling of aristocratic secrets for the profit and amusement of the lower classes.' Many are in agreement with him."

The room fell silent. The faces of his writers peered at him expectantly. Of course they would assume he would have a strategy or a scheme to exploit public opinion to their advantage or to otherwise ensure that *The London Weekly* was triumphant—and that their livelihoods and reputations were secure.

This thing with *The London Times* might be another newspaper's problem, or it could explode into an industrywide scandal and investigation. It looked like Marsden had a taste for blood, and intended more than the ruination of one reporter, or one newspaper.

The question was, how would *The London Weekly* fare in the midst of this crusade?

His writers routinely risked everything and anything for stories that had made *The London Weekly* great. Eliza had done numerous dangerous undercover stints, including disguising herself as a maid in a duke's household—the very exploits that had the ton riled up and calling for blood. Julianna routinely put her reputation on the line by exposing the scandals and foibles of her peers. Owens never met an assignment he didn't risk a stint in prison for, and no person or thing was too sacred for his ruthless investigating. What would become of Alistair or Grenville if they didn't have an outlet for their wit and discerning writing?

Knightly knew that he might own the newspaper, but it would be worthless without them. He couldn't let this scandal blow out of control, and definitely couldn't let his faithful and talented writers be sent to Newgate for their work, which served a city, both informing and entertaining the population.

He hadn't given much thought to Marsden's offer until this moment when it seemed he was the only thing standing between safety and disaster for the people he owed *everything* to.

Though the marquis dangled something he wanted very badly—entrée into high society with a strategic marriage—it conflicted with truth number three: *Be beholden to no one.*

But if it would protect his newspaper and his writers—while assuring his prominence in London society—hell, it was an offer worth entertaining. The New Earl would never be able to snub the man so connected to such a prominent marquis. This inquiry would turn a blind eye to his scandalous newspaper and the exploits of its writers.

It was an offer worth taking. Knightly made decisions quickly, and then abided by them. On the spot, he made up his mind to court Lady Lydia and probably marry her. He would take Marsden up on his offer to protect his paper and his writers.

"Rest assured, I'm doing everything in my power to ensure the authorities don't turn their attentions to *The Weekly*," Knightly said confidently. He could see them all visibly relax at the pronouncement, and he knew he'd made the right choice.

But speaking of turning one's attentions . . .

Knightly's eyes reluctantly flicked back to Annabelle. She did that strange thing with her very blue eyes again. Her lips were pursed into a pout that verged precariously on the side of ridiculous, and yet was strangely tempting all the same.

Grenville mercifully carried on about other, duller matters of government, and Damien Owens regaled everyone with that week's news of robberies, fires, murders, ridiculous wagers, and notable court cases. Knightly rushed everyone through, eager to conclude the meeting so that he might further investigate the burgeoning scandal with *The London Times*. And, frankly, so he could escape the distraction that Annabelle had suddenly, inexplicably, become.

He could kill Gage for suggesting the lowered bodice. But he suspected that damned actor wasn't the only one to send in that advice, and for good reason: it worked. Yea gods, it worked. Knightly couldn't stop looking—Annabelle and her décolletage was a sight to behold. That he'd forbidden himself made it all the more alluring.

She caught his eye again, and shyly looked down at her lap. He watched her lips murmur something incomprehensible, and then she glanced back at him. Eyelashes batting at a rapid pace. Lips pushed out. What the devil was she doing?

"Miss Swift, is there something in your eye?" he asked when he could restrain his curiosity no more.

"I am perfectly fine," she replied as a flush crept into her cheeks.

"Ah, it seemed you had something in your eye," he remarked, quizzically.

"No, nothing. I'm fine. Just fine." There was a hollow note in her voice. But he couldn't puzzle over that. Not when his empire was possibly under attack and it was up to him to protect it.

# Chapter 8

## A Writing Girl, Writing

### DEAR ANNABELLE

*In reply to Embarrassed in East End, I suggest fleeing
to America, praying fervently for the floorboards to
open up and swallow you whole, or do your best to
pretend the mortifying incident never occurred.*

*—Annabelle, who has herself addressed many
prayers to the floorboards and even investigated
the price of a one-way ticket to America*

*The London Weekly*

*Annabelle's attic bedroom*

**A**NNABELLE sat frozen at her writing desk, still
paralyzed with mortification hours after the Awful
Incident. Never in her entire life had she been more
embarrassed, including the occasion in her twelfth
year when she had unwittingly tucked her petti-
coats and skirts into her unmentionables and proceeded to church. Thomas had paid attention to her
then, and laughed heartily despite the chastising of
their parents.

The Awful Incident was even more horrifying than the time she accidentally sat on a freshly painted brown park bench whilst daydreaming . . . and en route to a weekly writers meeting. It was the only time she'd ever been thankful for her grayish dresses, though the paint was still visible. In attempting to keep her backside from view of anyone, particularly Knightly, she tripped over a chair and fell sprawled to the floor.

Annabelle groaned and replayed the worst of the Awful Incident again in her mind. The thrill of Knightly fixing his attentions upon her. The devastating realization of why. *Miss Swift, is there something in your eye?*

Her attempts to appear seductive were an unmitigated failure. If she couldn't even look at the man seductively, how was she to make him love her? After the success of the lowered bodice, she thought a sultry gaze would spark his interest, and perhaps he would start to fall in love with the mysterious Writing Girl in his midst. Intrigued, he would begin to seduce her and she would prettily resist his advances for the appropriate amount of time, at which point . . .

She sighed as the truth sunk in: it seemed she would have to seduce Mr. Knightly and that it would require a few more tricks from her readers.

Annabelle crossed the room to the mirror and tried her sultry gaze once more. Lowered eyelashes. Pouting lips. Smoldering thoughts. Oh very well, she did look ridiculous! In a fit of despair and humiliation, she flung herself on her bed.

She had gotten his attention, at least. But for looking like a fool of the first water! In her head she heard his voice echoing over and over, asking that wretched question: *Miss Swift, is there something in your eye? Miss Swift, is there something in your eye? Miss Swift, is there something in your eye?*

She groaned and flung an arm over her eyes.

Not even the pink roses from Lord Marsden could console her. Very well, they did, slightly. Annabelle lifted her arm and looked at the gorgeous, fragrant bouquet sitting proudly and so *pinkly* on her writing desk, reminding her that a gentleman, *a marquis*, paid attention to her and read her column and shared private jokes with her.

Not all hope was lost, sultry gazes notwithstanding.

No man had ever sent her flowers before. She bolted upright, needing advice. Was she to write a thank-you note? If so, what did one say? She was an advice columnist and thus she ought to know these things.

Oh, but what a problem to have! Annabelle smiled proudly and, Lord help her, a giggle escaped her lips. She was not so disconsolate that she couldn't appreciate such a lovely problem: whether or not to pen a thank-you note for an exquisite bouquet of hothouse flowers from an eligible gentleman.

Not like, say, the man of your dreams asking if you have something in your eye when you are attempting to throw sultry glances his way.

Best not try sultry glances on Lord Marsden. Or anyone she might ever wish to pursue.

It was now her noble duty to alert the female population of London not to heed the well-intentioned advice of a "Courtesan from Mayfair." Annabelle returned to her writing desk, this time with more focus. After another heavenly inhalation of the roses, she began to write her next column.

> *Ladies of London, beware! A Courtesan from Mayfair suggested that this author delivery sultry glances to the object of her affection. My attempts resulted in utter mortification! He—henceforth known as the Nodcock—merely inquired if I had something in my eye.*

Here Annabelle paused, and tapped the quill against her cheek as she thought about Knightly reading these very words. In an instant he would know that she had concocted a massive scheme involving the ten thousand regular readers of *The London Weekly* in a desperate attempt to gain his attention.

And that she called him a nodcock.

That was not acceptable. True, but unpublishable.

Her quill was poised above *nodcock,* ready to strike it out, when she meanly thought that Knightly wouldn't even read the column at all! The Nodcock.

However, it would do to make it just a touch more vague, because if she were to examine the contents of her heart and soul—as she was doing, in an effort to procrastinate, as one is wont to do—she would see that she wasn't ready to give up the jig just yet. In spite of the Awful Incident, she had made progress.

Her wardrobe had improved, and with it her confidence. A man had sent her flowers. She had managed a conversation with Knightly. Readers were responding with great favor to her column and to her quest. A New Annabelle was emerging; one who had adventures and flirtations to go along with Awful Incidences.

New Annabelle had much more fun than Old Annabelle, and being in possession of a great imagination and curiosity, she wondered where it would all lead. She wanted to know. She *could* know, so long as she did not allow one little Awful Incident to set her back. And as long as she composed her column to be vague enough so that Knightly might not put two and two together straight away.

Annabelle wanted his heart and she wanted his attention. But not from some slip of the pen. She wanted him to be drawn to her, interested in her, desperately in love with her. If she had to become a better version of herself, so be it. Frankly, it was much more exciting.

And so she rewrote the column to be a touch more vague, just in case Knightly did read it, and had a mind to place himself in it.

Then she rummaged through her assortment of reader letters for questions to answer, advice to dole out, and tricks to try to gain Knightly's attention.

"Ah, this one is perfect," she murmured. "Excellent idea, Sneaky From Southwark."

# Chapter 9

## Newspaper Proprietor Seeks Aristocratic Bride

### DEAR ANNABELLE

*I was eager to attempt to "seduce a man with naught
but the smoldering intensity of my love, revealed
wordlessly in a sultry gaze," as per the advice of a
Courtesan in Mayfair. Alas, dear readers, this led to
a mortifying disaster! Rather than succumb to the
fervor in my gaze, more than one person inquired if I
had something stuck in my eye.*

*The London Weekly*

*Home of Mrs. Delilah Knightly, Russell Square*

"**WELL** if it isn't my favorite son," Delilah Knightly
remarked with a laugh as Derek Knightly strolled
into the breakfast room unannounced. He was in
the habit of calling on his mother every Saturday
morning, like the good progeny that he was. Also,
her cook made the best breakfast biscuits and refused to share the recipe with his cook. Never mind
that he paid for them both.

"I'm your only son." This correction came with a
slight grin.

"That's what I said. You're so literal, Derek. How did that happen?" she asked. Her voice was loud—all the better to carry to the back of the theater—and there was always a note of mirth in her tone, whether she was scolding her young child or requesting more tea from a servant. No matter what, life was terribly amusing to Delilah Knightly.

"I believe you possess all the acting ability and inclination to fantasy in this family," he said. She was a renowned stage actress, and one of his guiding principles was to avoid drama, unless it was on the stage or the printed page. "I'm as straightforward as they come."

"I know, I'm you're mother," she said with a broad smile, pushing a basket of freshly baked biscuits in his direction. "How are you, my dear?"

"Business is good." He took a seat and poured himself a cup of steaming hot coffee.

"Which means that everything is good. Such devotion to your work!" She paused, smiled wickedly, and said: "I wish you'd employ some of that infamous work ethic of yours on providing me with grandbabies."

"Mother." The word was a statement, a protest, and an answer. She loved to vex him with the topic and he refused to react. He didn't see why she bothered bringing it up.

"Oh for Lord's sake, Derek, I can't help my natural inclinations. Tell me, how is Annabelle faring?"

"Annabelle?" This caught him off guard. So much so that it took a moment before he realized whom she was referring to. Dear Annabelle of the lowered bodices and sultry gazes who was on a quest to win the heart of some nodcock.

That his mother was mentioning this topic did not bode well.

Why the devil would his mother give a whit about one of his Writing Girls? Granted, she was tremendously proud of those girls and was known to say that hiring them was the best damn thing he'd ever done. Made your mum, proud, she'd say.

Which isn't why he did it. The chits were good for business.

And how had Annabelle—a chit he never gave much of a passing thought to—suddenly intruded upon his every thought and conversation? He brooded over this, sipping his coffee, as his mother explained.

"'Dear Annabelle.' The gal with the advice column. The one who is soliciting tips from readers on how to attract a man. You're really onto something with that one. I hadn't laughed so hard in an *age*." She chuckled again just thinking about it.

"Actually, I'm sure you have," he replied patiently. "You find humor in everything."

"It's an important life skill. But regardless, that girl is a doll. What is she really like?" His mum sipped her tea and then fixed her full attention upon him. The hair on the back of his neck stuck up in warning. When his mother took an interest in something . . . Things Happened.

"Annabelle?" He repeated her name in an effort to stall. And why was everyone asking him what Annabelle was like? He made a note to himself to read her columns more closely in the future.

His mother gave him a look that distinctly communicated *you dolt*.

"She's young. Pretty. Nice." The answer was de-

liberately evasive. The same answer he'd given to
Drummond and Gage, and for the same reason. If
Annabelle and this column didn't come across as
too interesting, his mother might lose interest. Like
playing dead to avoid a dog attack.

She yawned. Dramatically.

"You should include a picture with her column.
One of those illustrations." Knightly thought about
what the blokes in the coffeehouse had talked about.
Was she pretty? Were they advising a grandma
to show more cleavage? Some protective instinct
flared; he did not want those louts looking upon Annabelle's beauty. In some way, she belonged to him,
in that he had hired her and given her this platform
to enact her romantic schemes.

But a portrait of her would be damn good for
business. Pretty girls sold so well.

"That's a fine idea. Randolph can have it done
in an afternoon," he answered, and made a mental
note to make the request when he returned to the
office later.

"What did you think of her column? Wasn't it
hysterical?" his mother asked. "Is she unwell? What
a nodcock! Ha!"

It was not hysterical. He felt like an ass. She wrote
of her failed attempts to employ a sultry gaze and
that numerous people inquired if she had something in her eye. He took consolation in the fact that
he was not the only one to ask. But still—he felt like
an ass.

She must have been idly practicing in the meeting, or the man she was after was on staff. Definitely
not Grenville. She was set up for heartache if it were
Alistair. It had to be Owens. It mattered not to him.

But really, *Owens*? The man was young and talented but hotheaded, and with a habit of frequenting gaming hells and embarking on the most dangerous schemes to get stories. He spent most of his hours chasing down murders, investigating fires, and impersonating footmen and officers. When would he have time to court Annabelle? Or perhaps that was the point of her escapades.

"It was amusing," Knightly answered carefully. His mother's eyes narrowed. Bloody hell. She suspected something.

"You were one of the men to ask if she was unwell, were you not?" she asked, her eyes narrowing further. Damned intuition of mothers. Why they were not employed by the Bow Street Runners was a mystery to him.

She sighed heavily. "Oh, Derek, I do worry about you, taking everything so seriously. So literally. Then again, I do tend to the dramatic—"

"Overdramatic?"

"Oh, hush you," she said playfully and swatting at his hand. "Speaking of my flair for drama, I have a new show opening. I play the wicked fairy-godmother-like character. I love it."

"Sounds perfect for you," he said, grinning. "I shall be there opening night."

"You are a good son. A Great Son would bring that theater-reviewing employee of his. The one with the brilliantly colored waistcoats. If he gives me a bad review, you mustn't print it."

"I wouldn't dare. And I won't worry about it because you'll be fantastic," he said. And she would. For all her dramatics off the stage, Delilah Knightly had a gift and was a supremely talented actress.

"What will you do with the rest of your day? Back to the office?" his mother inquired, sipping her tea.

"Actually, I must pay a visit. Lord and Lady Marsden," Knightly said, sipping his coffee. Once he decided something, he acted. And he had decided to accept Marsden's offer. Thus, he would court Lady Marsden.

"Still angling to marry into the ton? I really don't know why," his mother said dismissively. It was an argument they'd had often over the years, ever since October 4, 1808, when he'd been forcibly ejected from his father's funeral. *Throw the bastard out. He doesn't belong here.*

But he did belong. And he would prove it.

She carried on with her condemnation of the ton, as she tended to do: "The lot of them are stiff and stuffy old bores with naught to do but make up silly rules and gossip viciously when they are broken. Except for your dear departed father, of course."

His father, the Earl of Harrowby, an esteemed member of Parliament and the ton. Respected peer of the realm. Beloved father.

There was a moment where they both fell silent, both thinking the same thing. There was someone missing from this scene. Even after all these years, *decades*, there was still a vague sense of incompletion. Like all the i's hadn't been dotted and the t's hadn't been crossed.

Her lover. His father. The late Earl of Harrow.

They had been *almost* the picture perfect family. Knightly remembered a home filled with warmth and laughter. His parents would dance around the drawing room to songs his mother would sing.

And inevitably his father would return to his other

family. The proper family. The family that wanted no part of the bastard by-blow. The brother that shared his blood but wouldn't look him in the eye.

"I am not cultivating this connection for amusement. Merely for business," Knightly answered curtly. The business of claiming what he deserved. What he had spent every moment since the funeral pursuing. He would not lose everything now.

"Oh, business! It's always business with you, Derek," his mother said with a huff and a pout.

How could he explain that amusement and work were one and the same for him? That everything he had ever wanted involved acceptance from the one person who wasn't alive to give it to him, and the next best thing was his half brother and the society that had claimed the late earl as one of its own.

And then there was his newspaper, which Knightly protected as if it were his own newborn. He couldn't explain these things; the words always died in his throat, if he was even able to articulate them in his mind at all. Funny, that being a man of words, there were so many unavailable to him.

*Berkeley Square*

KNIGHTLY discovered that the Marsden residence possessed many of the traits typical to an old ancestral home: it was drafty and vast with many wood paneled rooms and the air of being gently worn after a century of use. Marsden had invited Knightly to call upon him when Knightly sent a note indicating interest in discussing ways in which they might collaborate on the Inquiry, as it had become known.

From ballrooms to the coffeehouses it was fervently discussed in hushed whispers. What had the reporter uncovered? The rumors ranged from the benign to the horrific. What was to become of the newspapers?

Livelihoods were at stake. Knowledge, power, and wealth, too.

For Knightly, it was a simple matter of having everything he ever wanted: the success of *The Weekly* in addition to the aristocratic marriage that would assure him a prominent place in the high society that had rejected him.

Or risk it all . . . for what? There were too many livelihoods on the line, from his writers to the unfortunate boys selling newspapers on street corners. The more he thought about it—and sipped excellent brandy and enjoyed Marsden's conversation—the more saying no became unthinkable.

"Ah, Lydia, there you are," Marsden said as his younger sister appeared in the doorway a short while after her brother had sent a maid to fetch her.

She was beautiful not because of her features or her figure—both of which were admirable—but because Lady Lydia moved with a perfect grace. Where others might walk, she would glide. Her every movement, whether the incline of her head for a nod or the gentle waver of her fan in a heated ballroom, was a demonstration of perfect elegance. Her hair was dark and sleekly curled. Her eyes were dark and expressive. Her attire—from her sage green silk day gown to the ruby ear bobs—announced her status as A Person of Consequence.

She would look perfect on his arm. Save for the petulant pout. She was not pleased to have his company.

"We were just talking about the scandal at *The Times*," Marsden said.

"That's no surprise," she remarked dryly. The gentlemen stood as she strolled leisurely across the carpet. She was in no hurry to make his acquaintance. Knightly kept his emotions in check and reminded himself of the facts: she was the subject of gossip, and he was an infamous and influential newspaperman. Also, she was the sister to a marquis and he was a bastard. Literally.

"I'd like to introduce you to Mr. Knightly, of *The London Weekly*," Marsden said. "He's a new friend of mine."

"I recall that you've been singing his praises. Good afternoon, Mr. Knightly." She offered her hand languidly. The action was polite, and yet there was a stunning lack of interest motivating her. Knightly was intrigued.

"Pleased to meet you, Lady Marsden."

"Are you here for a story? Will we read about this in the gossip columns?" she inquired in the voice of a polite hostess, and yet there was an icy undercurrent not to be missed.

"Lydia—" Marsden said in a tone of lethal warning.

"It's a fair question, given the newspaper's *interest* in us," she said, gracefully lowering herself to sit upon the settee.

"I am pleased to let you know Knightly is on our side," Marsden said, with a glance at Knightly, who nodded to confirm that their understanding was in effect. Knightly would marry Lady Lydia, and Marsden's Inquiry wouldn't look too closely at the daring, questionable practices of *The London Weekly*.

"Really," she said, her voice dripping with disbelief. She stared hard at her brother.

"Really," Marsden said firmly, returning her stare.

Knightly sipped his drink and wondered if this was a typical sibling rivalry or if something else was afoot. He wouldn't know . . .

"The weather is very fine today. Would you care to walk with me, Lady Marsden?" Knightly offered, thinking he'd have better luck with her if he was not in the middle of some sibling battle. Also, should the New Earl happen upon the sight of him with Lady Lydia, the earl would be rankled and he would be pleased. Sibling rivalry was in full effect even if they'd never met.

"What a capital idea," Marsden said, clapping his hands. "It'll afford you both the opportunity to become better acquainted, and to perhaps see if you'll suit."

# Chapter 10

## An "Accidental" Encounter

Town Talk

TOWN TALK

*We hear that a certain marquis with a scandalous sister has been rather short on funds of late. We wonder: how does one lose a centuries-old fortune in under a year?*

The Morning Post

**I**N order to attempt the advice offered by Sneaky from Southwark, Annabelle enlisted the assistance of her own devious, meddlesome, and well-connected friends.

The tip: orchestrate an "accidental" encounter.

The trick: discovering when and where one might accidentally encounter Knightly. As far as anyone knew, he traveled from his home to *The Weekly* offices and back again—very early in the morning and very late at night.

However, thanks to Sophie and Julianna's machinations, the Writing Girls learned that he planned to visit Lord Marsden, probably to discuss the parliamentary inquiry into newspaper practices. The marquis conveniently lived near Sophie, between her house (which might more aptly be described as a castle, it was so massive) and Hyde Park.

The sun was shining. The birds were singing. Yes, they had snooped in Bryson's schedule for Knightly, but it was for the noble purpose of true love. Annabelle happily strolled along the neat streets of Mayfair with Sophie. Their pace was that of snails. The better to enjoy the atmosphere, of course.

"We have arrived at the park," Annabelle stated. Yet they had not encountered their quarry. This was not proceeding according to plan.

In her imagination, Annabelle would have seen Knightly as he strolled out the Marsdens' front door. They would laugh together at the marvel of meeting thusly. Then Knightly would suggest they take advantage of the fine day to stroll along the tree-lined paths of the park. They would stroll arm in arm, and at some point Sophie would discreetly vanish, leaving them alone. Perhaps a thunderous storm cloud would arise and they would seek shelter in an abandoned gazebo and he would gather her in his arms and say something devastatingly romantic, like—

"Come to think of it, I cannot believe I did not bring my parasol. I fear freckles," Sophie remarked, apropos of nothing.

"Since when do you care about freckles?" Annabelle asked, puzzled.

"I think we ought to return to the house for my parasol before we walk through the park," Sophie insisted. But Annabelle did not wish to spend a minute indoors, where they would certainly not see Knightly.

"You have your bonnet," Annabelle pointed out.

"I fear it may not be sufficient, and I'll be a social pariah if I get freckles," Sophie refuted.

"You're a duchess . . ." Not only that, she was extremely well regarded. She'd have to do a lot worse than freckles if society were to cut her.

"Oh, Annabelle," Sophie said with a giggle.

"Oh. That was just an excuse to walk past the Marsden home again, wasn't it? How silly of me. I'm just hopelessly distracted," Annabelle said as Sophie's intentions crystallized. She'd been so swept up in her imagined scene.

"Ah, young love," Sophie remarked lightly.

They continued their stroll. Annabelle began to marvel that what had seemed so simple on paper might be difficult to manage. At the very least, a stroll with her friend through the elegant cobblestone streets of Mayfair was vastly preferable to her usual afternoon activities of mending worn-out shirts, leading the children in their mathematics lessons, or writing her column solving everyone else's problems.

Sophie's exclamation jolted her from her thoughts.

"Mr. Knightly! What a coincidence!"

*It's really working!* It was Annabelle's first thought.

Then, second: *She is not supposed to be here.* Her brain registered a woman on Knightly's arm, and further cognitive function ground to a halt. Sneaky in Southwark hadn't mentioned that she might interrupt Mr. Knightly with another women. More to the point, a beautiful, graceful, elegant lady who made Annabelle feel like the most provincial spinster auntie, even in her fetching new day dress.

"May I present Lady Lydia Marsden," Knightly

said, and the perfect woman on his arm inclined
her head ever so slightly. "These are two of the infamous Writing Girls, The Duchess of Brandon and
Miss Annabelle Swift."

There was a flicker of recognition on Lady Lydia's
perfect features.

"My brother has been quite taken with you, Dear
Annabelle. Did you enjoy the roses he sent?" Lady
Lydia asked, much to Annabelle's surprise. She
glanced up at Knightly and saw him peering at her,
intrigued.

Her pulse quickened with a feeling that could
only be akin to triumph, for Knightly was now
curious to know that she was desirable, for other
gentlemen—marquises—had sent her roses.

She felt a surge of affection for Lady Lydia.

"Oh, they were absolutely beautiful," Annabelle
replied. "Although I am surprised your brother
finds my column of interest. He must have so many
greater concerns."

"He likes to know everything, however great or
small. Like a terrier with a rat, he is," Lady Lydia
said. "I myself don't bother much with the newspapers these days. I abhor the gossip columns."

Knightly grinned at Annabelle, and she smiled in
return, knowing the same thought had crossed their
minds: *Thank goodness Julianna isn't here!*

It was such a small thing, that knowing smile. But
she of the overlooked sighs and unrequited longing
was now sharing a private joke with Mr. Knightly
during an encounter of her own orchestration.

A heady rush of pleasure stole over Annabelle,
and it was as much Knightly's smile as it was the
sunshine warming her skin. Most of all it was that

she had made this moment occur. Fate had nothing on her.

"It's a lovely day for a walk, is it not?" Sophie said.

"Indeed," Lady Lydia replied. "We were just returning from a walk in Hyde Park."

Annabelle's hopes started to fade.

"There are matters at the office I must attend to after I see Lady Lydia home," Knightly added.

After politely wishing them a lovely afternoon, Sophie and Annabelle walked along in silence, until a safe distance had elapsed.

"Perhaps he is merely digging for gossip for Julianna," Sophie said. "She is like a hound at a foxhunt when it comes to that particular rumor of Lady Lydia's missing season."

"Ah yes, the missing second season. What are they saying?" Annabelle asked. Her pleasure in the exchange was starting to fade as she watched Knightly and Lady Lydia stroll off together.

"There are only three reasons a woman would miss her season," Sophie explained "A death in the family, which we know is not the case, or illness, or a baby."

"What does it matter?" Annabelle asked.

"It probably doesn't in the grand scheme of things. But everyone is desperate to know," Sophie said. "The ton does love their gossip."

"Do you think Knightly is courting her?" Annabelle asked, with a prayer the answer was no.

"It would appear to be so. Gentlemen generally do not escort marriageable misses for walks in the park if they are not considering something more," Sophie explained. She didn't need to add that it was doubly true for a man like Knightly, who did nothing that wouldn't ultimately benefit himself, his paper, or his empire.

"You do know what this means, Annabelle. It seems you have competition and must try a more ambitious scheme."

# Chapter 11

### Every Rogue Needs a Rival

FASHIONABLE INTELLIGENCE BY A LADY OF DISTINCTION
*With all of Dear Annabelle's delightful schemes, one
cannot help but wonder: How can the Nodcock be so
oblivious?*

The London Weekly

*Offices of* The London Weekly, *late*

**T**HIS was madness. This was dangerous. The suggestion of Careless in Camden Town had seemed clever and simple when it was just the few lines of a letter. Leave something behind. Return for it later. Find herself alone with Knightly. Allow romance to ensue.

Simple, no?

It had seemed imperative to Annabelle that she try something more daring after learning she had competition: Lady Lydia Marsden. It wasn't just the walk in the park. Julianna had learned that Lord Marsden was encouraging the courtship. They would have more walks in the park until they walked down the aisle.

Unless she managed to win his heart . . .

At the moment, however, Annabelle was having second thoughts about her quest, and in particular, this latest scheme. But it was too late to turn back, for she had already arrived at the offices of *The Weekly* after hours.

At the end of this week's staff meeting, Annabelle had left behind her shawl. Her nicest shawl, to add credence for her subsequent return for it. For the expedition, she wore her newly purchased day dress cut in a style that flattered her figure and in a shade of pale blue that enhanced her eyes. At the very least, she looked her best for this poorly planned adventure.

At home, Blanche would be wondering where she'd gotten off to—after realizing that the children hadn't had their lessons and fires hadn't been lit.

How was she to explain herself? She hadn't thought every aspect of this mad scheme all the way through because if she had, Old Annabelle would have concocted a million things that could go wrong and a million other reasons why she ought to stay home, safe.

New Annabelle prevailed.

And if anyone asked why she didn't wait until next week's writers' gathering, she had no good answer other than that dusk was much more romantic than daylight, and romance was more likely to occur in solitude rather than with the editorial staff of *The London Weekly* looking on.

Plus, she had a column due. She needed something to write about.

Thus, Annabelle slipped into the offices at the end of the day.

Knightly was still here, thank goodness, but he

wasn't alone. She lingered in the shadows outside of his office, waffling over her course of action but ultimately settling upon eavesdropping. Julianna would have her head if she didn't.

"What have you found out?" Knightly asked. She recognized the impatient tone of his voice. As if the earth didn't spin fast enough for him.

"Brinsley had kept up the ruse of doctor for months and ventured into many a proper woman's bedchamber," another man said.

Annabelle recognized the voice as belonging to Damien Owens. If Knightly had an heir to his empire, it would be Owens—young, brash, ruthless, and quite the charmer.

They could only be talking about the scandal with *The London Times*. Brinsley must be the reporter who had been arrested and now languished in Newgate.

"Bloody hell," Knightly swore. "What he must know . . ."

"My thoughts exactly," Owens agreed.

Annabelle dared to peek around the corner, glancing into Knightly's office, for the door remained ajar. She saw him pacing, hands clasped behind his back and brow furrowed in thought.

She bit back a sigh.

There was an intensity, depth, and energy about him that awed her and captivated her attentions. She noted the lock of hair that fell rakishly into his eyes, which he ruthlessly shoved back. How she wanted to run her own fingers through his hair . . .

His mouth was pressed into a hard line; she thought only of softening it by pressing her own lips to his.

"I want to talk to Brinsley," Knightly said briskly. "Our best angle is to portray it as a crime of one rogue reporter, not endemic of the entire newspaper industry," he added confidently.

"Understood, sir," Damien said.

She, too, understood that numerous articles would soon appear suggesting exactly that, then rumors to that effect would circulate. It was only a matter of time before Londoners believed it as the gospel—and marveled how *The London Weekly* was always so in tune with the heart of the city.

The conversation ended and Owens stepped out of the office, bumping right into Annabelle.

"Oof," she said. Again. For goodness sakes.

"Miss Swift! What are you doing here?" Owens asked, looking at her curiously.

"My shawl," she said. She became aware of Knightly glancing at them through the open door. "I had forgotten it here. It's my best one."

"You probably left it in the writers' room. I'll go look with you," Owens offered. Then he linked his arm with hers and led her along.

"What are you—" Annabelle started to ask in a hushed whisper, but Owens cut her off.

"Lovely weather today," he remarked. What did that have to do with anything? And didn't the man realize he ought to make his exit, leaving her alone with Knightly?

Owens followed her into the writer's room and then he *closed the door*, effectively shutting them alone, together.

"What are you doing?" she hissed, reaching for the doorknob.

Owens blocked her access by stepping in front of the doorway. For the first time, she noticed that he was quite tall, and his shoulders were rather broad.

His torso was flat and underneath his jacket he was probably well muscled from all of his dangerous exploits.

Her eyes locked with his. Dark brown. Long lashes. She had never noticed.

Annabelle's mind reeled. This was not what she had planned. What on earth was occurring?

"Is this one of your schemes?" Owens asked, a slight grin playing on his lips. There was no escaping and avoiding the question.

He leaned against the door. Lord save her from men who leaned.

"Whatever do you mean?" she asked. She didn't want to answer the question. She didn't quite know what was happening.

"Oh, come off it, Miss Swift. We're not all as dense as he is," Owens replied.

"So what if it is?" she asked, a bit miffed. "If so, you are standing in the way of my . . . story. My work. For the paper."

*Of true love,* she wanted to add. Instead, for emphasis, she uttered a certain three words for the first time in her life. "How dare you."

Owens laughed. "It's a good trick, Annabelle, leaving something behind. Classic. But how are you going to write about this without him discovering everything? He isn't stupid."

That was a good question. One she didn't have an answer for. Especially since Owens was right: she couldn't write about this without giving herself away. Again she realized that she hadn't thought this through. She blamed deadlines for her hasty actions. And the sad fact that if she thought about something too much, then she'd never do it.

"I'll come up with something," she replied. The room felt small all of a sudden. And warm. Owens peered down at her with dark, velvety brown eyes.

His response was unexpected.

"You're welcome," he said bluntly.

"I beg your pardon?" she asked, aghast. He was ruining her plans with every moment that he stood blocking the door with his tall and strong self and every second that he kept them mysteriously ensconced in this room. Together. Alone.

"Look, Annabelle, here is some free advice. Men thrive on rivalry. On the chase. On the challenge. And for the sake of your column, you need to raise some suspicions in his mind. If he's certain that he's the Nodcock, then it's too easy. But if it might be me," Owens let his voice trail off as the suggestion sank in.

Annabelle paused, allowing the words to sink in.

Making Knightly doubt would give her the liberty to write freely, without fear of betraying herself. It would make for better copy, which would make for better sales. And if there was one thing that caught Knightly's eye like nothing else, it was stellar sales.

People had written her letters suggesting that she encourage a rival and competition, but she'd dismissed it as impossible, for who would play such a part with her?

Owens, that's who. Owens who, she was now noticing, was a rather handsome young man.

"I see your point," she conceded. "But why would you do this to help me?"

"Because the sooner he gets married and starts having a life outside of this office, the sooner I get a promotion," Owens explained, as if it should have been obvious. "He's not the only one with ambitions around here."

"How does this work?" she asked.

"It's already working. Because now you can write about this and he'll wonder if you're after me or him. It'll make you interesting."

"Are you saying I'm dull?" she asked, aghast. Again.

"Not anymore, Annabelle," Owens said, grinning. "Not anymore."

"I'm not quite sure how to take that," she muttered, brow furrowing.

"I'm being helpful, Annabelle. And really, do something else with your hair," he said.

"Whatever do you mean?" she asked, aghast. Again. But her hands reached up to that tight bun held fast by a ribbon and pins.

"Allow me," Owens said softly, and reached out to expertly remove a hairpin or two, thus freeing a few wavy strands that fell softly around her cheeks. She watched him watching her. His gaze was warm and she saw something like wonder in his expression.

"Much better," he murmured. Her lips parted but no sound emerged. Something was happening—something far more than the removal of a few hairpins. Annabelle, always one to shy away from things, took a step back.

And promptly tripped over a chair.

She started to fall, but Owens moved quickly to catch her in his arms.

At that moment Knightly happened to open the door, discovering her in the arms of another man with her hair tussled and her lips parted. She knew it could only mean one thing to him: that she and Owens were up to something wicked.

"Is something amiss?" Knightly inquired.

"I forgot my shawl," Annabelle blurted out, which didn't explain anything, really.

Owens helped her to her feet and stood by her side. "I was assisting Miss Swift," he said smoothly.

It wasn't exactly a lie. Owens deviously let those words hang in the air, allowing Knightly to make assumptions. Annabelle watched Knightly process the scene with narrowed eyes and clenched jaw. Was Owens right? Was a rival just what she needed?

"I was just leaving to see about that thing we discussed," Owens said, affectionately touching Annabelle on the elbow before quitting the room, leaving her alone with Knightly.

Knightly leaned against the doorjamb. She bit back a sigh. She did so love it when he leaned.

"That must be quite the shawl," Knightly remarked.

"It's my best one," she replied, wrapping the blue cashmere around her even though she wasn't cold in the slightest. Quite the contrary, in fact.

"Is there a particular event you require it for?" he asked politely. Too politely. As if he suspected that she was up to her neck in some sort of scheme. She told herself she was oversensitive.

"Church on Sunday, of course," she said. But then she didn't stop there, as she ought to have done. Nerves got the better of her. Rambling Annabelle took over: "Which will come before our next weekly staff meeting, and I didn't dare risk forgetting to come another time. I must have my best shawl for church as it's the only one that matches my best dress and of course I have to wear my best dress to church. Do you attend church?"

"No," Knightly said flatly. "Not unless you count this."

By "this" she presumed he meant *The London Weekly*.

"Oh," Annabelle replied. She did not know if that counted. Didn't know how quite to reply, really. She loosened the shawl, for she was now quite hot. They really ought to open a window.

Knightly smiled at her in a way that made her heart race. Like he had a secret. Like they had a private joke. Like he knew she was up to something.

"I'm glad that you have your shawl," he said. "Given that it's June."

"Oh, you know the weather in England . . . so very fickle," Annabelle managed to reply.

"A second best shawl just wouldn't do," Knightly persisted, wickedly having fun at her expense, she was sure of it. This was not how this was supposed to go. And yet she was alone, with Knightly, when otherwise she would be sitting at home while her brother read the newspapers and Blanche read improving literature aloud to the family. Such was the unexciting life of Old Annabelle.

This was wicked good fun, and New Annabelle would enjoy it and play along.

"What makes you think I have a second best shawl?" She tried to sound perfectly natural, and thought she did an all right job of it.

"Your family owns a cloth importing business. If there is one thing you are lacking in, I would not put my money on it being shawls," Knightly replied as her mouth parted slightly in shock.

Some days she had wondered if he even knew her name, and yet he was aware of her family's business? Her jaw might have dropped open.

"How did you know that?"

"Miss Swift, it is my business to know," Knightly replied. Then, pushing off the doorjamb, he stood tall and said, "Come, let's take you home."

"Oh I couldn't impossibly intrude." The words—stupid words refusing such a coveted invitation—were off her tongue before she could stop them because she knew her home was impossibly out of the way.

That's what happened when one made a habit of being deferential and always thinking of others first. It became an automatic behavior that, in spite of her every effort, she still occasionally defaulted to.

"I couldn't call myself a gentleman and allow you to go off into the London night. Alone," Knightly said. She had come alone, for Spinster Aunties such as herself didn't have chaperones, they were chaperones.

"Well if you insist," Annabelle replied, quite possibly sounding coy for the first time in her life.

# Chapter 12

### Carriage Rides Ought to Be Chaperoned

**DEAR ANNABELLE**

*Some gentlemen are N.S.I.C. (Not Safe in Carriages). I*
*hope your nodcock is one them.*
*Frisky on Farringdon Road*
The London Weekly

**K**NIGHTLY couldn't say *why*, but the prospect of
this journey with Miss Swift intrigued him. Possibly because she was the last female in the world he
expected to find himself alone with, like this. Shy,
quiet, pretty, unassuming Annabelle. Seated nervously across from him in the dim, velvet interior
of his carriage.

She was a woman whom he'd barely given any
thought to for four years, and now she constantly
intruded upon his thoughts and conversations. Everyone, it seemed, was talking about Annabelle.

She was also a woman who by all accounts had
no romantic entanglements until just this week,
when he could link her to two unlikely prospects.

Lord Marsden, a bloody marquis and a notoriously charming one, sending her roses.

And then there was *something* between her and

Damien Owens. How else to explain her tussled hair, pink cheeks, and the fact that she was in his arms?

More irritating was why the thought of them together bothered him. So much so that he'd left his desk to investigate their lengthy silence behind a closed door. And when he opened it? The sight before him sent a surge of jealously, and a desire to plant a facer on Owens.

And now here he was, alone, with Annabelle.

"Where to, Miss Swift?" he asked once they were settled into his carriage. It was a very fine carriage, if he did say so himself: the newest design, comfortable forest green velvet seats, black lacquer detailing. He did enjoy the trappings of success: a stately home, the finest tailoring, and the best of anything money could buy.

"One hundred fifty Montague Street, Bloomsbury," she answered. "Or did you already know that?"

"I already knew. But it seemed prudent to confirm your destination in the event you planned to go elsewhere," Knightly said. *Like Lord Marsden's residence. Or Owens's flat.* The thought caused a knot to form in his gut.

"That is very considerate of you," she replied, and then paused, obviously debating whether to say what was on her mind. In the habit of snap decisions himself, it was intriguing to watch this internal debate.

"What else do you know about me?" Annabelle decided to ask. He watched her straighten her spine as she did, as if it required such determination to do so.

"You are six and twenty years of age," he answered.

"It's not polite to mention that," she replied, inadvertently confirming it.

"You live with your brother, the cloth merchant, and his wife. You have doled out advice to the curious, lovelorn, and unfortunate for about three years," Knightly told her.

It was an easy matter to accumulate basic facts about people, which often proved useful to have in hand.

Some other newly discovered facts would go unmentioned: Annabelle looked angelic with her tussled golden curls free of the knot she usually kept her hair in. And yet her mouth—all plump and red—hinted of sin. When she smiled, there was a slight dimple in her left cheek. She was prone to blushes and sighs, and he thought it fascinating that one should be able to feel so passionately and to show it.

He never could. But that was a woman for you. Most of them never had a thought or feeling they didn't share.

"I'm curious what you know of me," he said, turning the tables on her. She smiled, and thought for a moment, as if debating where to begin.

"I know that you are five and thirty years of age, that your mother is an actress, you have a town house in Mayfair, and your handwriting is an impossible scrawl," she replied pertly.

"And that my chest is firm," Knightly couldn't resist adding.

Annabelle only groaned in response. He couldn't quite see in the dim light of the carriage, but he would wager that a blush was creeping into her cheeks.

"You embarrass easily," he said, adding to his list of Facts About Annabelle.

"Did you know that already or are you only just discovering it?" she asked with a laugh.

"I'm learning," he said. He knew less about her than the other Writing Girls mainly because the others were in the habit of barging into his office, giving him a piece of their mind, and generally raising hell and causing trouble.

In fact, this might have been the longest conversation he and Annabelle had to date. Funny, that.

"I also know that your column has been the talk of the town," he added. Besides Drummond, Gage, and his mother, everyone seemed to be talking about Dear Annabelle's quest to win the Nodcock. (Owens? Or Marsden?) In every meeting he took, be it with a writer or fellow businessmen, they were discussing the matter. He'd even overheard his valet and butler in a heated discussion over just how low a woman's bodice should go.

"What do you think of my column lately?" she asked.

"It has been immensely popular," Knightly said. "You even have the blokes in the coffeehouses devoted to it. You should keep up the ruse as long as possible, because readers love it." Annabelle's Adventures in Love made for a great story. Great stories equaled great sales.

Also, the continuation of the ruse meant delayed satisfaction for Owens. Or was it Marsden? One of the two was surely the infamous Nodcock.

"I see," she said softly, and idly stroked the velvet

of the carriage seat. She looked out the window for a moment. It was as if a cloud passed over, for she suddenly was just a bit less vivacious. It was as if he'd said the wrong thing, which was confusing, as he had intended a compliment.

"The mail clerks have been complaining to me about the volume of letters you are receiving," he said, hoping that a mention of her popularity would bring back some brightness.

"They always complain about that," Annabelle said with a smile. "People do love to send their problems to me."

"You must have a knack for solving them. And giving good advice," he said idly. Her shawl had slipped off her shoulders, exposing her first trick in attracting that nodcock. Knightly was suddenly aware that he desired her, and that they were alone.

"I must have? Do you not *know*?" she asked, peering up at him with those big blue eyes of hers. He'd lost track of the conversation, distracted as he'd been by the swells of her breasts and a dawning awareness of his desire for Annabelle.

"I don't know how your readers fare after your suggestions. Or what constitutes good advice, which is why you won't see me penning your column. I have three truths I live by, that is all." And really, did a man need more? No.

"Scandal equals sales," Annabelle said, predictably sounding bored, as all the writers did when reciting that particular phrase. Yet it worked like a charm. They shared a grin over the shared knowledge.

"What is the next one?" she asked.

"Drama is for the page," he told her. Even though

he never actually said these truths aloud and he especially didn't talk about them. But with Dear Annabelle it felt safe to do so.

"Funny, given that your mother is an actress," Annabelle remarked.

"Or precisely because my mother is an actress," he countered.

"More drama *off* the page would be greatly welcomed by me," Annabelle said wistfully. "Of course, it must be different for men. There is very little adventure and excitement available to us unmarried females."

"Doesn't this count?" he asked. It was just a carriage ride. But there was nothing to stop him from tugging her into his lap and ravishing her completely. Nothing, that is, save for his self-restraint, which seemed to be eroding with every moment.

*It was just Annabelle,* or so he tried to tell himself. But it wasn't. He was discovering, slowly but surely, that Annabelle possessed a mouth he wished to taste, pale skin he wanted to touch, and breasts that—oh God, the wicked thoughts she inspired. How had he not noticed her all these years?

In his defense, she hadn't been wearing these revealing dresses until lately. She pulled the shawl up closer around her shoulders. Her best shawl, she had said. Or a ruse to meet privately with Owens?

"Oh, yes, this might count as an adventure," she replied with a smile that might actually be described as wicked. "Fortunately for you, I am not a Person of Consequence. Nor will my relatives ask you to declare your intentions."

"Why is that?" Knightly asked, because that was a deuced unusual attitude for relatives of unmarried females. Usually they were keen to foist off their sisters and daughters as early and as soon as possible. Look at Marsden, for instance.

"That would mean losing their free household help," Annabelle said. She forced a laughed that stabbed at his heart. She tried to be light about it but came just short of succeeding. "Blanche has actually done the math . . ."

Knightly assumed Blanche was her brother's wife, and that she must be horrid. The impulse to rescue Annabelle from this wretched situation stole over him; he chalked it up to some notion of ingrained gentlemanly behavior. Or too many hours at the theater.

*Drama is for the page. Repeat. Drama is for the page.*

"No wonder you crave adventure," he said, steering the conversation away from the apparently awful Swift household.

While the words still hung in the air a huge thud and a jolt rocked the carriage, sending Annabelle flying into his lap and bringing the vehicle to a halt. A loud commotion ensued just outside of the carriage. They must have collided with another vehicle.

He ought to go see what happened.

Knightly remained inside and discovered new things about Annabelle. She was warm. He knew this because he was suddenly, incredibly overheated. And she was luscious. He'd instinctively wrapped his arms around her to keep her steady. He felt the curve of her hips, the curve of her bottom, the curve of her breasts.

Fact: Annabelle was a tempting armful of woman. It wasn't just her mouth that tempted a man to sin. The rest of her, too.

Tempting as sin, that Angelic Annabelle.

How had he not discovered this about her before?

For one thing, he hadn't held her in his arms before. He certainly hadn't done so for longer than was necessary or proper.

Knightly also discovered that his body very much liked Annabelle on his lap. In fact, certain portions of his anatomy strained to display its fondness. It was positively indecent how much he liked it.

"I should go see what happened," he said, though it was another moment before either made an attempt to move.

As they disentangled themselves, he might have accidentally been less than concerned about the proper placement of his hands and might have unintentionally brushed his hand against certain round portions of her person.

He was a man, after all.

But it was wrong. She worked for him. Worked . . . for . . . him.

To play there would be to take unfair advantage. And it would be just a dalliance, given his impending betrothal to Lady Marsden. All of which would inevitably lead to hurt feelings, awkwardness, issues of pride, etc., etc., and the loss of one of his writers who was currently writing an increasingly popular column.

Annabelle was Off Limits.

As Knightly stepped out into the crisp evening air, his first thought had nothing to do with the melee before him. His first thought was: *Good thing Annabelle has her shawl.*

And then he focused on the situation at hand.

A collision had occurred between two carriages. One of them, unfortunately, belonged to him. The cattle were fine, thank God. No one was injured, save for some minor damage to his conveyance. The occupants of the offending vehicle were hollering and blustering and it took some time before Knightly's cool demeanor calmed them down, sorted out the mess, and sent everyone on their way.

Meanwhile, he was aware of Annabelle watching from the carriage windows. Which is why he did not take a swing at the man who accused his driver of ineptitude and hurled curses at everyone in vicinity. It was the reason why Knightly was in such a hurry to have the matter resolved. Not that he would have ever been inclined for a drawn-out scene, but knowing Annabelle waited in the dim confines of his carriage lent an urgency to the situation.

"There will be an article advocating traffic laws, will there not?" she asked when he finally rejoined her.

"Absolutely," he said with a grin. "And one lamenting other people's deplorable driving skills."

"It must be quite fun having your own newspaper to tell the world just what you think," she mused. "It must be wonderful to have so many people read it and agree with you. Is that why you work so much, Mr. Knightly?"

"I love the work. I love the success and what comes with it," Knightly replied frankly. He loved the challenge, and the chase, and the pride that came from his success. And all of the wealth and influence he had accumulated would soon deliver his ultimate goal.

*Throw the bastard out. He doesn't belong here.*

Oh, but he did. And they would soon have to accept him as one of their own.

"I can imagine. This is a very nice carriage," Annabelle remarked, sliding her hands along the plush velvet seat.

"It was a lot nicer an hour ago," he said, and Annabelle laughed.

Knightly added *Annabelle has a lovely laugh* to the list of things he knew about her.

"We are nearly there," she said, after a glance out the window. "Thank you very much for seeing me home. I hope I didn't keep you from anything important."

"Can't let my star columnist go gallivanting off in the night unescorted," Knightly said with a grin.

"Because this carriage ride with you wasn't dangerous or improper at all," she replied, smiling.

It wasn't. Nothing untoward had occurred . . . and yet now that he had this new knowledge of Annabelle, it felt dangerous for some reason.

When the carriage rolled to a stop before a neat little town house, the thought of taking Annabelle in his arms and tasting that sinful mouth of hers crossed his mind. He noted that she was thinking about it, too. How else to explain the nervousness in her pretty blue eyes? Or the flush across her cheeks? Or the way she nibbled at her plump lower lip.

*Why not kiss her?* The devil on his shoulder wanted to know.

*Why not, indeed,* logic countered, withering.

Because she worked for him. Had he not declared her Off Limits just a quarter hour ago? Clearly, he needed to remind himself why she was Off Limits.

Because she had her heart set on either Owens or Marsden. Because she had to keep up her quest to win one of those blockheads. Her column was the talk of the town, and if everyone was discussing Annabelle's adventures in love, they were not sparing a thought for the looming, sordid scandal brewing thanks to that damned inquiry. He'd like to keep it that way.

Because he would be courting and marrying Lady Lydia, because her hand in marriage would deliver him everything he'd always wanted: acceptance from the haute ton and protection for his newspapers. For his writers.

Because Annabelle was a sweet, innocent woman. And he was a ruthless, cold man who cared for nothing but his business and social climbing, as uncouth as that sounded. He didn't want to break the heart of a girl like her.

"You should go," he said. His voice was more hoarse than he would have liked.

# Chapter 13

## A Writing Girl's Lamentable Household

FASHIONABLE INTELLIGENCE BY A LADY OF DISTINCTION

*'Tis a small crowd in London that does not read* The
London Weekly. *What curious creatures.*

> The London Weekly

*The Swift Household*

**B**LANCHE descended upon Annabelle the moment she stepped into the drawing room. Blanche's bosom friend Mrs. Underwood, who Annabelle suspected might be a witch, hovered just behind Blanche. Privately, Annabelle thought they were both ghastly, though she felt pained to do so because she always made an effort to find the good in each person.

"How kind of you to grace us with your presence, Annabelle," Blanche remarked snidely. From the first, the woman had taken a dislike to her, and no amount of sweetness or helpfulness or anything else could dissuade her. Thomas had defended Annabelle once, when he declared his new wife would not cast out his thirteen-year-old sibling. Ever since, Annabelle had been left to manage her wicked sister-in-law on her own. For years Annabelle had tried to make Blanche happy with her choice to keep her on. Lately, she only tried to be at peace with her situation.

Blanche turned to her husband, who took refuge behind a newspaper. "Thomas, ask your sister where she has been this whole day.'"

"Where have you been, Annabelle?" Dear brother Thomas did not even lower his newspaper. It was *The Daily Financial Register*, and a duller publication Annabelle had never read. She didn't blame him for hiding behind it, given the company.

"I have spent the afternoon busy with charity work," Annabelle said, relying on her usual excuse. "And visiting some friends," she added, in the event that they saw Knightly's carriage and inquired about it.

Her family did not know about "Dear Annabelle." Her family did not read *The London Weekly* and must have been the only people in London not to do so. This suited Annabelle just fine.

Her family labored under the impression that she dedicated her time to a vast array of charitable works and committees, which explained her Wednesday outings and friendship with the other Writing Girls (who she might have declined to mention happened to be duchesses and a countess).

*The London Weekly* and the Writing Girls were her secret life. They were the only things that belong to her, and her alone. Well, other than those wicked silky unmentionables (she'd ordered more) and two fine dresses.

"I personally believe that charity starts at home," Blanche said stiffly. "Which reminds me, Cook may have set something aside for you. Or perhaps she was too vexed not to have your assistance in the kitchen this evening. You may go see for yourself."

"You're too kind, Blanche," Mrs. Underwood praised, and the two old birds clucked over their generosity. Annabelle was in too fine a mood to scowl or snort or otherwise express her disbelief.

Eat? She lived on love alone. Finally she had more than crumbs to sustain her. She sent up a silent prayer of thanks to Careless in Camden Town for such a brilliant suggestion. It was all she could do not to waltz across the foyer or burst into song.

What an adventure she'd had this afternoon!

"What, pray tell, is so amusing, Annabelle?" Blanche inquired.

For a second Annabelle considered telling her the truth. But why, when Blanche would not believe it? No, this would be her secret pleasure.

"There must be a man in the picture," Mrs. Underwood said.

"Hmm," Thomas murmured from behind his newspaper.

"That explains the prolonged absences. The flowers. The dresses like a dockside harpy." Blanche ticked these items off on her short fingers, much like the way she added up the accounts for the cloth business.

"Today I met with the Society for the Advancement of Female Literacy," Annabelle replied, which was her code for *The Weekly* staff meetings. Blanche, as the businesswoman behind the man, could not disagree with it.

"But you do not deny that there is a man in the picture," Mrs. Underwood said gleefully, as if this were a trial and she'd inadvertently made Annabelle confess to some heinous crime punishable by years of hard labor.

"Well let me inform you now that should you find yourself in a state of disgrace," Blanche lectured, "you won't darken this door with your presence. I shan't abide such an example in front of my children."

Watson, Mason, and Fleur, ages nine, seven, and five. They were miniature replicas of their parents and thus no friends of Annabelle's, no matter that she'd functioned as their nanny and governess for their whole lives.

"Do you not agree, Thomas? We cannot have your sister setting a poor example for our children," Blanche said loudly, as if he were deaf or as if newsprint effectively blocked sound.

"Yes, dear," he replied.

Old Annabelle would have blinked back tears to have her brother, her own flesh and blood, agree so blindly to his wife's cruelty. New Annabelle, however, knew that he likely hadn't been listening to the conversation and had no idea what he'd just agreed to.

New Annabelle was also overwhelmed by the urge to waltz around her bedroom and revel in raptures of delight.

Because some people—like Owens and Careless in Camden Town, and even A Courtesan in Mayfair—cared to help her. She'd been lonely until she worked up the courage (or desperation) to ask for help and discovered that people were more than willing to oblige.

Because this scheme had been the greatest risk of her life so far, and it was proving to be a success.

Because she had a carriage ride with Knightly. Alone. At dusk. It was the stuff Old Annabelle dreamed about late at night. New Annabelle lived it.

Because she had managed an entire conversation with Knightly, instead of her usual tendency to ramble or lose the ability to construct sentences— and even after tumbling awkwardly into his lap. (Although she had ceased to think, only to feel a million exquisite new sensations when that had happened.)

Because she had an adventure with Knightly.

Because Knightly had been about to kiss her, she just knew it.

Because New Annabelle was wicked good fun.

# Chapter 14

## A Lady's Lesson in Flirting

**PARLIAMENTARY INTELLIGENCE**
*London newspapers, beware! Lord Marsden's Inquiry
is gathering information and testimonies, all because
of the nefarious actions of* The London Times*'s rogue
reporter, Jack Brinsley, who is festering in Newgate,
awaiting trial.*

*The London Weekly*

*Offices of* The London Weekly

**W**EDNESDAYS had long been Annabelle's favorite day of the week. But this one made her smile a little more broadly, made her heart beat a little more quickly. The sky seemed bluer, the birdsong more pleasing. She herself was becoming a little more . . . alive or awake or in bloom or something lovely like that.

Knightly was no longer a remote figure with whom she'd never really conversed. She now knew the firmness of his chest (if only for one, exquisite and accidental instance) and what it felt like to have his arms around her (if only for one exquisite, accidental tumble in a carriage accident). She knew the truths he lived by, although it had occurred to her after their carriage ride that he'd only mentioned two of the three. She resolved to discover the third.

Yet it was Owens, not Knightly, who immediately sought her out upon her early arrival. She liked to allow for the possibility of drama or adventure to occur.

"Good afternoon, Miss Swift." Somehow Owens had managed to make it sound like he was saying something else entirely. Something very naughty. He affectionately touched her arm. It was lovely, that.

"Good afternoon, Mr. Owens," Annabelle said sweetly.

Heads turned in their direction. The other Writing Girls came up the stairs and looked at her very curiously as they passed by. Something about her company and her and Mr. Owens's pose must have told them not to interrupt.

Owens paid them no mind and leaned against the wall next to her, just outside of Knightly's office. Then a slow, lazy smile dawned upon his mouth and he took a slow, lazy, absolutely rakish look at her person. Her lips parted, slightly aghast. Her heartbeat quickened with the pressure to perform.

Owens was acting rakishly with her. Owens, who had said she'd never be wicked, was now looking at her as if she'd been very wicked *with* him. It was appalling. It was also part of the ruse and the sort of high jinks New Annabelle engaged in.

"I trust you are enjoying this fine weather, Miss Swift. With such warm temperatures, you needn't worry about leaving your shawl behind," Owens said with a knowing nod and wink of his velvety brown eyes. What unfairly long lashes the man possessed.

"It was so kind of you to help me . . . find my shawl," Annabelle replied. "I could never have done it without you." She hoped that sounded appropriately *something*.

"I live to serve—especially a beautiful girl like you, Miss Swift." Owens smiled at her again. She smiled back.

"I thought we were talking about the weather? And my shawl?" she asked in a whisper. Owens leaned in close to whisper directly in her ear.

"We are flirting," he explained.

"Oh," she gasped. She was so silly, needing to have a man explain flirting to her. And Owens of all the men in the world, too. She couldn't help it, she giggled.

"Don't giggle. Nothing terrifies men more," Owens said, fear creeping into his expression. "Men thrive on competition. And you need a rival, remember?"

"Oh, I remember," she said, and it even sounded a bit naughty.

"That's my girl. Now after you, Miss Swift." As they walked off toward the meeting, Owens placed his palm lightly, fleetingly, on the small of her back. She just happened to glance over her shoulder in the direction of Knightly's office. Just happened to see him looking her way with a dark expression.

"Dear Annabelle, do explain," Sophie said the second Annabelle took her seat. The other Writing Girls turned to give the full force of their attentions to her.

"Owens and I have an understanding," Annabelle said, and she didn't try to hush her voice. Across the room, she caught his eye and he flashed a grin and nodded in encouragement. He was rather boyishly handsome.

"What sort of understanding?" Julianna inquired.

"According to Owens, men thrive on rivalry. And that I ought to make Knightly wonder just whom I am writing about. Otherwise, how can I write freely about my exploits?"

"He does have a point," Eliza agreed. "I found it extraordinarily challenging to write about Wycliff without revealing my housemaid disguise."

"But do you not want Knightly to discover your feelings for him?" Sophie asked. It was a fair question.

"I want him to discover *me*. And fall in love with *me*. I don't wish for him to simply figure out whom I'm writing about because of a slip of the pen," Annabelle said. Then she added determinedly, "Besides, I am having more fun than I ever have and . . . *It's working.*"

It wasn't just that she was now on speaking terms with Knightly, but that she felt like a new person. One who was daring, adventurous, wore pretty dresses and wicked, silky undergarments. She liked New Annabelle.

The conversation then devolved into a flurry of whispers in which Annabelle related the lost shawl adventures. With their four heads bowed together, she almost didn't notice when Knightly arrived. Almost, for he was never far from her mind.

HE had caught them at it again—Miss Swift and *Owens*, of all the young, brash bucks in London. He saw them flirting. He saw Annabelle giggling. He did not miss the winks and smiles.

He couldn't say why it bothered him. Just that it did.

Next, he caught the Writing Girls with their heads bent together in some hushed conversation. Did they discuss his own innocent, gentlemanly carriage ride with Annabelle? But he couldn't very well let her go off into the London night alone, risking life and limb for her shawl.

He had done the right thing. The gentlemanly thing. He just hadn't felt remotely gentlemanly about it at the time, or since. The idea of ravishing Annabelle had begun to intrude on his thoughts with a stunning regularity.

"Ladies first," Knightly said as he strolled in. But instead of smiling, he scowled. What the devil did he care if Annabelle and Owens flirted and courted and married? He didn't care at all. They just should not engage in such behavior on work time.

But there they were, making eyes at each other across the room. Revolting.

"I have gossip," Julianna announced.

"I should hope so," he said dryly.

"It's about Lady Marsden's missing season," she said. Across the room, Grenville sighed. Knightly scowled at him, too, because he was intrigued by this, especially after making the acquaintance of the lady in question. During their walk, he'd learned that she despised newspapers, wished to leave London, and her favorite pastime was dancing.

They would be a horrible match. Nevertheless, he'd pursue her. For *The Weekly*. So he could quiet those damned words that haunted his every action: *Throw the bastard out. He doesn't belong here.*

"I have made inquiries, discreetly, of course," Julianna continued. "The official line is that she had been ill. But many are saying she had taken a lover—a scandalous one. It seems that her brother found a packet of love letters. He was livid. Positively outraged! He locked her in her room for a whole year."

"Who is her lover?" Sophie asked, a bit breathless in her eagerness to know.

"She still has not revealed his identity," Julianna replied dramatically.

"And yet she has been released from captivity," Eliza said, as dramatically.

"*If* he actually locked her in her bedchamber for a year," Knightly interjected. But this was dismissed by the group as not being as interesting.

"I suppose Lord Marsden gave up and decided the next best course of action was to marry her off," Julianna said. "Thus the whole matter would become another man's problem." She shrugged lightly. Clearly, she had not uncovered his discreet agreement with Marsden.

Another man's problem indeed. This shed new light on the matter, but did not change the fact that she was the sister to a powerful marquis, and ladies of such high standing were not exactly lining up to marry an illegitimate man who engaged in trade . . . fortune or not.

"Nothing like secret lovers, now is there?" Owens said from the other side of the room. And then he winked—*winked*—at Annabelle, who fluttered her lashes in his direction.

Sickening stuff. Truly. This was a place of business.

"One point to consider," Knightly said sharply, "is that Lord Marsden is leading the parliamentary inquiry into *The London Times* scandal. I would hate for him to have reason to turn his attentions to *The Weekly*."

"Oh, but the ton can speak of nothing else!" Julianna said passionately. "I have a feeling this scandal is going to explode."

"I don't care," he said. He especially wouldn't give a damn when his paper was shut down. Plus, Lady Lydia obviously held a particular loathing for newspapermen, and it would not help his suit if his own paper were printing salacious gossip about her.

"You would not believe the lengths I went to in order to obtain this information," Julianna argued. Knightly just shrugged.

"I'm quite sure that I don't want to know," he said. "When your husband finds out and comes storming in here in a rage, again, I would like to honestly say that I know nothing."

"Very well. Perhaps I shall just allude to it . . ." Lady Julianna pressed on, as she was wont to do.

"There should be no mention of the Marsdens in this paper," Knightly declared sharply. This elicited an audible gasp of shock from Julianna and an uncomfortable silence from the rest of the writers. He'd just violated one of the founding principles of the paper: *Everything and everyone was fodder.*

To hell with the lot of them, Knightly thought. But Annabelle's expression tugged hard at his heart. Some combination of dismay and betrayal was the only way he could describe the look in her big blue eyes. But he didn't want to know more. He'd made his decisions and now all that remained was following through.

Besides, she had Owens and his winks and smiles and all manner of romantic expressions and sickeningly sweet glances flying between them.

"Speaking of mystery lovers, Miss Swift, an update on your column this week, please," Knightly said dryly.

Bloody hell, had he just said *mystery lovers*? Bloody hell, he was getting soft. Except with Annabelle around, he wasn't soft at all. What the devil was happening?

"The letters keep pouring in, as you can see," she said, gesturing to another large stack before her. Letters full of inane suggestions from the likes of his friends Drummond and Gage. Letters full of dangerous suggestions like lowering her bodice to be positively distracting . . . and the devil only knew what else. He didn't want to know.

"I have seen in an increase in sales, not to mention all the talk about your column," he said. Annabelle was wearing another one of those low-cut bodices, and it took every ounce of his considerable willpower to lift his gaze a few inches higher. "Which means we have a good thing going, so draw this one out as long as you can."

Even if it killed him. Even if it slowly, excruciatingly tortured him. And then killed him. But he would endure, especially if it delayed and thwarted and slowed the budding romance between her and Owens, or perhaps Marsden, which he did not care about. Not at all.

No matter how many times he told himself that, however, the thought wouldn't stick.

"Yes, Mr. Knightly," Annabelle agreed softly.

He couldn't stop himself; he snuck one last glance at her bodice, and the generous swells of milky white skin rising just above the fabric. His mouth went dry. Where was her damn shawl when she really needed it?

THIS really was the happiest hour of her week, Annabelle thought. She propped her chin on her palm and just enjoyed being in the same room as Knightly. And her friends. And even her pretend-beau.

She battered her lashes at Owens for good measure. She even considered treating him to one of her sultry glances that were anything but seductive.

Knightly was in a terrible mood today. She wondered why, and if it was wrong that she thought the dark and broody look suited him.

Was it something with the newspaper, or another matter?

And what was this business with Lady Marsden? First, he'd been calling upon her and walking with her on sunny afternoons. And now he had banned her name from the pages of the newspaper. *It is probably nothing*, she told herself. She hoped it was naught but a strategic business decision that had nothing to do with his heart.

But still, it meant competition.

For the moment, though, there was nothing to do but enjoy this brooding version of Knightly in which he scowled, gazed darkly at his writers, raked his fingers through his hair and paced like some magnificent caged beast.

His gruff demeanor made her want to soothe his temper and smooth the rough edges. She wished to run her fingers through his hair, cradle his cheeks in her palms. Press her lips to his and kiss away that scowl . . .

Was it wrong that she wasn't paying attention in the slightest? It was. A Good Newspaper Woman would attend to the conversation.

"So let's get this straight," Owens said, brow furrowed. "A reporter for *The London Times* was caught impersonating a physician. Now he's imprisoned in Newgate, and Parliament and this parliamentary inquiry is looking into . . . what?"

"What exactly is the crime that merits such a massive investigation?" Eliza asked, puzzled. The methods of investigating were immoral, Annabelle thought. But it did seem like an isolated incident, as Knightly had said. It didn't seem to merit an investigation of the entire newspaper business.

"Why impersonate a physician anyway? That's an awful lot of risk and work," Grenville grumbled, and Annabelle quietly agreed with him.

"To get the story, of course," Eliza said, who thought nothing of adopting all manner of disguises for a story.

"What story?" Annabelle asked. The words were out of her mouth before she thought to censor them. And oh, she wished she had.

The room felt silent. Pin-drop silence. Pin drop on plush pile of sheepskin silence. Pin drop on plush sheepskin a country mile away.

The blush crept high onto her cheeks. Knightly focused on her intently. Had she thought his brooding stares were attractive? Because she could feel herself wilting under the intensity of his focus.

Would she *ever* stop humiliating herself in front of Knightly?

"What you're suggesting, Miss Swift, is that Brinsley didn't just wake up and decide to impersonate a doctor for amusement. He adopted that ruse because it enabled him to gain access and information to the *real* story."

"Just a means to an end," Owens added, thoughtful.

"Something like that," Annabelle mumbled.

"Brilliant," Knightly said, his voice rich with awe. Annabelle felt the warm heady rush of a rare, exquisite feeling: pride. She had impressed Knightly! "Miss Swift is right. What is the real story here?"

"Can we publish it if we uncover it?" Julianna dared to ask. "Given that Parliament is mucking into the practices of journalists . . ."

"Publish and be damned," Knightly said, with a grin that spoke of daring and danger.

# Chapter 15

## Newspapermen in Newgate

### ACCIDENTS & OFFENSE

*A fire at the offices of* The London Times *was deemed suspicious. A source informs that the editors were burning compromising files gathered by rogue reporter Jack Brinsley before Lord Marsden's Inquiry could collect them.*

The London Weekly

*Newgate*

**BRIBERY** was wonderful. Some men had compunctions about sort of thing, but not Knightly. He valued accomplishments and efficiency. Especially when one was at Newgate. It was not the sort of place where one wished to linger.

He was here because of Annabelle and her brilliant insight.

"It was only a matter of time before you showed up." Jack Brinsley, reporter and "physician" said gruffly upon Knightly's arrival. "At least one newspaper editor isn't afraid to show his face."

"Hardwicke has not visited?" Knightly inquired about the editor of *The London Times*.

"That patsy?" Brinsley spat on the floor.

"You have caused quite a scandal, you know," Knightly told him.

"You're welcome," Brinsley said with a smirk.

"It occurs to me that there's more to your story than the gossip or the paltry information I receive from the parliamentary inquiry." Knightly caught himself about to lean against the walls and then thought better of it.

"And I'm just supposed to tell you it, am I? I'm supposed to just tell-all to the rival newspaper," Brinsley said with a bemused expression.

"Aye, the rival newspaper that isn't turning its back on you," Knightly said pointedly. "Do you have a minute to talk?"

Brinsley snorted. Of course he had time, being in prison. He would talk. They always did with the hangman's noose swaying in the not-too-far future.

"Tell me about the day you woke up and thought 'I know! I'll pretend to be a physician to the aristocracy.'"

Brinsley took a long pause before answering: "It was a Tuesday. Foggy."

Knightly gave him A Look.

"I heard rumors about a particular lady. Hardwicke gave me orders to confirm them. And I thought, how the devil could I manage to confirm rumors about a pregnancy? Before anyone else did, that is."

"By impersonating a physician," Knightly surmised. Annabelle was right. Brinsley wasn't pulling this stunt on a lark, there had been a reason.

"Assisting one," Brinsley corrected. "But then the old blighter took ill himself and sent me on his calls. It proved to be rather informative. Lucrative, if you understand me."

It was a mad, genius scheme that definitely went beyond the pale, even for Knightly's bold tastes. He'd never support a reporter going to such *personal* lengths for a story.

But Damn, how lucrative it must have been. All newspapers made a small fortune in suppression fees when they obtained information the person in question did not wish to see in print. In this instance, it could be details of pregnancies or the pox or the devil only knew what else.

Some might say collecting those suppression fees was akin to blackmail. Others might say that's the newspaper publishing business. This was probably first on Marsden's list of practices to attack. One had to wonder, though, why he suddenly cared so much about an age-old practice?

"Whatever happened to bribing a housemaid?" Knightly mused.

"Child's play. Can't compete with *The Weekly* with those simpleton methods," Brinsley retorted.

"And the woman with the pregnancy rumors. Who was she?" Knightly asked. He had his suspicions.

"You're not stupid, Knightly, I'll give you that," Brinsley replied. "You're the only one to suspect I had a reason for this scheme. That I was after a lead and not just on a lark."

The credit was for Annabelle. He'd been as obtuse as the rest. But a more urgent matter persisted:

"Who is she?"

"I'm not just going to *tell* you," Brinsley said in an obvious play for cash. Knightly did love bribery. But he abhorred wasting money.

"Suit yourself. I'm confident I can discover it with a little sleuthing. I'm sure the ton will be riveted. Especially now that you and *The London Times* have so kindly set us up to reveal the details of such a riveting scandal."

"You're not going to publish this, are you?" Brinsley asked, jaw hanging open.

"I am," Knightly said. Publish and be damned.

"I take it back. You're not stupid. But damn, you are insane."

# Chapter 16

### Drama Is Not Just on the Stage

#### DEAR ANNABELLE

*Let the Nodcock know you care by a simple affection-
ate touch on his hand.*

> *Affectionate from All Saints Road*
> *The London Weekly*

*Covent Garden Theater*

**B**Y the end of Act One, Annabelle's cheeks were
as red as her crimson sash and she was thinking
some very uncharitable thoughts about Affectionate
from All Saints Road, whose well-meaning suggestion that a delicate caress or an affectionate gesture
would somehow make Knightly notice her, desire
her, love her.

This hint of affection was supposed to be a suggestion of *more*.

Who could predict that such a simple action
would be so fraught with peril?

First, she practiced upon Alistair Grey, who had
brought her as his guest to the opening night of
*Once Upon a Time*, featuring Delilah Knightly.

"Knightly's exact words to me were, 'My mother receives rave reviews or I find a new theater reviewer.' I understood this to mean I should attend," Alistair told her. "Of course, I always bring a guest. Given your situation and the assurance that you-know-who would attend, I thought to extend the invitation to you, Dear Annabelle. I expect a public display of gratitude in your next column."

"But of course," Annabelle replied, lightly touching her gloved hand to Alistair's forearm, clad in a deep mauve wool that set off his violet silk waistcoat to great effect.

Alistair did not take much notice of the gesture, but more importantly, he did not laugh or mock or ask her what the devil she was doing touching him thusly. *She could do this.*

She mustered her courage, straightened her spine, and quite nearly lost her nerve when Knightly arrived at the box appearing impossibly handsome in the stark black and white of his evening clothes.

If he was surprised to see her, he didn't show it. His eyes were as blue and focused as ever and his expression as aloof and inscrutable. She couldn't help it, a little sigh of longing and desire escaped her lips.

After greeting Alistair, Knightly took the seat beside her.

"How are you this evening, Annabelle?" he asked, leaning in toward her so his low voice might be heard over the din of the audience chattering before the start.

"Fine, thank you. And how are you?" Then she dared to brush her fingertips along the soft wool covering his arm, just for a second before snatching her hand away. Meanwhile, she kept her gaze upon him, so riveted was she by his blue eyes. That, and she was attempting to discern if that light touch had any effect upon him.

"I'm very well, thank you. Prepared for an evening of theatrics."

"Drama is for the page. Or the stage," she remarked, drawing a slight smile of recognition from him. She recognized an opportunity to seek an answer to a question that had been vexing her ever since their carriage ride. "Mr. Knightly, I don't think you ever mentioned your third truth."

Annabelle dared to punctuate this by placing her gloved hand upon his arm. In her head, she counted to three. Did he feel the warmth, the shivers? She felt positively electrified by the touch, however slight, and however much fabric separated his bare skin from hers.

Knightly leaned in closer. Her heart started to pound. She was sure her bosoms were heaving in anticipation, but in the dim light of the theater she couldn't tell if Knightly dared a glance or not.

"Be beholden to no one," he said in a low, heartbreaking voice.

"Oh," she replied, withdrawing her hand. That was the mantra of a man who refused love or attachment. The sort of man a woman ought not waste her time upon. That was a declaration of "Abandon all hope, ye who venture here."

But then she did catch Knightly glancing at her. And her bodice. She would swear that she felt his gaze like a caress. Her skin warmed. With the rush of pleasure from his attention was the satisfaction of knowing she had dared, she had achieved some small triumph.

The lights dimmed further. The audience hushed. The thick red velvet curtains were drawn apart, revealing a stage set to reveal a bedroom and a brightly dressed cast of characters ready to play.

The play was excellent, but couldn't fully capture her attention. Beside her, Knightly shifted and his soft wool coat brushed against her bare arms like the gentlest caress. She bit her lip, craving more.

Oh, it was just the brush of wool against her skin. It ought to have been nothing. But it was a tactile indication of all the affection she'd been lacking and all of her longing. It was an indication of how far she'd come, how close she was.

Old Annabelle never had moments like these, alone in the dark with Knightly, close enough to touch.

Throughout the performance, she'd kept her hands folded in her lap. But then she thought perhaps . . . perhaps she ought to try a little more.

She slid her hands across the pink silk of her skirts, over to the edge of her velvet chair just to where her fingers brushed with Knightly's, interlocking and then releasing for one exquisite and all-too-fleeting second.

In the middle of the first act Knightly leaned over to whisper in her ear some remark about the play. His voice was low, whisper quiet, and her attentions were distracted.

"What was that?" she asked at the exact moment when, as per the instructions of Affectionate from All Saints Road, she reached over intending just a brief gesture of affection on his arm, or his hand.

But he had shifted and she accidentally brushed her hand across a more personal and intimate and decidedly male portion of his anatomy. At the precise moment she had asked *What was that?*

Dear God, he would think—

That wasn't what she meant!

She just hadn't heard him!

All the words and explanations stuck in her throat. With cheeks flaming, Annabelle clasped her hands firmly on her lap and spent the second act regretting deeply the advice of Affectionate from All Saints Road and praying that she might disappear.

KNIGHTLY sincerely hoped that Alistair had paid excellent attention to the performance and planned to write an extensive, thorough, and meticulously detailed review, for he had not paid attention at all.

No, he'd been too damned distracted by Annabelle. First, it was those little flirtatious touches during their polite conversation, which fortunately consisted of just small talk. He'd had the devil of a time concentrating and instead wondered if Annabelle was *flirting* with him and if so, since when did Annabelle flirt?

It was probably for her column and probably practice for Owens or Marsden. But it tortured him all the same.

Especially when she had inadvertently touched him on a certain portion of his anatomy, which was far too pleased by it, given the circumstances. Such as a crowd of hundreds preventing him from *more.*

"Would you care for a glass of champagne?" Knightly asked Annabelle. Alistair had gone off to interview the actors backstage, leaving the two of them alone. He needed a drink, badly.

"Yes, *please,*" she replied, averting her gaze. Her cheeks were pink.

"Shall we?" He offered his arm and she entwined hers. It was the gentlemanly thing to do. But after all those little, taunting touches he wanted to feel more of her, feel her against him. With the slightest caress, she had started a craving.

With her tucked against him, he noticed Annabelle was taller than he expected—her head was just above his shoulder, and he towered over most men. He also noted that if he glanced down discreetly he was treated to a marvelous view of her breasts rising above the cut of her gown. God damn—or God bless?—that damn Gage and all the rest who made the suggestion that she lower her bodice. He hadn't been able to think of much other than Annabelle's breasts since.

He also noted that she gazed up at him with those wide blue eyes and caught him looking. She smiled shyly. Her cheeks were still pink.

They obtained the desperately needed glasses of champagne without further incident and sought refuge from the crowds in a private alcove near the lobby.

"Something is different about you, Annabelle," he remarked. It wasn't just the new dress or, now that he looked closely, a new way of wearing her hair that allowed a few golden curls to fall tantalizingly, gently, on her face.

"You noticed?" Her voice was soft and her blue eyes widened as she peered up at him.

"It's been hard not to, Annabelle." Every time

he saw her, there was something else to note. Even when she wasn't around, she managed to infiltrate his every conversation—and thoughts, and dreams. When he ought to have been planning his marriage to Lady Lydia, he instead thought of discovering Annabelle, inch by inch.

"Oh. I'm sorry—" she stammered, flustered, and he realized she must have thought he was referring to the, ahem, incident in Act One. What he couldn't tell her was that it worked. Or rather, he wouldn't tell her for it would only mortify her more (as adorable as that sight was, he couldn't torture her thus). And if he were practice for Owens or Marsden, then he took a perverse pleasure in denying them the pleasure of Annabelle's touch. However unintentional, however fleeting.

"No, don't be sorry," he said. For once he allowed himself a long, leisurely look at her, discovering all the tempting curves of Dear Annabelle, from the soft gold ringlets of her hair to the plump mouth, as if ripe for a kiss. The swell of her breasts, the narrow tapering of her waist, and the seductive flare of her lips made his mouth go dry.

Knightly was struck with the urge to claim her mouth with a kiss. He took another sip of his champagne instead.

"I don't know what inspired you, Annabelle. But I'm having the devil of a time watching your transformation." All that loveliness had been hidden away before. Idly he wondered, why now?

"In a good way, I hope," she ventured, nibbling her lower lip. Tempting. Knightly took a long swallow of his champagne, but it did nothing to quench his desire to taste her.

"Definitely in a good way," he told her. Good, yes. And also in an intriguing, tempting, beguiling, tormenting kind of way. In an interrupting-dreams-and-waking-thoughts kind of way. Annabelle was starting to happen, and for some reason, he was the lucky bastard who got to watch this bewitching transformation unfold.

She smiled, shyly. She gazed up at him like he was the whole damn world—sun, moon, and stars included. He stepped farther back into the shadows, drawing her close with the slightest grasp of her wrist. Kissing Annabelle suddenly became a necessity.

She tilted her head up. He lowered his mouth to hers.

Then Alistair interrupted, and Knightly thought of firing him for the offense.

# **Chapter 17**

## Writing Girls' Gossip

### THE MAN ABOUT TOWN

*The White's betting book is full of wagers on when Mr. London Weekly will propose to Lady "Missing Second Season" Marsden. All agree a betrothal announcement is imminent. He's been reported to call upon her regularly, and they have waltzed twice at each of the three balls they attended together this week.*

*The London Times*

**O**N Sunday afternoon Annabelle often volunteered her time with the Society for the Advancement of Female Literacy. Meaning, of course, that she escaped the domestic drudgery and dull company at home so that she might spend a few hours in the company of her fellow Writing Girls.

They most often gathered at Sophie's massive house to read periodicals, indulge in tea and cakes, and gossip shamelessly.

Sundays were definitely her second favorite part of the week, Annabelle thought as she curled up on the mulberry-colored upholstered settee in Sophie's drawing room. Last night at the theater, however, was certainly the highlight.

If she were not mistaken, it seemed that last night, Knightly noticed her. Was it her new hairstyle, thanks to Owens's strategic removal of a few hairpins? Or was it the silk dress that felt like a caress? Or the way those wicked silk underthings emboldened her?

Or was it the mortifying encounter with her hand and Knightly's anatomy?

At the thought, her cheeks flamed. But she took a deep breath and reminded herself that not only did Knightly notice her now, he had said so. And he had been about to kiss her, she was certain of it. If only Alistair hadn't interrupted.

"Annabelle, enough with the woolgathering," Eliza said. "We are desperately curious to know what has you lost in thought."

"And the reason for that dreamy smile and your blush," Sophie added.

Annabelle sighed, but this sign was one of utter delight. In spite of the most mortifying three seconds of her life, all was well. Funny, the power of an almost kiss. She went breathless imagining how it would feel to actually kiss him.

"I do believe that Knightly is beginning to notice me!" she exclaimed, in spite of all her efforts to be coy or demure or restrained. She saw the way he looked at her last night, as if it were the first time.

God bless Careless in Camden Town and even Affectionate from All Saints Road, and all the others who had written to her.

"Sophie, you were absolutely right about the dresses and the silky underthings. You have my everlasting gratitude," Annabelle vowed. "I daresay they have given me a new confidence."

"You are very welcome. In return, please tell that to Brandon when my modiste bills arrive," Sophie replied.

"Speaking of noticing you, Annabelle," Julianna, ever the gossip, said, "Knightly is not the only one, it seems. There is also Owens. And Marsden."

"You had said Owens was a ruse," Eliza added after a sip of tea. "But he seems genuine."

"He came up with the idea during the Forgotten Shawl Incident," Annabelle said. He'd also been extraordinarily attentive to her and affectionate. It might have begun as a ruse, but it was starting to feel like a friendship.

"A remarkably good idea and experiment," Eliza replied. "I daresay Knightly glowered every time Owens glanced in your direction during last week's meeting."

"Is that why he was scowling? I noticed he was brooding. Then my mind drifted, " Annabelle admitted with a sheepish smile. And she had been spending half of her attention on winks and smiles for Owens—even a sultry glance or two, for his amusement.

"Speaking of Knightly," Sophie said delicately, as she intently examined the lace trim on her dress sleeve, "they say that he is courting Lady Lydia. The Man About Town reported on it this morning."

"And that explains why Knightly forbade me to write about the Marsdens," Julianna grumbled. "I loathe when I am scooped by the Man About Town."

"It was just that one afternoon walk, was it not?" Annabelle asked. "Remember, Sophie?" One walk did not a courtship make. He couldn't possibly be courting another woman, not now. Not when she was finally coming out of her shell. Not after three years, seven months, and two days in which she languished in the shadows, only to emerge when it was too late.

"It's more than that, I'm afraid," Sophie said, wincing. Annabelle glanced from Sophie to Eliza to Julianna. Three dear faces with expressions of concern and anguish and worry, and even traces of pity.

"He's visited her on at least three other occasions," Julianna said. "Furthermore, they have waltzed twice at the Winthrop soiree."

Given that Knightly was not known to spend much time outside of *The Weekly*, three visits, two waltzes, and one afternoon walk were significant indicators of a courtship. Even Annabelle, ever the optimist in possession of an inventive imagination, could not see any other excuse. The truth left her breathless. A knot formed in her stomach. That warm glow of pleasure faded, leaving her cold.

She felt her shoulders rounding. She felt that familiar bleak hollowness as she contemplated a life without love; a life under the same roof as her brother and Blanche. A life just off to the side, in the shadows, forever handing props or whispering lines to the actors on stage.

"That is an interesting turn of events," Eliza said thoughtfully. "Perhaps it has nothing to do with the woman herself and everything to do with strengthening the relationship with Marsden and his blasted Inquiry looming over all of us."

"Are you suggesting it's some noble sacrifice to protect *The Weekly*?" Julianna asked.

"He would do that . . ." Annabelle said softly. "But Lady Lydia is also beautiful. And titled. And probably a lovely person."

"I've heard her dowry is paltry," Sophie said. "The Marsdens have recently fallen on hard times."

"Knightly has a fortune of his own," Julianna said. "He has no need of a wealthy bride. Though it sounds like she needs a wealthy husband."

"What she has is an immensely powerful brother," Sophie said. "Brandon works with him frequently in Parliament. Given this Inquiry, and the practices of *The Weekly*, Knightly needs all the allies he can get. Marsden is stirring up many, many supporters. He is so popular, and charming, and righteously outraged over the matter, no one is able to refuse pledging their support to his cause."

"And then there are the rumors," Julianna said, with such relish that Annabelle felt a spark of hope after the sinking feeling in her stomach following Sophie's appraisal of the situation.

"Have you discovered her mystery lover yet?" Eliza asked, leaning forward, intrigued.

"No. But the latest *on dit* is that her illness was the sort that lasts only nine months," Julianna shared, pausing for effect and to sip her tea.

"Knightly probably doesn't care one whit about the rumors," Sophie said with a shrug. One should never believe in rumors, especially disparaging ones. How many times had Annabelle counseled her readers thusly?

"She is quite the competition," she said softly. A battle of tug of war erupted in her soul. *Give up*, Old Annabelle whispered. *Fight for him*, New Annabelle urged. The conflict made her stomach ache. "I did not realize that he had set his cap for someone else when I started my campaign to win him."

"So what if he has?" Julianna asked, shrugging. "What does that have to do with anything?" Not for the first time, Annabelle wished she possessed some of her friend's brazen spirit. Or her ability to *not* consider the contents of Lady Lydia's heart or her lifelong happiness when considering what to do.

"I shouldn't want to steal him," Annabelle said softly. "Or make anyone unhappy." That was the thing about always seeking the good in everyone, and doling out advice for years. Her point of view always focused on how to make everyone else happy.

It pleased her to do so. Truly. How could she even enjoy Knightly's love if it came at the expense of another woman's happiness?

"It's not 'stealing,'" Eliza said. "He would be exercising his free will."

"Annabelle, you have loved him for years—" Sophie began.

"Three years, seven months, and two days. Give or take," Annabelle replied. She gave a shrug of her shoulders as if to suggest it mattered not. But it did. Her heart had beat just for him for all those days . . . and all those nights.

"Precisely. You have loved him for quite some time, and now, finally, he is showing signs of returning your affections," Sophie pointed out, bolstering Annabelle's confidence.

"He is beginning to notice me. I know he is," she said fiercely. But she now realized that noticing was only the first step. She wanted his love. She wanted his undying devotion and eternal passion. She had wanted it for three years, seven months, and two days.

"Until a few weeks ago, you'd never quite had a conversation with him," Eliza pointed out, "and now you two are gallivanting all over town in a closed carriage and sipping champagne together at the theater. You cannot give up now."

"But how can I compete with Lady Lydia?" Annabelle cried.

The woman was a formidable opponent. Lady Lydia owned numerous gorgeous gowns, all in the first stare of fashion, whilst she had only two nice dresses and a wardrobe that demonstrated the different shades of brown and gray.

Lady Lydia's every movement was elegance itself. Annabelle had, in an attempt to be flirtatious and affectionate, placed her hand where no lady would dare, while asking, "What was that?"

Lady Lydia indulged in the social whirl, and she was oft found busying herself with other people's problems.

Lady Lydia's brother held the fate of *The London Weekly* in his hands. Annabelle's brother never looked up from his newspaper and didn't even read *The Weekly*.

The competition was fierce. Swifts were not known for being fierce.

"Just be you, Annabelle. Or the you that you are becoming," Sophie urged gently.

"If he doesn't notice and fall madly in love, then to hell with him," Julianna declared.

What she wouldn't give to possess Julianna's fiery streak. Or Sophie's confidence. Or Eliza's daring.

The words "to hell with him" didn't just stick

in Annabelle's throat, she couldn't fathom uttering such a phrase. Not for Knightly. Not for love.

"What have your readers suggested you try next?" Eliza asked, slightly changing the subject.

"Oh . . ." Annabelle sighed evasively. That was another issue. She had tried all the easy things. Each week the suggestions grew more and more outrageous.

"Annabelle, what do the heroines of the novels you like to read do?" Sophie asked.

"That's just the thing, you see. The most compelling suggestion from a reader is to faint into Knightly's arms, but no heroine worth her smelling salts would ever *faint*."

And that was precisely what Swooning on Seymour Street had advised her to do: feign a faint and hope the man who never noticed her would catch her when she fell.

# Chapter 18

## Impossible Advice

### DEAR ANNABELLE

*Fetch the smelling salts!*

*The London Weekly*

*Annabelle's attic bedchamber*

**O**F all the letters Annabelle had received in her
years as an advice columnist, of those hundreds
upon thousands of questions and pleas, not one had
tugged at her conscious, tormented soul or broke
her heart quite like this one.

It quite took her breath away, this letter. Squeezed
the air right out of her lungs.

It came from Lady Lydia Marsden. Not that she
signed her name; Annabelle recognized the crest on
the sealing wax. It was the same crest that accom-
panied the note that had been tucked into the bouquet of pink roses her brother sent. This little slip
revealed oh so much more than the author intended.

If Annabelle hadn't noticed that detail, she would
have easily composed a reply urging one to pursue
true love at all costs. But Annabelle had noticed,

and thought twice about encouraging her rival to increase her efforts to ensnare the man she herself loved.

After she finally completed her domestic drudgery for the day—tending to the children's bedtime routine, dusting Blanche's collection of breakable porcelain shepherdesses with a scrap of white flannel, mending her brother's shirts—Annabelle returned to her bedchamber to practice fainting, along with reading her letters and drafting her next column.

Now she actually did feel faint, thanks to this letter. Who needed air, anyway? Who needed to breathe when her heart was torn in two?

Where were the smelling salts when a girl needed them?

The letter began *Dear Annabelle*, as all letters to her did. It read:

> *I am in love with an unsuitable man, for his station is far below mine. My brother wishes me to marry another. Surely you, Dear Annabelle, believe in the love match! My dear brother will listen to you. Perhaps you might advocate for true love as the primary consideration in marriage?*
>
> *Scandalously in Love in Mayfair*

Annabelle understood, plain as day: Lady Lydia had fallen in love with Knightly. Given that she was the sister of a marquis and he was the son of an actress . . . of course they could not be together.

How on earth was she to advise Lady Lydia without compromising her own ideals (true love!) or without compromising her own aims (Knightly!)?

Annabelle believed in love the way the Pope believed in the holy trinity or physicists believed in gravity. She could not, in good conscience, advise Lydia *not* to pursue true love. Yet to encourage Lady Lydia was to thwart her own aims. Could she so willingly thwart herself?

A heroine would fight for her love, Annabelle thought as she tucked the letter into her copy of *Belinda* and stuck the novel high on the shelf.

A heroine would also never be so lily-livered as to faint, and certainly not deliberately. And yet . . .

Annabelle stood next to her bed for a soft landing. She wavered on her feet. The waver had to be essential, so that Knightly would have a moment to, oh, notice she was unsteady and prepare to catch her. For dramatic effect, she tenderly draped the back of her hand across her brow.

And then she let go . . .

Let herself simply collapse . . .

No more strained effort to keep her spine straight and proud. No more tense muscles, awaiting some kiss or heated gaze that never came her way. She allowed her knees to be weak (for that happened to heroines all the time). She allowed herself to stop trying so darned hard to be still and strong in a world with all odds stacked high against her.

She fell softly on her feather mattress. Her breath escaped in a whoosh.

She had let go and landed unharmed.

She stood again, and closed her eyes this time. She released all of the problems that came her way—those of her readers, Lady Lydia's, and those of her own creation. Just let them, let herself, go.

This time when she faux fainted she let her arms

splay out. Her hair started to escape from its confines and it felt so pleasant to be so unrestrained. She thought of Owens, and that he was right to risk such an intimate gesture to loosen those hairpins. To let her hair down. To let herself go.

Again and again Annabelle practiced her swoon. Again and again she discovered the pleasure of letting go.

# Chapter 19

### A Lady's Guide to Feigning Faints

THE MAN ABOUT TOWN
*Lord Harrowby has pledged his support of Lord
Marsden's Inquiry.*
The London Times

*Offices of* The London Weekly

THE meeting passed as all the others did. Her heart
thudded, the butterflies in her stomach fluttered, her
eyelashes batted. And above all Annabelle admired.
Even his rumored courtship of Lady Lydia, while
troubling, was not sufficient to thwart her passion
for him.

In fact, for the first time in her life, Annabelle felt
. . . competitive. Old Annabelle put everyone else's
needs first. New Annabelle fought for her beliefs,
and loves, and desires.

Oh, yes, desires.

The meeting proceeded, and she didn't hear a
word.

When Knightly wasn't leaning like some devil-
may-care rogue with all the time in the world for

some Grand Seduction, he stood tall with his wide shoulders thrown back. As someone who usually turned in on herself as if to take shelter from the world, she admired how he always seemed poised to manage anything. And everything.

Knightly was so controlled, too, from the lift of his brow to the tug of a grin. He did not tap his fingers or his foot in idle energy. He didn't run his fingers through his hair rakishly, or fidget in any way. His every movement was restrained and possessed by purpose.

She could only imagine if they made love, what it would be like to have that energy—his blue eyes, his strong hands—harnessed and focused upon herself. In bed. Making love. With Knightly. Honestly, she didn't think she'd survive that.

"Annabelle, are you overheated?" Knightly interrupted the meeting to ask.

She sighed, so mortified there was no point in pretending otherwise. There was no denying the telltale redness of her cheeks.

"Perhaps you should remove your shawl," Owens suggested with a rakish grin and a suggestive nod of his head. Knightly scowled at him.

"I'm not feeling quite myself," Annabelle said, to foreshadow what was to come. But wasn't that the truth! Her own thoughts were making her feel faint. Perhaps a feigned swoon wasn't necessary. She'd just have to keep imagining Knightly. Making Love. In bed. With her.

The clothing would have to go. Each layer stripped off. She vividly recalled how warm and firm his chest was. She could only imagine it uncovered . . . could only imagine his hot, naked skin next to her own. Could only imagine how that faint stubble upon his jaw would feel against her cheek as they kissed and . . .

She did imagine. In great detail. Her face positively flamed.

Other parts of her were rather warm as well, starting in her belly and fanning out. Warm and aching for something . . . she knew not what, exactly. Just that she'd do anything to find satisfaction for this craving.

For one thing, she'd start by fainting into Knightly's arms this very afternoon.

Knightly glanced at her, concerned.

"Owens, open the window," he ordered. Owens did and a rush of cool air stole over her scorching skin. She almost sighed from the pleasure of it.

"Are you quite all right? Should we abandon the mission?" Julianna whispered.

"I'm fine. Just warm," Annabelle replied briskly. It had nothing to do with the temperature in the room, and everything to do with the scorching thoughts in her head. Her. Knightly. Limbs tangled. His lips upon her skin.

"I wonder why . . ." Julianna murmured.

"You wonder no such thing, Julianna," Annabelle hissed. No one could know that she was entertaining the most wanton, lustful fantasies when she ought to be occupying her brain with serious thoughts.

"Oh, Knightly, if I might have a word with you . . ." Julianna requested at the end of the meeting as the other writers were quitting the room. Annabelle lingered by her friend's side.

This was all part of the plan to faint into his arms. She realized now what an extraordinary leap of faith this required. To expect the man who never noticed her to catch her when she fell. This was madness.

What was the worst that could happen? Julianna would catch her. Or she might collapse on the floor, possibly doing herself an injury. Yet she would certainly survive it, and Lord knows she'd already survived embarrassment in front of Knightly.

Like this afternoon, when she thought about him hot and naked, entwined with her . . . His kiss. His touch.

"Oooh," she groaned again. Really, this must stop. Knightly glanced at her, his blue eyes narrowed in concern.

"What is it, Julianna?" he asked. He stood close enough to Annabelle that she thought her plan might just work. His arm brushed against hers as he folded his arms over his chest. She recalled the last time she'd been so close to him—at the theater—and the mortifying brush of her hand upon his . . .

Oh, her skin felt positively aflame.

"It's about Lady Marsden," Julianna said, her voice low. Knightly leaned in. Annabelle groaned again—this time it had nothing to do with her feigned faint or explicit romantic thoughts.

That cursed letter still remained, unanswered, and tucked in a volume of *Belinda* on the highest shelf in her bedroom.

"I told you, no mentions of the Marsdens," Knightly said firmly. Impatiently. He loves her, Annabelle thought wildly, and Lady Lydia loves him. They were star-crossed lovers, with cruel brothers and society conspiring against them! Every reader of romantic novels knew it was a recipe for some Grand Gesture and Bold Romantic Display.

"What if the Man About Town scoops us?" Julianna questioned sharply.

"It won't happen because Hardwicke is quaking in his boots in fear of Marsden and his Inquiry," Knightly said, becoming visibly irritated. That was not part of her plan, but there was no stopping Julianna once she pounced upon a subject.

"Of course that silly man is. But are you?" Julianna challenged.

"Julianna." Knightly and Annabelle said this at the same time, both adopting tones of warning.

Knightly glanced at Annabelle. She wavered on her feet. This was her moment. She knew it like she knew the earth revolved around the sun, like spring follows winter, like the sun rises in the east.

*Be bold,* she told herself. *Let go. Have faith in Knightly and in the advice of Swooning on Seymour Street.*

She fluttered her lashes. In order to bring a feverish blush to her cheeks, she imagined how it would feel to be embraced by Knightly with his strong arms holding her against the muscled planes of his hot, firm chest.

"Are you all right?" he asked, looking closely at her. He pressed his palm on the small of her back. It was amazing how such a small gesture could be felt so intensely and all over.

"No, I don't think I am," Annabelle replied truthfully. She loved him, and he courted another, while she could not restrain the most wicked and wanton thoughts. She was not all right. She was the very definition of wretched, hopelessly in love, desperate to win his heart. "I feel . . ."

*Faint.*

And then she fainted.

Or pretended to.

She let her knees go weak, her eyelashes flutter and close, and then let herself fall.

She even managed to languorously drape a hand across her brow for dramatic effect.

The next thing she knew, she had landed right in Knightly's arms. Right where she had always wanted to be.

She had dreamed of this, and the reality far surpassed it.

The man was all muscle—from his arms to his chest—hard and strong. She inhaled the clean scent of wool suit, the indescribable scent that was just him and that she'd only recently gotten close enough to know. Heaven couldn't possibly be better than this.

When she opened her eyes, his vivid blue eyes were fixed upon her face and Knightly gazed at her intently. The blue had darkened considerably. His lips parted slightly.

When he looked at her like that, she *felt* it. Everywhere. It made her skin feel feverish.

"Annabelle?" he said, and there was a rough quality to his voice. His gaze roamed over her, as if searching for answers. Her lips parted to explain . . . but there was nothing she could say.

Her heart began to pound.

Was this *actually working*? She'd been so accustomed to being overlooked that she hadn't quite considered that this mad scheme of hers might actual succeed.

And yet here she was, in Knightly's arms, as he lifted her up and carried her away, like a princess. He carried her over the threshold to his office, like a bride. He held her like a woman he noticed.

# Chapter 20

## The Dangers of Fainting

TOWN TALK

*Mr. Knightly's courtship of Lady Marsden continues.
She has confided to friends that she expects a proposal soon.*

    *The Morning Post*

No one actually fainted so prettily, complete with
the hand over the forehead. In fact, women did not
actually faint as much as the stories would have one
believe. Knightly might have allowed that her corset
was laced tightly, depriving her of air, for he had
noted that her waist was narrow and her breasts
were marvelously high and nearly spilling out of
her gown.

But he knew a fake faint when he saw one, especially when it swooned delicately into his arms,
bringing an end to the world as he had known it.

It was just Annabelle, he tried to convince himself.

Just Annabelle, lovely and luscious in his arms
with her soft gold curls escaping from restraint and
tumbling down around the soft curve of her cheeks.

Just Annabelle, with her lips slightly parted while he thought of nothing—*nothing*—else but pressing his mouth to hers to discover, to taste, to know, and to claim.

For the first time he truly noticed her blue eyes and dark lashes. He saw the depths of emotion there. Desire. Uncertainty. Hope and fear.

He thought this was how she must appear in the throes of pleasure—tussled hair, desiring eyes, lips slightly parted to share sighs of pleasure. His body responded to the vision as if it were real. As if he had inspired that blush, made her lips part for gasps of pleasure . . .

Knightly wanted to lay her down, have his way with her, and give her that pleasure.

Now that he'd seen Annabelle like this . . .

He knew he wouldn't be able to look at her again without seeing her thusly. That wicked, seductive, wanton, and sensual image was now seared into his brain forevermore.

In the far recesses of his brain shards of logic remained and alerted him to the facts: this was a ruse for her column, for her elaborate seduction. But was this moment just practice? In other words, was this the closest he would ever be to witnessing Annabelle as if in the throes of pleasure?

Or . . .

Was he the infamous object of her affections? Otherwise known, lamentably, as the Nodcock. To that, his heart, his brain, every fiber of his being firmly declared . . .

*No.* No.

"Where are you taking me?" Annabelle asked. He forced a slight smile, even though the world as he knew it was coming to an end. She'd been "the quiet one," and now he wanted to lay her on his office floor and have his wicked way with her.

"I'm taking you to my office," he said. Where we might have some privacy, he thought. *Wrong.* Wrong!

They were going to his office, where she might recover herself and he might have a drink and restore sense and reason in his brain. *Think of Lady Lydia,* he ordered himself. *Think of that damned New Earl and everything you've ever wanted.* Then he promptly ignored the command.

"I'm certain I can walk," she said. Probably because all the other writers were staring as he made his way to his office with Annabelle in his arms. She did seem to have an aversion to being the center of attention.

"Let's not risk it," he said, because he couldn't actually say that he rather liked the feel of her in his arms and in a moment would set her down and probably never hold her thusly again.

*Lady Lydia. Everything he'd ever wanted.*

He set her down in one of the large plush chairs before his desk and proceeded to pour himself a brandy. He took a large sip and tried to convince himself that it was truly Owens she was after, not him.

What the devil did he do now, with Annabelle gazing up at him expectantly?

"How are you feeling?" he asked. That was a safe question.

"Oh . . . I'm fine. Truly. I feel a bit silly," she said sheepishly.

*She had made him see . . .*

Knightly eyed her now. Blond curls pulled back.

Blue eyes full of questions. Her sinfully full mouth making him think of kissing, which made him think of how she'd appeared in his arms just a moment ago. As if in the midst of a damn good ravishing.

Knightly moved behind his desk so she would not see that he was in a state to give her a damn good ravishing.

He'd never thought Dear Annabelle would torture him thusly. Two could play that game, he thought with a slight grin. And speaking of playing the game, he ought to act as if she had actually fainted. Pretending to be obtuse and oblivious to the scheme would afford him time to figure something out.

"We should send for a doctor," he said gravely.

Her eyes widened significantly. Perhaps he'd inherited some of his mother's flair for acting after all.

"Oh no, I feel significantly improved. I'm sure I'll be fine," she said. Which wasn't fair, because he wasn't sure he'd ever erase the image of Annabelle, as if in the throes of passion, out of his head. It was going to drive him mad.

"A real doctor, I promise," he said, and she laughed. It was a girlish laugh, very sweet. She didn't laugh enough—or had he never really paid attention before? What else had he missed over the years? Why did he have to notice now?

"I don't want to cause any more trouble. I've inconvenienced you enough already . . ." Before his eyes, Knightly watched Annabelle in retreat. Her shoulders curved and her voice dropped to nearly a whisper.

"I do hate to be a bother," she said softly. Said the woman who had just faked a swoon into his outstretched arms. It didn't entirely add up.

His gaze locked with hers for one intense second before she looked away. Knightly watched her look around the room, as if looking for some shadows to blend in with.

Had he not noticed her before because she didn't let him?

"You're not a bother, Annabelle." She flashed a shy glance in his direction. She didn't believe him. And why should she? She had just faux fainted directly into his arms and was now keeping him from his work, and life as he had known it.

But he saw daring Annabelle starting to retreat, and he sought to cajole her out of hiding.

"Very well, you are a bother. But I don't mind being given the opportunity to demonstrate my strength and quick reflexes."

And then she treated him to that lovely girlish laugh again. It was shy and nervous and happy all at once. Damn, if it wasn't a powerful feeling to have teased her out of the shadows. But did that mean . . . ? Knightly took another sip of his drink.

"It's important that the other staff be aware of my many talents, including my physical prowess," he continued. "So I do believe thanks are in order."

He raised his glass in cheers to her and took another sip to drown out the words *besides, there are worse things than holding a beautiful woman*. While he didn't want her to feel wretched—and she was clearly the romantic, dramatic sort who would mope for days on end—he couldn't bring himself to say anything that would make things awkward.

And since she was clearly the romantic, dramatic sort who would puzzle over every word for days on end, he did not want to give her Ideas. Not when he had to continue his courtship of Lady Lydia and ensure that Annabelle's column remained the smashing success that it was, so that he didn't lose everything, starting with *The London Weekly*.

At that thought, Knightly took another sip and savored the burn.

"Should I have some of that?" Annabelle asked, and he choked.

"Brandy?" he sputtered.

"In novels, the heroes always force the heroines to drink brandy after they have fainted. Apparently, it is very restorative," she informed him.

"It burns like the devil and will likely make you ill," he lectured. But damn, did he want to laugh. Especially when she pouted so adorably at him. Where had this Annabelle been all these years? And why did she have to appear now?

"I should still like to try," she said.

"I'm not giving you brandy," he told her. It seemed like something done by the vile seducer character in a novel. He would not play that part.

"Very well. What if it was research for my column?" She smiled, pleased with her strategy of selecting the excuse he could not refuse.

"Oh, Dear Annabelle . . ." he said, laughing, and handing over his glass. One small sip remained.

She lifted the glass to her mouth. After one whiff she wrinkled her nose.

"Perhaps I needn't try it," she said. "And pray do not say I told you so."

Knightly grinned, enjoying her company tremendously, even though that was the road to ruin. *Think of Lady Lydia. Think of everything you ever wanted.* But he didn't.

"Come on, Annabelle, let's take you home. No, do not protest," he said to her as much as to himself. "I cannot send you off in a hired hack after you've just fainted. What kind of gentleman would that make me?"

# Chapter 21

### What *Not* to Ask a Woman

THE MAN ABOUT TOWN

*Lord Marsden was joined by an unlikely guest at
White's—Derek Knightly, owner of* The London
Weekly. *The two gentlemen were in deep discussion.
Was it about Marsden's Inquiry into the reporting
methods of the press, or Knightly's courtship of Mars-
den's sister?*

The London Times

**A**NNABELLE had done it again—she somehow con-
trived to find herself alone with Knightly and to indulge in the tortured pleasures of his presence. Had
she known what to do years ago . . .

She still wouldn't have done a thing, because she
wouldn't have been desperate enough to ask for help
or to risk taking the advice of Sneaky in Southwark
or Careless in Camden Town and especially Swooning in Mayfair.

"Thank you for taking me home," she said. "I am
sorry to inconvenience you. Well, a little bit. But this,
with you, is far preferable to a hired hack or a long
walk. But I sincerely hope this isn't too much trouble

for you." She was a bit awed, truth be told, at these situations that she had conjured up. Like she possessed magical powers and was only just discovering it.

"You don't like to ask for things for yourself, do you?" Knightly questioned. "You just fainted, Annabelle. I can't let you walk across town alone. Back in the office, you didn't want me to send for a doctor because you might be a bother."

This was Knightly seeing her. Seeing into her soul, even. Seeing into the dark, quiet parts of her. The part that was forever afraid of being too much of a nuisance and left behind accordingly.

Annabelle was afraid that if she didn't prove useful around the house, Blanche would cast her out, as she had threatened shortly after the marriage. What bride wanted her husband's awkward, orphaned sister lurking around the house? Why pay to send her to finishing school when she could earn her keep—and save household funds—by acting as a servant?

She was afraid that if her column was late or not good enough, she'd demand too much of Knightly's limited time and he'd decide to find a better advice columnist. She labored over each column as if her hopes and dreams depended on each word being perfect.

She was afraid to burden her fellow Writing Girls with these fears in case they found her tedious or hopeless and then cast her aside for more fascinating and fashionable friends.

Having Knightly glimpse these fears was wonderful and terrifying all at once. Before, she could dismiss any slight as simple carelessness or obliviousness. But now that he was learning about her, she had opened herself up to all kinds of hurt and vulnerabilities.

"I hate to cause trouble," Annabelle said softly, finding herself still too tongue-tied around Knightly to say any more.

"How do you get ahead?" he asked, perplexed. The question was blunt; her answer was, too.

"I don't. I get by." She said this with a sigh, of course.

"That's no way to live, Annabelle." Knightly drawled the word in a way that tempted her— forever shy, forever cautious—to throw all caution to the wind and try to be great instead of ducking her head and hoping to get through the day.

"I'm improving," she said, proud, and also relieved to be able to say so truthfully. Yet it was a constant effort to let go of Old Annabelle and adopt New Annabelle. Even now, after having done the most dramatic, daring thing of her life—fainting into his arms—she found herself retreating to more familiar safer, calmer waters.

"You are improving," Knightly said, "thanks to this column of yours." He noticed! Again!

"See, it's taking all of London to instruct me on how to be a bother," she said with a little laugh. Across the carriage, Knightly smiled.

He looked like he wanted to say something, but he didn't. She wondered, desperately, what he was holding back.

"I trust you are succeeding? Is the Nodcock noticing you?" Knightly asked.

How, oh, how to answer! Her heart started to thud because she wanted to declare, *You are the Nod-*

*cock and here we are!* and launch herself into his arms. But she did no such thing, because she was not yet sure how he would take it. Would he kiss her passionately? Or awkwardly untangle their limbs and stop the carriage?

She was still the "Annabelle that just gets by," even though she was slowly, agonizingly becoming bold New Annabelle.

And she also didn't tell him if she was succeeding with "the Nodcock" because that wasn't how she dreamed the moment would be. She had not yet given up her hopes and dreams in which he declared his love for her.

"I am making progress," she allowed. And then she gave voice to the vexing truth. "But not too much . . . you said it's very popular and you'd like it to continue."

"It's the saving grace of *The Weekly* right now. With all eyes focused on the scandal at *The Times*, it's only a matter of time until they examine the journalistic practices at *The Weekly*," he said, plainly stating the facts.

"And then we are doomed," Annabelle said dramatically.

"Not if I have anything to do with it," Knightly said. His voice was calm, but his intentions were fierce. Oh, to be loved the way Knightly loved his newspaper!

Quietly, but steadfast and strong, with a relentless, daily devotion. To know that your beloved would fight to death to protect you. Knightly had taken bullets for the paper.

"You love this newspaper more than anything." Annabelle said the truth aloud.

"It's mine." Plain. Simple. Fact. But there was a world of emotion in that little phrase, *it's mine.*

Knightly might be remote or apparently unfeeling, but if he could say those words, *it's mine,* like that, for a newspaper, then he could love a woman tremendously. She wanted to be that woman more than anything.

"A man. A newspaper. A love story: a novel in three parts," Annabelle said, and Knightly laughed, which gave her the confidence to say more. "What is your story? How did you fall in love with *The Weekly*?"

"It was a second-rate newspaper—yesterday's news, poorly edited—and it was for sale. The editor had married a woman of means and wished to retire. I wanted it, and I had the means to acquire it."

"Starting right at the top," she remarked.

"Actually, I was one of the writers," Knightly said, surprising her. "Before that I worked the printing presses, and before that I delivered them to all the aristocratic households."

Annabelle smiled at the image of a young Knightly standing before a Mayfair mansion with a hot-off-the-presses edition of *The London Weekly* in his hand. Had he known or dreamed then that he would one day live in such a grand home?

"No one knew that paper like I did. The owner offered me the opportunity to buy it," Knightly explained, and she marveled that there was no note of apology in his voice, as there would have been in hers in detailing an accomplishment. That was another reason why she adored him.

That, and the way he made her heart beat a bit faster and heightened her awareness of her every breath, of the rustle of silk against her skin.

When he looked at her, when Knightly noticed her, she felt like she existed.

And she could see the woman she wanted to become.

Starting with not being afraid to ask questions.

"But how did you have money to buy a newspaper? Which isn't to say that writers are not paid enough. But if . . ." Oh, how to ask the question without insulting her wages and the man who paid them? "I do not mean to suggest that you compensate your writers inadequately . . ."

"It was cheap," Knightly said bluntly.

"Not *that* cheap, I'm sure," Annabelle said, daring to contradict him.

He shrugged then, and looked out the window. Drummed his fingers on the seat next to him. Things the calm, cool, utterly self-possessed Mr. Knightly ordinarily Did Not Do.

Had she discovered a vulnerability? Was Knightly *not* perfect? She had thought she'd known him over the years, but apparently there was more to discover. This only made her more enthralled with the man seated across from her in the carriage.

"I had an inheritance, from my father." The way he said it, it sounded like a confession.

In the years, seven months, and a few days since she had loved Knightly, she'd always kept an ear out for information about him. Not even Julianna mentioned much about their employer's family or past. His father had been a peer; Annabelle knew that much. She also knew he was illegitimate. Julianna had told the Writing Girls one day, in the strictest confidence.

"If it was enough to buy a business, wasn't it

enough to just live off of?" she asked now. That's what her brother would do, if he could. Just sit in his library chair with a stack of newspapers and pay no attention to the world around him.

"I could not idly go through life, watching my bank account dwindle and not do something with my time. I have to build and create," he said passionately. "And now I have accomplished something: a successful business. And a bloody fortune, every penny of which I earned my damned self."

"And yet you do not retire," she pointed out.

"It would kill me," he said simply. Knightly paused, fixed his blue eyes on hers, and she knew that what he would say next would be vitally important. "I haven't yet accomplished everything that I intend to."

"What is left?" she asked, her breath hitching as she awaited his response.

He stared at her for a moment, as if debating whether to tell her.

"I want my place in society," he said, and she dearly wished he hadn't. The facts aligned swiftly to reveal a heartbreaking truth. Lady Lydia was high society. Marriage to her—and his bloody fortune— would all but assure his impeachable status in the ton.

"You can't lose your paper now, can you?" she said, referring to the threat of the parliamentary Inquiry. It was the only thing that could ruin *The Weekly*. "Not when you are so close to the ton and everything you ever wanted."

"So close I can taste it," he said, his voice rough.

Annabelle smiled wryly, for they were more alike in this moment than ever before, yet in the most wretched way. Each of them so close to attaining that one thing. Though she had found herself alone with Knightly, and even managed to gain his attention, he had just effectively told her they could have no future together—unless she wanted him to give up his life's dream and burning ambition.

Just for her. Little old Overlooked Annabelle.

She nearly laughed. It was either that or cry.

"Speaking of high society," Knightly began slowly, building up to something. "Lord Marsden has taken a liking to you."

"I suppose he has," Annabelle said carefully, so that she might not betray one of the decoys. She knew, too, what Marsden was to the newspaper at this moment. Possibly its savior; possibly the destroyer.

"He sent you flowers," Knightly stated slowly.

"A gorgeous bouquet of pink roses," Annabelle added, suddenly keen to show that she was *wanted*. Wanted by high society, too.

Perhaps she might even make Knightly jealous.

Also, she wanted him to know she liked pink roses, if he should ever think to send her flowers.

"I have the distinct impression that it is his affection for you and your advice column that has him thinking favorably of *The Weekly*," Knightly said, his meaning becoming plain. Gut-wrenchingly, heartbreakingly plain. "If you encouraged him, Annabelle, it would be a tremendous boon for *The Weekly*. And it would be a great favor to me."

Her heartbeat slowed. The simple act of breathing became impossible.

*Do not ask this of me*, she wanted to plead. But all the words died in her throat.

It was because he loved his newspaper. She knew that. Because he was so close to attaining his life's ambitions, and to lose *The Weekly* was to lose everything. She could make sense of the request, but she could not deny the hurt.

He didn't know her feelings, she rationalized. Otherwise he wouldn't ask this wretched *favor* of her. If he did . . . she couldn't even contemplate such a thing. Not now, in this small, dark, confining carriage with Knightly's blue eyes fixed upon her.

He was waiting for her answer. Waiting for her to say *of course,* because that's what Annabelle did: she solved other people's problems with no regard to the expense to her own heart and soul.

"Annabelle . . ." He seemed pained. Good, she thought. He didn't know from pain.

"I understand, Mr. Knightly." And she did. But that didn't mean she liked it, or would do it, or that it didn't feel like a cold knife blade to her warm beating heart.

The rest of the carriage ride progressed in silence. She was achingly aware of his fleeting glances in her direction. Old Annabelle would have tried to soothe his conscience, even as he'd asked this despicable thing. To hell with Old Annabelle.

"Annabelle . . ." Knightly spoke her name, breaking the silence. He even reached for her hand. She glanced down at that long awaited sight. Her small, delicate hand in his, which was large and warm and strong. But the moment wasn't quite as she had dreamed. She felt deprived, though still wanted her hand lovingly in his.

*If* she were to do this thing he asked . . . it would make him beholden to her. She would no longer be just Dear Old Annabelle, but the savior of *The London Weekly*. How tempting.

"Annabelle . . ." he said again, his voice rough, trailing off as if there were more to say. Vaguely she was aware of her lips parting. *If he kisses me I'll forgive anything . . .*

The carriage rolled to a stop in front of her house.

He wasn't going to kiss her. It didn't feel right. He was probably going to say something wretched and heartbreaking and possibly about Lady Lydia or Lord Marsden or how he loved *The London Weekly* above all else. She knew all of these things.

She also knew that Blanche was likely watching from behind the drawing room drapes.

"I must go," she said, recognizing her moment to employ Mysterious in Chelsea's advice to "leave the Nodcock wanting more."

# Chapter 22

### Newspaper Tycoon Sighted in the Most Unlikely of Places

**DEAR ANNABELLE**

*I'm glad Remorseful in Richmond asked for the best way to apologize to a woman. 'Tis information many men need to know. Flowers wouldn't be remiss; this author is partial to pink roses (in the event the Nodcock is reading this).*

*The London Weekly*

*The warehouse*

**H**E was not brooding. Knightly preferred to view it as thinking logically and rationally about a frustrating situation. Brooding men paced like caged lions or drank whiskey to intensify the burn.

Instead, he went down to the warehouse and printing presses. Nothing cleared a man's mind like the sweat and strain of manual labor and the roar of machines so loud that thought became almost impossible.

Almost.

The noise of the steam-powered printing presses

generally had a way of drowning out all distractions. Except for Annabelle and that awful thing he'd asked of her.

With a crew of laborers, Knightly lifted and tossed reams of paper that would be fed into the printing press. The warehouse was so hot it felt like an inner circle of hell. The work was tedious. After a while, a long while, his muscles start to holler in protest at him. It was a feeling he craved. Pain. Agony. But damn good all at once.

This soothed more than brandy or boxing.

Usually.

Even over the shout of his muscles and the din of the presses, some damn pesky thoughts persevered. They nipped and nagged at his conscience.

He should not have asked Annabelle to encourage Marsden. Not for him, not for the paper. It was just plain wrong. He resolved to remedy the situation later and then he put the matter aside.

Or tried.

Annabelle. The clang of the machines seemed to rap out her name.

The hiss of the steam engine, sounding like *Miss.* The deep clank of the cast iron upon cast iron: *An . . . na . . . belle.* The rush of paper through the machine sounding like *Swift.*

Knightly bent to lift the next ream of paper and hurled it to the bloke on his right.

He thought of Annabelle.

*I know it was wrong to ask,* Knightly told himself. *It's inappropriate and taking unfair advantage. I will even concede that it might be morally reprehensible.*

Hell, he knew it was wrong the moment he'd said it. And he'd tried to amend it on the spot but the words died in his throat. Her sweet smile had faded. Her sparkling blue eyes dimmed and then she had averted from his gaze. Right before his eyes she seemed to shrink and fade in a desperate attempt to disappear. He'd been the one to extinguish her with his selfish, brutal request.

The fact remained: an apology was in order. He resolved to do it this afternoon.

Thus, at the moment there was no point in thinking about it further.

And yet, he was still bothered, like a stone in his boot or a wasp trapped under his shirt. The damned machines kept it up, churning out issues of *The London Weekly* and sounding out her name.

*An . . . na . . . belle.*

His muscles began to burn from the exertion. He'd been here hours by now. Sweat soaked though his white linen shirt, flattening it to his chest and abdomen. The exhaustion weakened his mental defenses, so the truth was now unavoidable.

It was the way she felt in his arms. Like ravishment waiting to happen. His mouth went dry thinking of her in his arms: warm, luscious, and pure. A man could lose himself in those curves. Spend a lifetime exploring every wondrous inch of her.

It was that innocence. He wanted to taste it. Touch it. Love it. Be redeemed by it.

And he had tainted it with that loathsome request. Sent her off to seduce another man when he wanted to claim that ripe, red mouth of hers for himself. To capture Annabelle's sighs before they escaped her lips.

Knightly wanted to know that purity, that innocence, the sweetness that was Annabelle. He wanted to know every last inch of her pure milky white skin.

Each and every curve, from the swells of her breasts rising above those newly lowered bodices to the less obvious but just as tantalizing dip in her lower back. There was the tilt at the outer corners of her eyes, catlike, with lashes reaching high. Eyes he had seen closed as she swooned. As she might appear in a real swoon of pleasure. As she might appear in a thoroughly satiated sleep.

That damned faint really did a number on him. Making him see her thus.

*Miss. An . . . na . . . belle. Swift.*

He knew it was wrong to ask Annabelle to appeal to Marsden, but that wasn't what made him feel like a damned devil. He didn't get to where he was by worrying about the delicate sensibilities and bloody feelings of others.

He understood now.

The request he'd made was driving him mad because he wanted her for himself.

Wanted her in a wicked, sinful way.

Her innocence and sweetness was like a breath of fresh air, and here he was in the polluted stench of the factories.

Strange, that. Wanting Annabelle all of a sudden with a profoundly unsettling intensity . . . after all these years when she had been around, under his nose, shrinking back and not wanting to be a bother.

Well, she was a damned bother now, though he'd wager she had no idea about it.

On his way out of the warehouse, Knightly passed a group of workers gathered around the new issue of *The Weekly*, steaming hot off the presses, ink smearing under their already dirty fingertips. One worker read aloud to the others as they shifted around, smoking and listening to the news. Seven or eight men, one newspaper.

Knightly slowed, listening, allowing himself to be drawn into their conversation of the news of the day. This might distract him. He might learn something. He listened to the gruff voice of the man reading, and the thoughtful silence of the other men who listened. It occurred to him in an instant: pictures.

If there were more pictures so even the illiterate could understand if no one was around to read the words to them. It would require some advances to the printing press, some experiments.

"That's Knightly. That's the owner," one of them said roughly as he nodded and picked up his pace, now eager to return to the offices. But first: he owed Annabelle an apology.

# Chapter 23

## Writing Girls, Enraged

### DEAR ANNABELLE

*Perhaps you might do the Nodcock a favor. He'll have
to pay attention to you then.*
*Helpful from Holburn*
The London Weekly

*Roxbury House, teatime*

**"H**E asked you to do *what*?" Julianna gasped.
Annabelle shrank back against the settee. One
minute she had been delightfully retelling her fainting adventures and subsequent carriage ride with
Knightly. The next moment an uncomfortable silence had fallen over her fellow Writing Girls when
she mentioned Knightly's request that she encourage
Lord Marsden's attentions for the good of the paper.

"It makes perfect sense if you think about it," Annabelle said defensively. She did understand Knightly's motives, his logic. She had been hurt by it, but he
didn't know how she felt about him, which lessened
the sting. And should she succeed, she might just
get his attention. And everlasting gratitude.

Julianna, even more brash and fiery than usual, scoffed openly. Sophie and Eliza exchanged nervous glances.

"Explain to me how this is anything but a horribly offensive, inconsiderate thing to ask of you," Julianna said sharply. So sharply it hurt, like a knife to the heart. Annabelle was taken aback by this sudden attack. A second ago they were all laughing over her request to taste Knightly's whiskey.

"He loves his newspaper and it's in trouble. He merely asked for help. People help those whom they love," Annabelle explained. Really, it did make sense. Did it not? She didn't like that he had asked this of her, but understood that it came from a place of love or passion. Or something like it.

"Perhaps," Julianna retorted. "But one does not ask them to encourage the affections of another man. That is not love."

"It's not like that. It's not that simple," Annabelle said, because . . . because . . . of course there was a reason why this was all fine. She just couldn't think of it at the moment. Her urge to help him, to demonstrate her usefulness and love, surpassed all else, but she couldn't quite find the words to explain.

"Annabelle, why don't you explain again," Sophie said gently, resting her hand on hers. "Perhaps Julianna is misunderstanding the situation."

Annabelle recognized the diplomacy; it was usually her role. She wasn't usually the one in the thick of drama. With three grave, concerned faces peering at her, she felt like she was on trial. Her crime: idiocy. Her defense: love. Being helpful. Generally trying to prove she wasn't a nitwit.

She wasn't. Right?

"Knightly noted that Marsden seems to have an interest in me, and asked that I encourage it. My column is also a bit of a success, so he asked that I keep up the ruse. It's business and it's Knightly," she said, as if that *explained* everything. The man thought of nothing else.

But did it excuse his behavior?

Doubts began to creep in, like the dampness in a drafty house on a cold wet winter day. Even under Julianna's scorching glare.

"He doesn't know . . . how I feel," Annabelle added, nervously sipping from the teacup she held in her hands, even though she had no idea what Knightly knew. Or didn't.

"How do you know that, Annabelle?" Sophie asked gently. "How did this make you feel?"

"If he knew, he wouldn't ask this of me," she said stubbornly, even though she was well aware that this was based firmly upon the flimsy foundation of her own wishes. Not hard fact.

The doubts continued their march.

Why was she defending him?

What did she know, anyway? The truth began to dawn: where she had thought herself a noble maiden on a quest for true love, she was probably, in fact, an foolish lovesick girl who was so blinded by the stars in her eyes that she'd hand her murderer the weapon.

Annabelle's head began to throb. A headache.

"Annabelle, he cares about nothing but his paper. Remember when he cast me out—when everyone had turned their back on me?" Julianna persisted, hacking away at Annabelle's illusions, and removing obstacles for the army of doubt to come in, and conquer.

"Because of Knightly's ruthless devotion to *The Weekly*, I almost lost Wycliff," Eliza added. Annabelle glanced sharply at her. Whose side was Eliza on? Julianna's or hers? The shattering of dreams or the preservation of hope?

The throbbing in her head worsened. Her eyes became hot. She would not cry. She would *not* show weakness.

"It just means that he cares. There is nothing wrong with caring," Annabelle said firmly. Yet her hand trembled, and the teacup she held clattered tellingly against the saucer. She had a feeling her friends were right and that she was wrong.

She had feared this moment, in which her friends grew tired of her optimistic infatuation. Of her. Where they no longer thought her sweet, but stupid. She could see it in their pitying gazes and in the worried glances they exchanged amongst themselves.

"Yes, he cares for his newspaper, Annabelle. Not for anyone or anything else," Julianna persisted, driving the point home. Beautiful and bold Julianna. Annabelle felt herself pale and shrink beside her friend, a tower of strength and assurance.

"How did it make you feel when he asked this of you?" Sophie asked gently, again.

"I didn't like it, of course," she said, caving in to pressure because that is what she did. And a little bit of her hadn't liked it. "But he doesn't know how I feel about him, and if he did, I have every confidence he never would have made this request."

She had been confident. Now, thanks to Julianna's

persistent, artful interrogation, she was no longer certain of anything other than her foolishness to persist in loving a man who obviously cared so little for her.

Annabelle leveled a glare in Julianna's direction.

"How can you love a man that would ask that of a woman? No decent man would ask this of a woman, love aside," Julianna said, because she never knew when to stop. If there were a line, Julianna would stomp right across it, turn around and implore you to hurry up and come along.

*What about me?*

Well, maybe it was time she crossed the line. Maybe it was time she defend herself instead of Knightly.

"What is the purpose of this conversation?" Annabelle asked, and her voice had a bold quality to it that sounded strange to her ears. Eliza straightened, Sophie's lips parted, and Julianna fixed her green eyes upon her. "I love Knightly and I have since I first saw him. It's just a part of me and you have known that and now suddenly it's wrong?"

"It was all fine until he asked you to practically prostitute yourself for his bloody newspaper," Julianna replied.

"Julianna!" Sophie and Eliza gasped.

Annabelle took a deep breath. She could do this. She could defend herself.

"What if I want to?" Annabelle challenged. But her hand wavered and tea sloshed over the cup, spilling into the saucer.

"What if you don't, but you have so defined yourself as She Who Loves Knightly that you cannot say no?" Julianna retorted. In the midst of battle, Annabelle recognized that it was a fair question. One she would explore later, on her own.

"Is that what you think of me? That I am nothing more than a foolish girl in love with a heartless man? Perhaps you're right." Annabelle laughed bitterly for the very first time in her six and twenty years. "Look at me—trying to get his attention with ideas from strangers because I have no idea what to do. And now he is starting to notice me and it's suddenly all wrong and—"

"I only want you to be happy, Annabelle, and I'm afraid that—" Julianna said, trying to reach for her hand. Annabelle set the teacup on the tray and stood to go.

"No, you are a know-it-all, Julianna. You may know all the gossip of the ton, but you do not know the contents of my heart nor do you know what is best for me."

And then Annabelle did the unthinkable. She stormed out without even a backward glance.

# Chapter 24

## A Gentleman's Apology

TOWN TALK

*Lord Marsden has succeeded in rallying his peers to support his Inquiry. If you enjoy reading a newspaper, enjoy it now, for it seems our days are numbered.*

*The Morning Post*

AFTER Knightly knocked on the door to the Swift residence, a meek servant opened it and mutely led him to the drawing room where he might await Annabelle.

The room was sparsely furnished. Everything was useful and plain. No thought seemed to have been spared to comfort, just practicality. He thought of his own home, also simple but designed for ease and comfort, with plush carpets and richly upholstered furniture. Everything was expensive, yet nothing was ostentatious.

This room, however, was thrifty to an extreme.

And then there was Annabelle, standing in the doorway. She wore a shapeless brown dress with a white apron pinned to the front. White flour covered her hands, spotted the brown dress, and there was even a smudge on her cheek.

Her eyes, though . . . instead of sparkling, they were dull. In fact, he suspected she had been crying when he noted her eyes were reddish and puffy, too. He felt like he had been punched in the gut.

"What are you doing here?" she asked flatly. When she did not sound pleased to see him, he realized he had expected her to be, which made him feel like an ass. Like a nodcock.

"Why are you wearing an apron?" he asked. She should not be dressed like a servant.

"Cook and I were baking bread," she answered.

"Don't you have help for that?" She was the sister to a prosperous cloth merchant. They should have a fleet of household help. A woman of Annabelle's position should be occupied with friends and finding a husband, not domestic drudgery.

"I am the help," she answered flatly. This was not the Annabelle he knew; she seemed to be missing her sense of magic and wonder. Something was wrong. Was it the awful request he'd made of her? Probably. He was glad he'd come to apologize.

"Why are you here, Mr. Knightly?" she asked.

"Would you like to sit?" As a gentleman, he could not take a seat until she did.

Mutely, she sat upon the settee. He took a place next to her on the most uncomfortable piece of furniture he'd ever encountered. He reached for her hand and held it in his. Her hand was cold.

"I owe you an apology, Annabelle. It was wrong of me to ask you to encourage Marsden on behalf of the newspaper. Or as a favor to me."

Knightly had expected to find his conscience

soothed upon uttering those words. He had traveled across London, all the way from the Fleet Street office to Bloomsbury to deliver them. He thought she would thank him and say not to worry, for she had understood his request was one of a desperate idiot. A nodcock.

Annabelle narrowed her blue eyes and titled her head questioningly. His breath hitched in his throat.

"Julianna put you up to this, didn't she?" she asked. He could not miss the note of accusation in her tone.

"I beg your pardon?"

"You have come to apologize because Julianna thinks it's wrong of you to ask and *pathetic* of me to agree to it," she said, spitting out the words. At least as much as Annabelle could do. Then she took a deep breath that foretold doom and proceeded to say more to him than she ever had in the years he'd known her. "We all know that the only thing you care about is the newspaper. No one is under any illusions here, Mr. Knightly. Not even me, who has a foolish propensity toward flights of fancy and always seeks the bloody goodness in everyone."

Knightly's jaw dropped. *Annabelle had uttered a swear word.* What next—unicorns pulling hackneys and the King in dresses?

"I knew what you were asking of me. And why. I'm not stupid," she added. Her chin jutted forward. She lifted her head high. Angry Annabelle was impish and magnificent all at the same time. Thinking had suddenly become impossible when all the truths he'd ever known seemed null. This was Annabelle as he had never seen her—and, he suspected, as she'd never even been seen.

"It was wrong of me to ask," he said, because that was all he knew in a world that had just turned upside down.

"It was wrong. You really ought to think beyond yourself and your newspaper for once," she lectured. "I ought to have said so at the moment you asked. I'm very sorry you have come all this way to hear me say that. And listen to me! You are in the wrong and I have just apologized. I am such a . . . a . . . nodcock!"

"Annabelle, what is this all about?" he asked in a calm, measured tone.

She took a deep breath to calm herself. She fixed her pretty blue eyes on him.

"You really do not know," she said, awed. He had no idea what she was talking about. It must have shown in his expression. "Oh . . . oh . . . oh . . . bloody hell!"

She flung herself back on the wretchedly uncomfortable settee and just laughed her pretty blond head off while he marveled that Annabelle, who barely spoke, had just uttered the words "bloody hell."

He did not know what was so funny.

He was about to ask when the laughter ceased and the tears began.

Knightly glanced in the direction of the heavens, seeking guidance. Like many a man, nothing flummoxed him like a woman's tears. With some mixture of horror and terror, he watched as Annabelle wept beside him.

Although she looked tragic and adorable, something had to be done to stop this madness. First, he pressed a clean handkerchief into her palm and she pressed it to her eyes. Her pretty shoulders shook as she cried.

Horrors. Curses.

"Bloody hell," he muttered; then, with a sigh, he pulled her into his arms.

Annabelle burrowed her face into his shoulder. No doubt soaking his jacket and cravat with tears. It didn't matter. He could feel her become calm and still in his embrace.

He also felt her soft curls brushing against his fingertips. He felt her breasts pressing against his chest. He felt powerful for having soothed her. It felt right to hold her so close. Above all he craved more. All he wanted was more Annabelle.

He whispered her name.

They were interrupted before anything untoward could occur. A dowdy, hatchet-faced woman stood in the drawing room entry and cleared her throat. Loudly.

"Would someone like to explain this scene to me?" she asked in a sharp voice. Annabelle recoiled from his embrace and took up the smallest possible amount of space on the far end of the settee.

Knightly replied in kind. He did not take orders anywhere, from anyone. "Perhaps introductions might be in order," he stated after rising to his feet.

The woman lifted one brow at his command, in her house.

Annabelle, on the other hand, interrupted in the softest voice.

"This is my sister-in-law, Mrs. Blanche Swift," she said dully. And then with a pleading glance at him, she added, "This is Mr. Knightly, with whom I work on the Society for the Advancement of Female Literacy."

Society for the Advancement of Female Literacy? *Oh, Annabelle.*

Knightly ached to turn to her and ask a thousand questions. But he recognized a scene when he was in the midst of it. He did his best to play his part.

He schooled his features into what he hoped was a charitable expression; he had not inherited his mother's gift for acting.

"Ah, yes. Your charity work," Mrs. Mean Swift said in a glacial tone to Annabelle. "When I suggested that charity begins at home, this was not at all what I had in mind. Who is supervising the children? Have they been fed? What of the bread?"

Annabelle stood a step or two behind Knightly, as if he might protect her from her hatchet-faced sister-in-law. Frankly, he wanted to.

"Nancy is with them," Annabelle answered, even though Knightly thought she ought to reply that governesses and servants existed for those sorts of tasks, not sisters.

"I see." To emphasize her point, Mrs. Swift glared at Annabelle, who took a step back. She then glared at Knightly, who only squared his shoulders, stood taller, and looked down his nose at her. Intimidating with one's size was a juvenile maneuver, but really, sometimes the situation just called for it.

"Mrs. Swift, I would like to conclude my conversation with Miss Swift," he stated. He paused for emphasis and added, "Privately."

Never mind that he was a guest. In her house.

She stared at him with narrowed eyes.

Knightly confidently met her gaze and held it. Unblinkingly. Really, one did not attain his level of success without the ability to win a staring contest.

"I will insist the drawing room door remains open," she said harshly. "The last thing I need is a moral lapse that results in a poor example for my own children." She turned quickly and quit the room. No one was sorry to see her go.

Had he not been fully in the mode of Haughty Commander of All He Surveyed, his jaw might have dropped open.

Did this woman not know Annabelle? He'd wager his fortune she was the *last* person in the world who might corrupt an innocent youth. She was probably the last woman in the world who set a poor example. She was a paragon.

Or did *he* not know her?

Speaking of the little minx, she'd been hiding behind him during that strange introduction, and he turned to face her now. He smiled. And took a seat on the damned uncomfortable sofa.

"My dear Annabelle, you have some explaining to do."

# Chapter 25

## A First Kiss

### DOMESTIC INTELLIGENCE

*The Duke of Kent dismissed his secretary upon dis-covering the man was bribed to relay information to writers of* The Morning Chronicle. *The editor and re-porter's arrests are imminent.*

*The London Weekly*

IN the history of bad days, Annabelle was certain this one would rank in the top one hundred. Perhaps even the top ten. It was certainly one of the worst days in her own life, along with the death and funeral of her parents and the day Blanche married her brother.

There was the horrible fight with her fellow Writing Girls earlier that morning. All these years, she'd been afraid they would find her tedious or foolish. Today her fears were confirmed. It was everything she had dreaded, and more.

Even worse, Knightly had asked her to debase herself for him. While she had not agreed, she had not refused. In fact, she had defended him when she ought to have stood up for herself. That he was here in her drawing room, apologizing, only confirmed that Julianna was correct and she had been a fool.

Had she not been so fixated upon Knightly, to the exclusion of all sense, reason, and eligible bachelors, she might have married another by now. She could be a mother of a darling brood with a home of her own. Annabelle thought of Mr. Nathan Smythe and his bakery down the road. She was baking bread anyway; why not in her own kitchen instead of slaving for the ever-unappreciative Blanche?

Worst of all, she had imagined Knightly calling upon her at home a time or two or twenty. But not like this. Not when she wore her worst dress and her eyes were red after sobbing in a hired hack all the way from Mayfair to Bloomsbury.

Not when she ungraciously ignored his apology, bickered, burst into tears, buried her face in his shoulder and sobbed.

He had held her; it was lovely beyond words to have a man's strong arms holding her close and secure, as if protecting her from the world. She had wanted to savor it more but was all too aware that she was soaking his fine white linen shirt. All too aware that a dream of hers was coming true—Knightly, embracing her—but she was too distraught to enjoy a second of it.

Cruel, cruel world!

Then Blanche interrupted and mortified her. Treating her like a servant was one thing, but to do so in front of Knightly? Words could not describe the humiliation of having him see just how worthless and unloved she was by her own family, in her own home.

He could never love her now. She had a prodigious imagination, but even she could not envision how a man so strong and commanding as he could ever fall for a delusional, foolish, and unappreciated girl like her.

"Miss Swift," Knightly said sternly as he sat on the settee. She stood before him, emotionally distraught and utterly exhausted.

"My dear Annabelle," he said, and she wondered if he was mocking her.

She heaved a sigh.

"You have some explaining to do," Knightly commanded. It was as if the Swift drawing room was his office at *The London Weekly*. Well, it wasn't and she didn't have to explain anything. She told him just that.

"This is not your office. I don't have to explain anything to you," she said. For emphasis, she folded her arms over her chest. Was it her imagination, or did his gaze stray to her décolletage?

"Annabelle, you intrigue me more each day," he said, and her lips parted in shock.

"What do you mean?"

"The Society for the Advancement of Female Literacy?" he questioned with a lift of his brow. She sighed again and sat beside him.

"They do not know the truth," she confessed quietly.

"You've kept that secret for three years?" he asked incredulously.

"Three years, seven months, and five days," she clarified out of habit. "They do not read *The Weekly*. I did not care to encourage them. I fear they would not approve of me writing and would forbid me from doing so."

And it was something that belonged to her, and her alone. Writing for *The Weekly* had been her secret, happy life. Advising and helping other people was the one thing she was good at, and it satisfied her deeply to be recognized for her talent. Much as she assisted at home, her family never gave her much credit for it.

"How did you keep such a secret for so long?" Knightly asked, his blue eyes searching hers for more answers.

"Mr. Knightly," she began impatiently. She moved away and began to pace about the sparsely decorated room. "I exist in the shadows, overlooked. I do not bother people. I live to serve. I am a professional solver of other people's problems, often at the expense of my own. And above all, expectations for me are low. Even if you told Blanche now who you are and what I write, it would take a quarter hour, at least, to convince her you told the truth."

"I see," he said after a long silence.

"Do you? Do you really?"

"I'm beginning to," he said. He glanced over at the open door. "And why do you think Julianna motivated my apology?"

"You know, it's awfully audacious of you to call upon me for this interrogation," Annabelle replied, because she didn't want to answer that question and say that Julianna meddled terribly and that she didn't have faith that Knightly would recognize what a wretched position his request placed her in.

"I came only to apologize. This interrogation was inspired by the oceans of domestic drama I have witnessed in your drawing room. Besides, I didn't become so successful by standing aside," he said, to the girl who was an expert at taking one step to the left—or right, you pick!—and generally getting out of the way.

"What's that supposed to mean?" she asked.

"Be bold, Annabelle," Knightly said, his voice all low and urgent and making her want to do just that, in spite of herself. "I like it. And it probably suits you more than you realize."

"I've been trying," she replied, and there was anguish in her voice. Because this boldness didn't come naturally to her. It was a conscious thought, a deliberate action. For every success, she encountered some sort of trouble Old Annabelle never would have succumbed to.

Old Annabelle never fought with her friends. But then again, Knightly never called upon Old Annabelle.

"I know you've been trying. Trying to the tune of four thousand extra copies each week," Knightly replied with a grin. A usual printing was around ten or twelve thousand. This was really good. She allowed herself to enjoy the rush of enjoyment upon the news.

They both cringed at a massive clattering in the kitchen and paused to identify the unmistakable sound of Blanche, grumbling and storming off to the back of the house.

Knightly stood, walked over to the drawing room door and shut it.

Annabelle did not protest.

"You have not answered my question," Knightly persisted as he strolled toward her. "About Julianna. My apology."

"I fought with them," Annabelle said with a shrug. "They think I am a fool. They are probably right. I certainly feel like one. And I don't want to talk about it with you. I cannot."

Knightly took a step closer to her, closing the distance. With his fingertip, he gently tilted her chin so her face was peering up at him.

"So don't talk, Annabelle," he murmured. And then he lowered his mouth to hers.

And then he kissed her.

Knightly. Kissing. Her.

On one of the top five worst days of her life.

She felt the heat first, of his lips upon hers. Of him being near her. It was a particular sort of heat—smoldering and building up to a crackling fire—and now that she basked in it, Annabelle realized she'd been so very cold for so very long.

This heat: a man's warm palm cradling her cheek, the warmth from his body enveloping hers, and the warmth from his mouth upon hers.

At first it was just the gentle touch of his lips against hers. She felt sparks, she felt fireworks. Her first kiss. A once in a lifetime kiss. With the man she loved. This alone was worth waiting for.

Aye, there was a surge of triumph with this kiss, along with the sparks and shivers of pleasure. She had waited for this. She had *fought* for this. She *earned* this. She was going to enjoy every exquisite second of it.

And then it became something else entirely. His lips parting hers. Her, yielding. Knightly urged her to open to him, and because she trusted him implicitly, she followed his lead with utter abandon. She had no idea where this would go, but she knew she would not go there alone.

This kiss was not at all like she had imagined—she hadn't *known* the possibilities—it was so much more magical. She let him in. She dared the same. She tasted him. Let him taste her.

A sigh escaped her lips, and it did not travel far. This sigh was one of contentment. No, she was not at all content. This was a sigh of utter pleasure, experienced for the first time. This was a sigh that only Knightly's kiss could elicit.

He placed his hand upon her waist, just above the curve of her hip. It was a possessive caress. She wanted to be possessed. She clasped the fabric of his jacket. Her whole world was spinning wildly—in a magical way—and she was dizzy with the delight of it. But still, she needed to hold on. Needed to ground this moment in physical, earthly sensations so she'd know it wasn't some flight of her own fancy.

There was the wool of his coat in her palms.

His cheek against hers. A little bit rough. So very male.

The scent of him, so indescribable but intoxicating all the same. She wanted to breathe him in forever.

The sound of his breathing, the rushed whisper of her own sighs. Little sounds, to be sure, ones that spoke of intimacy and passion.

The pounding of her heart.

The taste of him . . .

His mouth, firm, determined, generous, hot, and possessive against her own. She melted against him. Whatever he wanted, she would indulge. And she wanted, needed, him to know, how much this kiss meant to her. How she had waited her whole life for this kiss. She kissed him with years' worth of pent-up desire. And the amazing, wonderful, exhilarating thing was . . . he kissed her with a passion to match.

# Chapter 26

## The Nodcock Begins to Wonder if
## He Is the Nodcock

### DEAR ANNABELLE

*While many readers have written with encourage-
ment and advice for my quest to attract the love of the
Nodcock, many have challenged me to explain why
I bother. I confess, this author does wonder if he is
deserving of my efforts, or if I should give up. But just
when I am ready to admit defeat, some magic occurs
to convince me to carry on. Dear readers, please
advise! How far does one go for love?*

   *The London Weekly*

*Galloway's Coffeehouse*

KNIGHTLY sat with a newspaper and a hot coffee
at Galloway's coffeehouse, as he did every Saturday morning. His love of newspapers extended
beyond his own. He loved, too, the atmosphere in
the coffeehouse—the rich smell of coffee mingling
with the smoke of cigars and cheroots. The rustle of
newsprint. The hum of conversations.

   He badly needed the coffee, for he had not slept.

He badly needed a distraction, but this was not to be.

He had kissed Annabelle.

Shy, quiet, Writing Girl number four. Annabelle. Just weeks ago he'd barely spared a thought for her, and now . . .

He had kissed Annabelle.

What madness had impelled him, he knew not. But some force beyond his control had him strolling across her horrible drawing room and tilting her chin to his, lowering his mouth to hers.

It had been a good kiss.

So good he had the damnedest time thinking of anything else since it happened. She tasted sweet, dear Annabelle. She kissed with an artlessness and enthusiasm that undid him.

It was not calculated to please, like that of a mistress, and it was all the more seductive because of it. It was a kiss for the sake of it. Purely for the love of it.

Knightly had discovered all these truths in the moments when her tongue tangled with his, just as he had known then that it was her first kiss. The implications of that kind of kiss made his chest feel tight and deprived of air.

But to hell with the implications, if a certain part of him had its way. The memory of the taste, the touch, kept him awake at night, inspiring wicked dreams. He sought relief. He attained it. And yet still, he craved Annabelle.

In an attempt to restore his world to rights, he would coolly consider the facts:

*Fact: Annabelle was in his employ.* No law prohibited him from ravishing his workforce should he so choose, but it just felt . . . wrong. Like taking advantage. That was not the pleasure he sought—and he had given extensive thought to the pleasures he might have with Annabelle.

*Fact: Annabelle lived with strong contenders for the dubious distinction of London's Worst Relatives.* Her family treated her like a servant. Right before his eyes Annabelle shriveled under the menacing glare of the Mean Mrs. Swift, who put him in mind of a particularly nasty school warden.

Annabelle was no servant. She was a beautiful woman and a talented writer—which all of London seemed to know except her family.

Society for the Advancement of Female Literacy, indeed. Of course they never questioned her—likely never paid her that much mind. As she said, they probably wouldn't even believe her if he commissioned her illustration, placed it on the front page along with a statement confirming her as Dear Annabelle, and had a cartload delivered to their front door.

Knightly was of half a mind to do just that, except . . .

*Fact: Annabelle was delicate.* In the course one afternoon, he watched her act boldly, then retreat. Blossom and then wilt. All right before his eyes. Something was happening with Annabelle. He liked Bold Annabelle, and was glad he told her so, even though Bold Annabelle stalked his thoughts and seduced him with a kiss that was a heady mixture of enthusiasm and innocence. Old Annabelle made his life easy. Bold Annabelle set his life on fire.

Something was happening, something glorious, and he didn't want to wreck it. A picture began to emerge of a woman who possessed hope and optimism and gumption in spades in spite of wretched relatives and a world that never took much notice of her—in real life anyway. On the pages of *The London Weekly*, Dear Annabelle was something else: a delightful minx, a sweetheart of a hellion.

It was bloody impossible to concentrate on facts when Drummond and Gage were having the most infuriating conversation about Dear Annabelle, as they were now. Knightly pretended to read *The Morning Post* while eavesdropping on their idiotic chatter.

"You know, I don't think this nodcock deserves Annabelle," Drummond declared as he set down this week's issue. He paused and sipped his coffee, brow furrowed as if he pondered Annabelle's love life in the same way Newton must have puzzled over calculus.

"Though it pains me to agree with you, Drummond, I reckon you're right. And 'Nodcock' is not a strong enough name for the bloody ungrateful, cork-brained jackanape she's set her cap for," Gage added thoughtfully.

"Obviously, he has bruised her soul and is testing her faith in love," Drummond said, jamming his finger at that particular page of *The London Weekly*. "Positively criminal, that is."

Knightly snorted. Faith in love? Bruised her soul? What sentimental rubbish. But what else would one expect from a playwright? All the same, he shrunk back in his chair and lifted his own newspaper higher.

He had read her column, holding his breath the whole damn time. He had his suspicions. But the cost of confirming those suspicions was too high. He would either give up his lifelong quest to prove he belonged with his peers or break Annabelle's heart.

He was not prepared to do either.

"It sounds like she has attracted his attention but he just took advantage of her, if you know what I mean," Gage said. Knightly's gut knotted.

"It does, doesn't it? You're right. 'Nodcock' is not a strong enough word. You know, I wish I knew who he was only so I could plant a right facer on him," Drummond practically growled.

For years Knightly read the papers and drank coffee with these old friends, and in all that time he'd never heard Drummond react so bloody passionately to a single item in any newspaper. It was worse than when *The London Chronicle* described one of his plays as "entertaining as a severe bout of smallpox" after he'd shelled out six pounds in puff money.

"While you're doing that, I'm going to whisk Dear Annabelle off to Gretna Green and along the way show her the love of a good man," Gage said with a rakish grin that made Knightly want to plant a right facer on *him*.

Knightly concluded it was up to him to bring logic and rationality to this conversation—before his temper flared and he revealed far too much.

"You cannot be serious," he said flatly, lowering the newspaper he'd been pretending to read.

"Oh, I am," Drummond said solemnly, hands clasped upon the rough-hewn table.

"I as well," Gage added with equal gravity. He pounded the table for emphasis.

"You don't even know her," Knightly pointed out.

"Aye, but you do. Fancy introducing us?" Gage asked with suggestive lift of his brow.

"No," Knightly replied firmly. In the name of all that was holy, no.

"Why not? She's obviously a lovely chit who is lonely and looking for love," Gage said.

"And young, pretty, and quiet," Drummond added in a way that could only be described as dreamily, even though it pained Knightly to do so.

"Do you not think she deserves love?" Gage demanded.

"It's her own business," Knightly said, snapping the newspaper shut and setting it on the table.

"Maybe it *was*. But once she started writing about it in the newspaper it became everyone's business," Drummond said. Unfortunately, he had a point.

"Given that it's your newspaper," Gage said, "I'd think you'd be more interested it. Being your business and all."

"Annabelle is . . ." And here Knightly's description faltered. She was shy, except for when she was bold. She was beautiful. Adorable, even when her eyes were red with tears. She was a mystery, ever unfolding before his eyes, which both fascinated and terrified him.

And he had kissed her.

He'd choke before he said any of those things aloud, and he'd choke to death before uttering such sentiments to the likes of Drummond and Gage.

"Annabelle is a very nice person," he finally said. His companions stared at him, slack-jawed. And then they both burst into raucous laughter, slapping each other hard on the back and pounding the table with their fists. Old Man Galloway himself hollered at them to shut their traps.

"It's you, isn't it? You're the Nodcock!" Drummond shouted, and pointed, in the midst of roaring laughter. The rest of the coffeehouse quieted, heads lifted up from newsprint pages to stare at him.

"I'm not the Nodcock," Knightly said hotly, feeling like quite the . . . Nodcock. He cursed that damn faint. Until that moment he could exist in a blissful ignorance, caring only about the Nodcock's affect on sales and not his identity. He could assume it was Lord Marsden or Owens (it could *still* be Owens) and carry on with his plans.

He cursed Drummond and Gage for their laughter and accusations because they brought to the fore an issue he wanted to ignore. He wasn't ready to make that fateful decision. *Belong. Be beholden to no one. Break Annabelle's heart.*

The entire situation was impossible. Their laughter was irritating. Yet Knightly retained a cool demeanor nonetheless, because that's what he did. That's who he was: cool verging on cold. Always in control. The laughter of some louts rolled right off his back, like water off a duck.

But he suddenly thought of Annabelle, and the day Owens declared her too well behaved to be wicked and thus *unworthy* of investigation. They had all laughed.

Shame and remorse kicked him in the gut as Knightly realized, belatedly, how devastating that must have been for her. Was that the day she started to blossom? Had that been the moment she resolved to capture Owens's attentions?

Was their kiss something meaningful, or sweet

Annabelle's determination to be wicked? Was he the Nodcock or just another man she practiced her tricks upon?

So many questions and none of them mattered. He had decided his fate years ago, on an October day in 1808. When he made decisions, he acted and abided by them.

# Chapter 27

### Missing: One Loving Sigh from the Lips
### of Dear Annabelle

TOWN TALK

*Mr. Knightly's proposal to Lady Marsden must be im-*
*minent. We have it on good authority that he visited a*
*jeweler in Burlington Arcade. However, he left with-*
*out making a purchase.*

*The Morning Post*

*Offices of* The London Weekly

THE first thing Knightly noticed upon entering the
writers' room: Annabelle did *not* sigh. The second
thing he finally noticed: she had always sighed
when he strolled into the weekly gathering of writers. It was this routine, like clockwork, that he never
realized until the watch broke.

For a moment he faltered. She had sighed; he had
kissed her; now she did not sigh. The facts explained
nothing. Logic and reason failed him. He wracked
his brain thinking back over her columns—had
there been clues he missed? He tried to tell himself
it mattered not.

But his mind wandered to Annabelle.

His gaze strayed to Annabelle.

He craved Annabelle.

Yet his decision had been made and obligations remained. Both Lord *and* Lady Marsden were becoming impatient with him. He drank tea with the lady, drank brandy with the gentleman. He visited the jeweler but found himself unable to find something suitable. Something that declared, *I belong. You can't ignore me.* None of the diamonds, rubies, or sapphires were large enough.

This morning he'd learned that the editor of *The London Chronicle* had been arrested for printing an editorial that questioned the Inquiry . . . and that relied on facts gleaned from penny-a-liners employed as footmen.

It was clear to Knightly what he must do—would do, because he was a man of action.

Given all that, he should not care in the slightest about a sigh, or lack of one. And yet here he was, standing mutely in front of his staff, pondering the absence of a sigh.

He scowled, mightily.

He would not be undone by the absence of a pretty girl's sigh.

He glared at the room.

That's when he noticed that Annabelle wasn't where she was supposed to be, or where she always was.

They had a routine, he and his staff, and today she had disrupted it, tremendously. He would walk in. Annabelle would sigh. He said, "Ladies first," and then meeting would commence with the Writing Girls rattling off their reports one after another, seated side by side in a neat row.

Today Annabelle sat between Owens and Grenville. Knightly narrowed his eyes—was Owens the Nodcock? How else to explain why Annabelle sat beside him, and touched his hand when he leaned over to whisper something in her ear? Something that made her blush and smile.

"What the devil is going on?" He asked, irritated, and itching to put his fist through the wall. Or into Owens's jaw. No one answered. "Miss Swift, why are you over there?"

Then he remembered how she preferred the sidelines to the center of attention and resolved to not make her uncomfortable before the other writers.

"Never mind," he said gruffly. And then the meeting proceeded mostly as usual. His staff chattered. They debated the Scandal at *The Times*. He stole glances at Annabelle, her lowered bodice. Her lowered gaze.

At the conclusion of the meeting, he clasped Annabelle by the arm as she attempted to slink past him, arm in arm with Owens. He had questions—he didn't know quite what they were—and he suspected she had answers.

It had been his plan to act even more imperiously to remind them both of the Right Order in the world. But when he said her name, "Annabelle," he heard the questions, the sleeplessness, and something like feelings in his voice.

"If you're going to apologize again, I'd rather you wouldn't," she said, stunning him.

"Why would I apologize, Annabelle?" He leaned against the doorway.

"For the kiss," she whispered, and she leaned toward him to keep the words private. He breathed deep, breathing in Annabelle.

He ought to apologize, probably. For taking advantage of a woman in a state of despair, and who was in his employ and thus could not risk rebuffing his advances. But he had tasted her wanting, her desire—along with that intoxicating sweetness. There was no way in hell he'd apologize because he wasn't the slightest bit sorry.

And as anyone could attest, he hadn't become so damned successful by issuing apologies. So he leaned in closer to her and murmured:

"Oh, I'm not sorry for that kiss, Annabelle."

It was the truth. He was bewildered by it, wanted it again, couldn't make sense of it, craved it . . . he had a million thoughts and feelings about that kiss, but regret was not one of them.

"You're not?" she asked. Her expectation didn't surprise him, but it bothered him. She had no idea how beautiful and alluring she was, did she? But then again, why should she if she loved a man from afar, for years, and he never paid attention to her?

"Are you sorry?" he asked.

"You didn't mean to do it, did you?" she questioned. She must have spent hours fretting over what it meant and what his intentions were. When was a kiss not just a kiss? When it was with Annabelle. He meant that in the very best and worst ways. The best answer he could give her was plain honesty.

"I did not drive from Fleet Street to Bloomsbury with the intention, no. But it's not as if I tripped and fell and our mouths collided."

She couldn't help it; she giggled. Progress. He grinned.

The words "Am I the Nodcock" were just there in the back of his throat, waiting to be spoken aloud. But it sounded too ridiculous to actually say aloud. Frankly, he did not want to know.

Because if he knew . . . .

If it was he . . . .

If she had been pining after him all these years and he was only just noticing her now, when he intended to marry another woman, then fate was a cruel mistress indeed. Knightly could not think of this here, now. Instead he snuck another glance at her bodice to clear his mind. And then his gaze fell on a thick packet of letters in her hands.

"What scheme are you up to this week?" he inquired. What did he have to watch out for? he wondered. Or was it none of his concern? He couldn't rule out Owens—not with those damned winks and whispers they shared throughout the meeting.

"I can't tell you yet," she said, with a nervous laugh. He lifted one brow, questioning. "Because . . . I haven't read them through, all of them. The suggestions are becoming more and more outlandish. Like this one: compose a song and hire a group of singers to serenade him."

"I don't know if that's the way to appeal to men," Knightly said frankly. But it surely would put to rest the matter of who she was after. *Which he did not want to know. Why did he not want to know?*

"I don't know that I'd have time to write my column after composing a song, hiring and training singers, and finding a moment when they might perform for the Nodcock."

"Your advice column must come first," he insisted.

"Then I shan't take this reader's advice to commission a portrait of myself in a suggestive pose and have it delivered to the Nodcock or displayed at the National Gallery. Just imagine those hours of sitting still and not writing. Nor shall I fling myself in front of an oncoming carriage while the Nodcock looks on and presumably rescues me. If he notices me . . ."

It was on the tip of his tongue to say, *Have that put on my schedule, it would make great copy,* but he felt like an ass for presuming it was he, and that she wanted him enough to risk life and limb like that for him. That was the thing; he could not *ask* without sounding like the most pompous, presumptuous nodcock.

"I am appalled at these suggestions," he stated. "And like these readers, the blokes down at the coffeehouse are full of idiotic ideas. They also fancy themselves in love with you."

"Are they suitable gentlemen?" Annabelle inquired, and his jealousy flared. "If so, I may wish to meet them."

"They are not suitable at all," Knightly said flatly. And then he could not resist inquiring further— because one did not attain his level of success without always inquiring further. "More to the point, I thought you were quite taken with the Nodcock, as you call him."

"It's a funny thing, really," Annabelle said in a thoughtful tone. He caught himself holding his breath, hanging off her every word. Because what she was saying wasn't what he expected. He didn't like it either, and he didn't know why, and deliberately avoided a thorough examination of his heart and mind.

"I suppose the question is, is the Nodcock taken with me?" she asked. "And how far is this scheme supposed to go? But don't worry, Mr. Knightly. I'll turn in good copy, as befitting *The London Weekly*."

Bryson, the secretary, stood off to the left and cleared his throat.

"Yes, what is it?" Knightly asked. He didn't take his eyes off Annabelle.

"Mr. Knightly, you asked that I remind you of your afternoon appointments. Mr. Skelly is here to see you about the new factory acquisitions, Mr. Mitchell requested an interview, and you had promised to visit with Lady Marsden this afternoon."

"Thank you, Bryson. I'll just be a moment," Knightly said. He didn't once take his eyes off Annabelle.

*Fact:* Annabelle did that thing where she tried to make herself invisible. She took a step away from him. She developed a sudden fascination with the hem of her dress. She clasped her arms over her chest, turning in on herself.

It had been the mention of Lady Marsden, no? What else might it be?

*Fact:* He was stricken with the preference to spend the afternoon with Annabelle, rather than call upon Lady Marsden. Rather than issue the proposal that would assure him the success he'd sought all his life. Since the moment the New Earl uttered those crushing words:

*Throw the bastard out. He doesn't belong here.*

*Fact:* Lady Marsden was the golden ticket to all

of his long-held plans. Success. Power. Vindication. Recognition—especially from the New Earl.

*Fact:* Men in their right mind didn't throw the lot of that away, and he'd always prided himself on logical, rational behavior.

"You have a busy afternoon. I shan't keep you any longer," Annabelle said, and she bid him a good afternoon.

*Fact:* He wanted her to keep him longer.

# Chapter 28

## Lady Roxbury's Apology

FASHIONABLE INTELLIGENCE BY A LADY OF DISTINCTION
*The identity of Dear Annabelle's nodcock is the best kept secret in London, and apparently a secret from the Nodcock himself. But how much longer must she—and her readers—wait for him to come to his senses?*

*The London Weekly*

AFTER the meeting in which Annabelle cowardly avoided her friends, Julianna clasped her arm and tugged her down the stairs and out to her awaiting carriage. The Roxbury crest was emblazoned on the side in bright gold. A bullet hole pierced the very center of it, courtesy of an irate Julianna. Unlike this version of Julianna, sitting opposite her in the carriage. She appeared to be making a concerted effort to appear woeful and contrite.

"I owe you an apology," Julianna stated, presumably in reference to their argument the previous week. Annabelle had been in a wretched mood ever since. It had even dulled the lovely glow from Knightly's kiss, which was an unforgivable sin.

Old Annabelle didn't have these problems. New Annabelle had considered reverting to her previous ways.

"So much talk of apologies lately," Annabelle mused.

"Who else . . . ? Was it . . . ?" Julianna leaned forward eagerly. Then, remembering herself, she leaned back and folded her hands primly in her lap. "No, that is not the point. I behaved abominably toward you, Annabelle, and it was horrid of me to do so. I am so very sorry. You love Knightly. He just doesn't realize what a treasure your love is, and that angers me."

Annabelle eyed her cautiously. She did seem sorry. Julianna did have the unfortunate habit of shooting her mouth off (and actually shooting— Annabelle took a moment to be grateful it hadn't come to that).

"If you must know, Knightly also apologized. That should answer the question you remarkably restrained yourself from asking. Which means you were right, that it was wrong of him to ask me to encourage Marsden. Upon that we all agree. It's funny, though: I was a fool, and yet everyone is groveling to me."

"I'm sorry that I was right," Julianna said, and Annabelle laughed at the sentence least likely ever to be uttered by her friend.

"Let's not get carried away, Julianna," she cautioned, but a smile tugged at her mouth.

"No, truly. I want you to be happy, and Knightly, too. But only if his happiness is found with you. And yes, I know that's probably the wrong thing to say. But I'm not as goodhearted as you, Annabelle.

And my own experiences with Knightly have been . . . difficult."

"Is that because of him, or because of you?" Annabelle asked.

"Eliza also— What is your point?"

"My point is that it was simple before. I adored, he ignored . . ." Annabelle paused to marvel on the poetry of that. "But now it seems that not only is he beginning to see me, but I am also beginning to see him as he is and not how I have imagined him to be."

"Do you still love him?" Julianna asked.

"Does it even matter?" Annabelle mused, shrugging. "He kissed me, Julianna. And yet now he is calling upon Lady Marsden and probably proposing marriage to her this very moment. I do not know how much more I can bear."

Her love of Knightly, the thrill of her successes, the terror of still losing, was beginning to exact a toll on Annabelle. This past week, after the fight with her friends and Knightly's kiss had lead to hours of musing, pondering, wondering. In the end, she'd barely ate or slept and was none the wiser.

And know Knightly was still going to call upon Lady Marsden after he had kissed her. The Nodcock.

"Did you love the kiss? Was the kiss just delicious?" Julianna asked, eyes aglow.

"Yes," Annabelle replied. The exact details—the taste of him, the heat of his touch—those were hers to savor and hers alone. And yet . . . "However, I fear I may go mad trying to puzzle out what it all means. What do you know about him and Lady Marsden?"

"Would you believe me if I said nothing?" Julianna asked, cringing.

"Not at all," Annabelle retorted. Perhaps she wasn't a fool after all.

"This is part of the reason I behaved so horribly. Everyone believes a proposal is imminent. It was in *The Morning Post* that he was sighted perusing jewelry at Burlington Arcade. He did not purchase anything."

Another matter that had weighed heavily upon Annabelle's conscience was that Letter from Lady Marsden, which had spent days and nights tucked away in a novel, on a very high shelf. It remained unanswered.

But Annabelle knew the contents well: *I am pressured to marry but I love someone far below my station . . .*

She really ought to give her an answer. Or admit that she didn't know what to do. Or do the *right* thing and suggest she hold out for true love.

"Will her brother allow it?" Annabelle asked. Lord Marsden had sent her flowers, and might just forbid the marriage that would destroy her hopes and dreams. She liked him.

"He is encouraging the match! He covets Knightly's fortune and influence, you see. I am so vexed that I can't publish a word of all this drama," Julianna said, scowling and wringing her hands. "And of course, one can't avoid the conclusion that Knightly certainly stands to gain protection for the paper if he makes this match."

She no longer liked Lord Marsden very much. There were not enough pink roses in the world to console her if he forced his sister to marry her own true love . . . lest Knightly risk losing everything he valued most.

But wait . . .

Annabelle frowned, puzzling over these two contradictory pieces of information. Lady Lydia loved one man and was pressured to marry another . . . She had just assumed she loved Knightly because . . . well, of course she did. She found him extremely deserving of that fine emotion.

But Lady Lydia also said she was pressured to marry a man she didn't love. If her brother was pressuring her to marry Knightly . . . it meant that she didn't love Knightly.

Which mattered because . . .

"Who is her lover, then?" Annabelle asked. If her hunch was correct, Knightly was about to shackle himself in a loveless marriage. This struck her as terribly sad.

"What do you mean?" Julianna queried, tilting her slightly.

"She loves someone. But not Knightly. Who?" Annabelle questioned.

"How do you know that?" Julianna asked.

"Never mind how," Annabelle said, waving off the question. "I suppose it doesn't change anything, really. He is still courting her. Lord Marsden is approving of the match. Knightly shall marry her and they'll be so very posh and fashionable and aristocratic and I shall slog out the rest of my days helping Blanche and everyone else."

"Here is what you must know, Annabelle," Julianna said earnestly, leaning forward and clasping Annabelle's hands in hers. " If you love him you must fight for him."

"But what if I want him to fight for me?"

And then she understood why she couldn't derive supreme satisfaction from the kiss or her progress thus far. She had teased and tugged him along. She stalked and hunted, when she wanted him to chase her.

"Why all the talk of fighting when we are speaking of love? You must admit, Annabelle, that you have waited and waited and nothing came of it. And now you've set your cap for him, pursued him, and he has kissed you. Frankly, I do not see why you are wavering."

"I am chasing him and he is chasing Lady Lydia," Annabelle stated plainly.

"And may the best woman win," Julianna urged. "You have a duty to your readers, Annabelle, to see this through, if nothing else. Now tomorrow evening is the charity ball for the Society to Benefit Unfortunate Women. Knightly will be there."

"How do you know that? How do you know *everything*?" Annabelle asked.

"Because I know that he gives a sizable contribution. Secretly he's charitable, that Mr. Knightly. Also, I assisted the hostess, Lady Wroth, with the invitations, so I knew he was invited. And then I may have peeked at Bryson's calendar that he keeps for Knightly, so I confirmed he would be attending."

"Julianna!"

"Can I help it if he left it unattended to investigate the smell of smoke?" Julianna asked with feigned innocence and a delicate shrug. Obviously one could not help it at all.

"There was no smoke, was there?" Annabelle questioned; Julianna's reply was an impish grin, and Annabelle supplied the words: "Of course there wasn't. How do you manage these things, Julianna? If I had half the gumption you did—"

"You are writing about your own trials and tribulations in love for all of London to read. I'd say that's gumption in spades. The whole city is cheering for you to succeed, Annabelle."

Tears stung at Annabelle's eyes. It wouldn't do to disappoint the entire population of London by giving up when she had gotten so far. If Knightly was going to marry Lady Lydia, she vowed that he would at least know how she felt before he did so.

# Chapter 29

## Lady Lydia's Secret, Revealed

KNIGHTLY thought of Annabelle as he traveled to the Marsden residence. To be more specific, he thought about how he wished to be traveling to the Swift residence. More to the point, he really wanted Annabelle here, in this carriage, with him.

Why the devil did she think he would apologize for that kiss?

What kind of man did she think he was, anyway? Whatever she thought, he was not the kind that apologized for pleasuring them both.

In the far recesses of his mind—the part devoted to decency, which was currently largely overruled by the part devoted to thoughts of lust—it occurred to him that he was planning a seduction of one woman while on his way to court another. It also occurred to him that this wasn't the best example of decent, gentlemanly behavior.

Rather caddish of him, really.

But the facts were thus:

*Fact: The London Weekly* was the most important thing to him.

*Fact:* Lady Lydia's hand in marriage would ensure that Marsden didn't crack down on the nefarious reporting tactics of his reporters. Another one had been arrested—this time a reporter from *The Daily Register.*

*Fact:* Lady Lydia's hand in marriage would also assure his prominent place in high society. Like his father before him. The New Earl would not be able to ignore him.

*Fact:* Annabelle's kiss made him want to throw thirty-five years worth of facts aside and ravish her thoroughly, completely, utterly.

*Fact:* He was not going to throw away thirty-five years worth of facts, truths, and plans for a kiss. That was the rash action of madmen. He was the epitome of a sane, logical, practical man.

Or he used to be. Knightly exited the carriage, strolled up to the Marsden's residence, and generally made an effort to ignore the sense of dread in his gut.

"My brother is not at home," Lady Lydia declared when she received him in the drawing room. It was a fair enough slight, for he'd often combined his calls to her with visits with Marsden.

"Actually, I have come to visit with you, Lady Lydia," he replied.

"Of course you have," she said with a sigh.

"Would you care for a walk, Mr. Knightly? I've been sitting here all day, chattering and drinking tea. I fear I shall go mad if I don't get a breath of fresh air. I first must fetch my shawl."

Women and their blasted shawls, he thought. He knew Annabelle had left hers behind as some sort of ploy. But had it been for Owens . . . or another? He did not dare entertain that thought. Not with Lady Lydia present.

"Lord Marsden is with Parliament," she began as they strolled along the streets of Mayfair in the direction of the park. "I suppose you shall wish for an update."

It irked him, that. While their courtship and relationship was never based upon affection, she didn't need to be so obvious about it. Though any romantic streak he possessed was buried deep, Knightly was the product of a love match (if not a marriage), and this cool detachment was uneasy to him. How he planned to endure it for a lifetime of holy matrimony had not been considered in great depth. He thought only of immediate threats, not long-term happiness.

Status, he reminded himself. His peers. He'd be a damned earl if it weren't for a few twists of fate. *Throw the bastard out. He doesn't belong here.*

He did belong, though. Knightly gritted his teeth. He would prove it.

"Would you believe it if my intentions to you went beyond digging for gossip?" he asked Lady Lydia. "I'll ask Marsden myself. Just to confirm if his reports matched those of my reporters."

That was the other thing. Marsden wasn't the only one with information. Owens was on the case, and Grenville, too. The details they unearthed were ... intriguing. Incriminating. Hints of blackmail and bribery. It seems Marsden had been paying enormous suppression fees ... until the money started running out.

Those explosive, expensive secrets that consistently eluded him.

Lady Lydia treated Knightly to a long look with those large brown eyes that put him in mind of a startled doe.

"You are not afraid of him. Most people are," she said, and it was clear he had impressed her.

"Most people don't have something that he wants," Knightly replied easily.

"And what might that be?" Lady Lydia inquired. What could the tradesman possibly possess that a peer of the realm could want? He could hear the derision in her voice, and it only made him want to marry her more so he might prove to her, and everyone, that he was not any less than they.

"I have a fortune," Knightly answered. "And influence."

There was a pause, in which undoubtedly they both thought of the rumors that plagued the Marsdens, from her missing season to their evaporating funds, and the ability to stop it.

"Most of the newspapers are terrified of him," she replied, but did not correct his presumption that his wealth was appealing. So much so that his lower status could perhaps be overlooked.

"No one of any sense reads that rubbish," he replied, and Lady Lydia laughed.

"So if you are not here to talk about newspapers and my brother and his mad schemes, then what brings you?" she asked. She paused under a tree and pulled her shawl close around her shoulders. "I know my brother wants me to marry you. But what of my wishes on the matter?" she asked. And there was something desperate in her voice: *What about me?*

"What are they?" he asked.

Lady Lydia paused. Her jaw dropped open. She remembered she was a lady and closed it. Obviously he was the first man to inquire about her wishes.

"My wishes would not be supported by society," she said stiffly.

"Does this have anything to do with your extended stay in the country?" he asked. The reporter in him didn't shy away from questions, even the insensitive ones. Besides, Lady Lydia seemed to respond well to direct and open conversation. He liked that about her.

"Perhaps. You do know, of course, that *The Times* reporter was after me," she told him. He did not know that . . . but he stitched that fact together with what he had learned from Brinsley. Rumors of a pregnancy. An extended stay in the country. A missing season. It was now clear to him what her secret was.

Knightly said none of that. Instead he asked, "Whatever do you mean?"

"Do not play obtuse, Knightly. It doesn't suit you. There were rumors about me, being with child. What better way to confirm them than by disguising oneself as a physician?"

"Other than time?"

"Time will tell, usually. But that is not as lucrative. The rumors were bad enough, but it was the blackmail and suppression fees that have nearly bankrupted us. And still, in spite of that . . . the gossip has been horrendous. I had to go away." She shuddered, and Knightly actually felt a strong stab of guilt for all the gossip peddling he'd done in his day. It had earned him a fortune, which might be the Marsdens' salvation. Funny, that.

"You're intriguing, Lady Marsden," he said. And wasn't that the truth. The web of secrets and gossip was woven thick around him. He imagined Julianna would be beside herself to have this conversation.

"You might as well call me Lydia. Though it will certainly set tongues a-wagging," she replied with a wry smile.

"You never did answer about your wishes on the matter of my courtship," Knightly replied.

"I'm agog that you would mention it again after what I just confessed to you."

"I'll be frank with you, Lady Lydia. There is no pretense that it is a love match. You and your brother would benefit from my fortune, and your brother's political career particularly would benefit from my influence. I want an entrée into the ton. This would be a marriage of convenience, but we could get along."

As far as proposals went, it was certainly a contender for "least romantic" or "the worst." But it was the truth.

It wasn't what she wanted to hear.

Lady Lydia blinked and asked, "What if I want a love match?"

# Chapter 30

## The Hero, at Work

**DOMESTIC INTELLIGENCE**

*Two newspapers have folded—*The Society Chronicle *and* Title Tattle *—for lack of staff after too many writers were arrested for questionable journalistic practices by Lord Marsden's Inquiry.*

*The London Weekly*

*Offices of* The London Weekly

**L**ADY LYDIA hadn't said yes. But Lady Lydia hadn't said no either. His fate hung suspended in the hands of a noblewoman in need of a fortune who wished for a love match, presumably with some impoverished mystery lover.

And then there was Annabelle . . .

His thoughts kept returning to Annabelle.

He kept tasting her on his lips, no matter how much wine or brandy he drank.

The hour was late, and Knightly was still at his desk. Candles burned low. A stack of articles begged for his attention, but he couldn't give it. One sheet of paper in particular haunted him. Dear Annabelle.

Dear God, Annabelle.

*It was just a newspaper article.* Some femalecentric fluff that appeared on page seventeen, between adverts for medications of dubious efficacy and haberdashery. Or so he told himself, even though he was well aware that Dear Annabelle contained hopes and dreams of a beautiful woman. It was a fleet of devastating words in her girlish script. It was a love story that had nearly all of London riveted.

He picked up the sheet of paper, determined to see only grammar and spelling.

Would she write of their kiss? he wondered. And if she did . . . he leaned back and raked his fingers through his hair.

It all came down to one question, didn't it?

Was he the Nodcock?

Suspicions remained. They lurked in the back of his head, and Knightly did his damnedest to ignore them.

He edited Grenville's twelve-page transcription of parliamentary debates. He corrected the grammar in Owens's news reports on fires, robberies, and other crimes. He edited out the libelous statements from Lady Julianna's "Fashionable Intelligence." He poured a brandy and did the rest.

And it all came back to Annabelle.

Amongst all the articles was a quick portrait of her that he'd requested done, partially inspired by Drummond's and Gage's obsession and curiosity, partly inspired by seeing the men who couldn't read listening to the paper being read aloud. In this sketch she looked pretty. Quiet. Shy. He set it aside, knowing what trouble it would cause her if this were printed and her horrible relatives witnessed such undeniable proof of her Writing Girl status. Knightly placed it in the top drawer of his desk. And when he could avoid it no more, he gave his attention to the newest installment of Dear Annabelle.

*Dear readers, your suggestions are becoming more outrageous by the day, much to the amusement of my fellow Writing Girls and myself. From moonlit serenades to specially commissioned portraits or even a simple declaration in these pages . . . Yet one writer writes with a suggestion that is utterly simple and unbelievably risky: Do nothing . . .*

Oh no, she did not get to do nothing when he desperately needed a clue, a confirmation. When he wondered what he was to Annabelle. Wondered when he *wanted* to be something to her.

They had kissed, and the whole world seemed askew, like it shifted on its axis and started spinning in the other direction. This new world intrigued him, even though Knightly could see it meant letting go of the old world . . .

*What if I want a love match?* Lady Lydia's question was pointed, the implications devastating. If she married him, it would be reluctantly and he would never again taste Annabelle on his lips. If they did not marry, *The London Weekly* would have to survive on wits and popularity alone in a climate when every printed word risked imprisonment for the writer. These were the tangible things that he could wrap his muddled brain around.

Knightly closed up the offices and set out for home. A walk in the cool night air would clear his head, and somewhere between Fleet Street and Mayfair he would figure out what was to be done about Lydia's love match, his newspaper, and the constant craving for the sweet taste of Annabelle's kiss.

The houses in Mayfair were lit up, with balls and soirees in full swing. Knightly wove his way through streets congested with carriages and drunken revelers until he came to one house in particular.

The one belonging to all the Earls of Harrowby, and where the earl had lived with his other family. Knightly had never graced the halls. He had never been summoned before the desk in his father's study to report on his lessons or receive a punishment. He had never strolled through the portrait gallery to observe the paintings of centuries of relatives whose names and stories were still a mystery to him. He had never slept in the nursery, climbed a tree in the garden, or explored the attics. There was an entire life he had never lived.

As things stood now, he would never dine with his brother in the family home. Nor would they smoke cigars and sip port and make stupid wagers whilst the ladies took tea in the drawing room. They would not reminisce about their father. They wouldn't speak at all.

It was likely they never would, unless he married well.

If he were the Nodcock . . . then he'd have to break Annabelle's heart in order to obtain entry to his father's house.

It was just one kiss. He tried to convince himself of this, and failed. It was so much more than just a meeting of lips one afternoon. If he was the Nodcock, then Annabelle was the price he'd have to pay to live out his life-long dream.

# Chapter 31

## Annabelle Truly Falls in Love

### THE MAN ABOUT TOWN

*It is a small consolation that Lady Harrowby is no longer alive to witness her husband's illegitimate child swiftly climbing the rungs of the social ladder. How mortifying it would have been for the countess to be confronted by her husband's transgression at something so civilized as a soiree. One must sympathize with Earl Harrowby, who must encounter this family shame with an appallingly increasing frequency.*

*The London Times*

**A**NNABELLE arrived at the ball with Julianna and was quickly left to her own devices as her friend spent more time trolling the private alcoves and other dimly lit areas where gossip and scandal lurked. Awkwardly on her own, Annabelle stood next to a potted palm while she tried to identify which corner belonged to the wallflowers and spinsters, and thus where she would go.

A conversation happening just to her left intrigued her. Temporarily abandoning plans to spend the ball in a state of hopeful desperation with other imperfect girls, she retreated into the protection afforded by the large plant and eavesdropped.

"They let anyone in these days, do they not?" The man who made this remark was tall, with dark hair brushed back from his face and deep blue eyes. Everything about him screamed overbearing aristocrat, from the perfect cut of his evening clothes to his rigid posture.

"It is a charity ball, Harrowby. Anyone who can afford a significant donation is welcome to attend," the friend said, with a notable emphasis on *afford*.

Annabelle peered out to look at these . . . snobs. But her gaze was drawn to Knightly, standing just behind them. His mouth was pressed in a firm line and the hand holding his drink was a fist. He must have heard. He must have assumed they were speaking about him. Her gaze shifted between the two men and she noticed a similarity in their appearance.

"What is this world coming to?" the man named Harrowby said to his friend, but it was Knightly who replied.

"Welcome to the future, Harrowby, when talent supersedes nitwits with nothing to recommend them other than the name of long dead ancestors," he said easily. But still, Annabelle saw the fierce grip he kept on his drink. She wouldn't have been shocked if he cracked the cut crystal glass with his bare hands.

"A name you'd do anything to have," Harrowby replied with such disdain that Annabelle recoiled behind a palm frond. "I cannot believe you have the audacity to speak to me."

Harrowby glanced uneasily around to see who might be witnessing the exchange. Annabelle shrank back even farther into the refuge afforded by the potted palm.

"Nothing like family, though is there?" Knightly mused in a jovial tone likely designed to be particularly provoking. Annabelle continued to watch his hands, still gripping the glass so hard his knuckles were white. He was anything but relaxed, no matter how he might seem.

"Apparently not," Harrowby said, his voice like ice. "As my father abandoned his *real* family for some doxy and her bastard."

If she understood the conversation correctly— Annabelle never presumed things of that nature— then it seemed that Knightly had a brother. Or if one wanted to be precise, a half brother. Had she heard anything about his family? He didn't seem like a man who had one. It seemed that Knightly had been born all-powerful and fully formed.

"Talk about me all you like, but leave my mother out of it," Knightly said. Or so Annabelle thought he'd said. His voice was low and his expression menacing. But he stood his ground as she shrank back and away from the conflict.

"You are a stain on the Harrowby name," Harrowby uttered viciously. She gasped. But Knightly stood tall, shoulders back, as if he wasn't bothered. Annabelle stood in awe.

"Out, out damn spot," the third man quipped. Both men turned to glare at him. When they realized their identical reactions, both stalked off in opposite directions and pushed their way through the crowd.

It was a miracle to Annabelle that Knightly had

been able to coolly stand there and trade cutting remarks with the half brother who so obviously loathed him. She would have slinked off, or never even approached him, and bent over backward to make sure no one ever felt the same way toward her.

But not Knightly. He was a tower of calm strength, of self-possession. He dared to venture where she never might, and with wit and grace, too.

It was why she loved him.

"Why are you seeking refuge in a potted plant, Miss Swift?"

"Oh! Lord Marsden! Good evening," she replied, a blush staining her cheeks.

"Perhaps you would like to waltz instead?" Marsden offered his hand, and Annabelle accepted.

*On the terrace, in the moonlight*

LATER that evening, Annabelle strolled past Knightly and gave him a flippant glance over her shoulder— or what she hoped seemed a flippant, coy, inviting glance as Flirtatious in Finchley Road had instructed.

Knightly's gaze locked with hers for that brief, potent second. Her skin seemed to tingle with a strange delight, like awakening. Or anticipation. Her heart began to beat faster. Would he follow?

She sauntered outside, where all manner of danger and romance might befall her, if the stories were to be believed. She attempted to lean casually against the cool stone balustrade, as she had seen Knightly do. And then he stood before her and she didn't notice much else.

"Annabelle." Knightly said her name softly. It was

a statement, a greeting, and a question all at once. "I did not realize you would be in attendance this evening."

"I came with Julianna and Roxbury. Yet I seem to have lost them, for it has been some time since I've seen either of them . . ."

"I saw you waltzing with Lord Marsden," Knightly said flatly. Annabelle thought of the advice to cultivate a rival. Or another reader's advice to hold herself at a distance and not throw her heart and soul at his mercy. And another's suggestion to play coy.

"I imagine most of the guests here this evening did as well," New Annabelle remarked.

"It was a stupid suggestion, Annabelle. And I'm sorry I asked you to encourage him to protect the paper," Knightly said urgently, still fixated on his wretched suggestion from days ago. Weeks ago! She had moved past it after his sincere apology. Quite forgotten all about it, really, after he had kissed her. She was forgiving like that.

"Who says I'm encouraging him for you or *The Weekly*, Mr. Knightly? What does it matter, anyway?" she asked. He had apologized, she accepted it, and they had moved on, hadn't they? Or was there another reason?

"I don't know, Annabelle, I don't know," he said, sounding awfully frustrated.

She took a deep breath and straightened her spine, as if it might give her the courage to ask a certain vexing question.

"Is it for the newspaper that you are courting Lady Lydia? So that she will plead your cause with her brother?"

"It's more complicated than that," Knightly replied, which only raised more questions. Did he love her? She wished to express her skepticism, her curiosity, with the lift of one brow arched.

"I really wish I had the ability to raise one eyebrow," she said wistfully, and Knightly laughed. The conversation had been taking a turn for the far-too-serious anyway. "You can do it. Julianna can. All the heroes and heroines in novels can do it."

"It's easy. You just have to look all haughty and superior. Like this." Knightly's demonstration looked remarkably like . . . Knightly did all the time. Lofty, unattainable, wickedly handsome, mysterious.

"Who is Harrowby?" she asked, and Knightly's shock was evident. But how could she not ask, after what she had heard? "I saw you speaking to him. And when I say 'I saw,' I might actually mean that I happened to overhear your conversation with him. I'm sorry."

"I didn't see you," Knightly replied, and Annabelle smiled wryly at that. She gazed at his face, which she knew and loved so well—the slanting cheekbones, firm jaw, dark hair, and piercing blue eyes and dark lashes.

"Haven't I told you that I am Miss Overlooked Swift? There might have been a potted fern standing between myself and the rest of the ballroom," she replied, a touch ruefully. "I understand you and that Lord Harrowby fellow are related in some fashion?"

"You've an awful lot of personal questions this evening, my dear Annabelle." Knightly brushed a wayward curl away from her face. His fingers grazed her cheek, ever so slightly. It was the familiarity of the gesture that made heart beat faster, and it was the possessive *my* in *my dear Annabelle* that thrilled her.

She remembered a time when he addressed a letter to her as "Miss Swift." How far they'd come!

She was his Dear Annabelle, wasn't she? Always had been since he'd named the column she was to write, and named it after her, thus bestowing an identity beyond Spinster Auntie or unfortunate, destitute relation.

Dear Annabelle was a girl of his own creation. She belonged to him and had for three years, seven months, one week, and five days. And now he was finally starting to see.

"It is Julianna's terrible influence, you see," Annabelle explained. "She is encouraging me to have more gumption."

"And how does it feel, Annabelle?" Knightly leaned upon the balustrade. She did so love it when he leaned, for he appeared at ease even though she knew he wasn't. What would it be like to see him truly at ease? To slumber beside him, to wake with him . . .

Really, she had to stop imagining these things when he was right there. Or at least blushing at the thoughts. Because Knightly leaned in close, observed her every blush and grinned wickedly as if he could read her mind.

"It feels exhilarating. Constantly. But don't worry, I shall write all about it," she told him.

"Speaking of your writing, how fares your progress in attracting the attentions of the Nodcock?" Knightly inquired. Wasn't that the question of the hour, the week, the month, the year, the moment?

Annabelle smiled, and her cheeks burned, utterly at a loss about how to answer *that* question. And in her silence, she thought she might have detected caring in the way his breath hitched. As if he were holding it, awaiting her answer. Only she would notice such a thing, thanks to all those novels loaded with such details, and thanks to all those hours in which she was so utterly devoted to loving and knowing him.

But one's breath only hitched like that if they cared. And why should Knightly care about the identity of the Nodcock, unless . . .

Unless he had a wager on the outcome, or something. No, she ought to give him more credit than that.

Unless he suspected that he was the Nodcock? How on earth could she ever tell him now, after that awful nickname? She ought to never write in a fit of pique again.

Annabelle found herself leaning in toward Knightly, drawn to his warmth. She dared to brush an invisible piece of lint from the lapel of his jacket as Affectionate from All Saints Road had told her to, in a letter weeks ago.

"Are you not reading my articles, Mr. Knightly?"

"Of course I am, " he replied, in a tone that affectionately called her silly, and ducking his head a bit closer to hers so he might whisper in her ear. "Perhaps I want to know the secret, Annabelle. Perhaps I want the unpublished version of the truth."

"That's awfully demanding of you, Knightly," she said softly. Oh, he was closer to her now. Their mouths, just inches away, quite possibly close enough to kiss.

"That's how I am, Dear Annabelle," he murmured, and Lord above if she didn't feel the vibrations from his voice all over and deep down inside.

"You told me to keep up the ruse," she reminded him, a bit breathless. He traced one finger along her jaw, down the slender column of her neck. Knightly, touching her. Such a light touch, such a little thing, but she felt it in spades.

"What if I said to hell with it?" he asked. He lifted one brow, and she couldn't help but smile even as her heart was thundering from the thrill of his touch.

"What if I am enjoying it, Mr. Knightly?"

She did not want this moment to end. She wanted to stay here, suspended between knowing and not knowing, where everything was lovely. The final risk she was not yet ready to take.

Knightly traced along her collarbone, dared to trace his fingertip lower, along the edge of her bodice where lace rested against her skin. It was the smallest caress, but so possessive. Her skin felt feverish, and she wondered if he could tell.

"Do you like all that waiting, wanting, anticipation?" he asked. "Do you not want satisfaction?" His voice was low and rough.

"When I am assured of it," she whispered. This moment was magical and lovely. She had an idea of the kind of satisfaction he spoke of, and it was one she mostly dwelled on very late at night.

But there were other kinds of satisfaction, and though she was well aware that beggars shouldn't be choosers, she wanted him to fall in love with her. Not just to discover she was in love with him.

Knightly dropped his touch, and Annabelle missed it intensely, immediately.

"What about Marsden? Was that part of the ruse?" Her heart thumped hard in her chest. Knightly was asking an awful lot of questions that were homing in on the truth. Did he know . . . ?

"Perhaps I enjoy his conversation and take pleasure in his company," Annabelle replied. "And the pink roses he sent me."

But she thought she was allowed to ask questions, too. "Who is Harrowby?"

"Harrowby is my half brother," Knightly said plainly, and then added, "I hope Julianna's influence hasn't rubbed off on you too much because I wouldn't want that talked about."

Annabelle counted to three, summoning up her courage to ask the question she knew would cut to the heart of the matter.

"*You* wouldn't like it, or *he* wouldn't like it?" A quiet rush of mocking laughter escaped him.

"Is there a difference?' he asked skeptically.

"There's a world of difference," she replied. Everything she'd seen and heard—that Knightly had even confided in her—told her that he would declare the news on the front page of *The London Weekly* were it not for Harrowby's refusal to acknowledge the relationship.

If there was one thing she knew even better than the back of her own hand, it was the desperate, driving need to seek approval and acceptance. All these years she had thought Knightly didn't need that. He carried himself like he didn't give a damn.

And now she'd learned that Knightly was not immune to seeking acceptance and recognition, as she was. He was not an impossible, remote god, but a man who was perhaps more similar to her than she'd thought.

He wanted to belong, just as much as she.

This was the moment that she really, truly fell in love with Knightly.

The for better or for worse kind of love. A love based on acceptance of the real person, and not some imagined fantasy.

"I don't want to talk about Harrowby," he said bluntly, and it took Annabelle a moment to place the name and recall their conversation. Once she caught up, she suspected that what Knightly really didn't want to discuss was his humanity, despite all of his efforts to portray himself as above the worldly fray.

"I'm sorry for mentioning it," she said automatically. "No, I'm not. Well, 'I'm sorry' is just a thing to say, you see. I'm trying not to be so apologetic and obsequious all the time. It's just such a habit and—"

"Annabelle?"

"Yes?" She looked up at him, and he pressed his hand against the small of her back and then pressed her close to him. Then Knightly's mouth claimed hers for a kiss. In the moonlight. Oh Lord above, the romance.

Annabelle closed her eyes, blocking out the ballroom behind her and the moonlight above them so that the only thing she was aware of was Knightly's mouth upon hers, hot, searching, and wanting. She was aware, too, of those sparks and shivers at an ever-growing intensity that threatened to overwhelm her, except . . .

She wondered if he was only kissing her because she'd been rambling on a subject he didn't wish to discuss and he wanted to stop her from talking. Or was he overwhelmed by passion? Did the intentions of the kiss matter? Why the devil could she not just enjoy it? How did one turn their brain off?

Knightly pulled back, just a bit. He cradled her head in his hands, his fingers entwined in her mass of curls. Her coiffure would be wrecked. She didn't care. Knightly looked her firmly in the eyes. They were so blue, even in the moonlight.

"Just so we're clear, Annabelle," he said in the calm, self-assured way in which he stated facts and gave orders, "I'm kissing you because I want to, not to make you stop talking, or to avoid the conversation. And you need to stop thinking."

"How did you know that I was—"

"I'm learning you, Annabelle," he said with a knowing smile, and she wondered if there were any words more magical than those: *I'm learning you, Annabelle.* "Now enjoy this because I've been at war with myself over it and I'd like to thoroughly enjoy the spoils."

His lips were firm against hers, his intentions clear. Annabelle could not think this kiss was accident or that he was overtaken by the moonlight.

Could anything possibly matter more than Knightly's arms wound around her, holding her in a haven she had only dreamed of?

He urged her to open to him, deepening the kiss. She responded with a fervor that came from years of longing and loneliness. Knightly wrapped his arms around her, tighter, pressing her close to him. She slid her arms around him, holding onto not just the man but this moment. She had dreamed of this.

This moment, this real moment, was better.

She tasted him, let him taste her. His every touch set her aflame. A slow, ever-growing heat that pooled in her belly and radiated to every inch of her. With her silk-clad body pressed against his, she felt his arousal pressing hard against her, there. Her cheeks flushed, and that blush crept all over her skin, leaving her feeling feverish in a wickedly wonderful way.

"Oh, Derek . . ." She sighed his name. There was so much she wanted him to know—her love for him, this hot, surging desire he was awakening within her, that she wanted to do *everything* with him—but words were impossible. She contented herself with a sigh of his name.

She sighed his name again.

KNIGHTLY tasted that sigh, and understood all the unspoken thoughts and feelings it conveyed. He felt that sigh deeply. He'd never felt so wanted, and because he now did, he could just savor all these little moments adding up to this soul-altering kiss. There was no need to seduce or impress or win; he just needed to kiss like it was the first and last thing in the world.

Or so he tried to reason, but then logic fled, leaving one thought in its wake: no one would ever kiss him with the passion that Annabelle did. No woman would ever sigh his name the same way, and if she did, it wouldn't mean anything. This kiss meant something. What, he knew not. Thinking was impossible. He desperately needed to taste the soft skin where Annabelle's neck curved gracefully into her shoulder, so he pressed his mouth there for a kiss. She murmured her pleasure. He felt like a king.

He ran his fingers through her hair. He caressed the curve in her hip, slid his hands lower still and pressed her close. There was something about Annabelle that required delicacy and there was something about restraining himself that made him feel every little touch, and sigh a thousand times more intensely.

He wanted to feel her, everywhere. Feel her, without this silk dress, without anything at all . . . but enough higher brain functioning remained to tell him they were at a ball. They were in public. He needed to stop this.

But he didn't want to.

# Chapter 32

## Angry Women Storm *The London Weekly* Offices

### THE MAN ABOUT TOWN

*At long last, a clue to the true identity of the Nodcock.*

The London Times

*The following day*

**K**NIGHTLY was pretty damn sure that other newspaper proprietors were not plagued by females
storming into their offices with all sorts of dramatics, such as he was.

*Drama is for the page.*

Apparently rules do not apply to females, he
thought dryly.

Julianna arrived first, a fiery haired, sharp-
tongued hurricane in a green dress. This was a habit
of hers. Today he was not inclined to deal with such
dramatics, which is to say that he was in a bloody
good mood. Whistling while he walked down the
street kind of mood. It was the effect of Annabelle
and her kiss.

Well, one of them. The other effect was a rampant,
relentless desire. Nevertheless, his eyes had been

opened and he wanted what he saw. He knew, too, that he wanted to know more about Annabelle, and what that knowledge would cost him. The question was, would he pay the price of throwing off Lady Lydia and enraging Lord Marsden?

It was one hell of a question, and he preferred, instead, to whistle and think of kissing Annabelle.

"Really, Knightly. Really," Julianna said, with buckets of sarcasm, anger, and disappointment dripping from each syllable. She threw a newspaper on his desk; it landed with a *thwat*.

Knightly stopped whistling. He looked at the paper.

"*The London Times*, Julianna. Really? No wonder you're upset, if you're reading this second-rate rubbish."

"Read it." Her tone was that of ice, covered with frost.

Intrigued, he picked up the paper.

*At Lady Wroth's Charity Ball to benefit the Society of Unfortunate Women*, The London Weekly's proprietor Derek Knightly was glimpsed in an extended moonlit interlude with a woman identified as The London Weekly's own Dear Annabelle. Readers of that gimmick-laden news rag will know that she is engaged in a public scheme to win the attentions of a man now known by all of London as the Nodcock.

*The Man About Town* wouldn't care in the least about the goings on of two Grub Street hacks, were it not for Knightly's well-known courtship of Lady Lydia Marsden. Or has this scandal-plagued female lost yet another suitor, this one with very unsuitable connections (for his suitable ones will not claim him)?

*Which woman is this by-blow newspaper tycoon after? Will either chit want him now that he is so openly pursuing the affections of two different women? Or is his ton blood showing true, for what aristo is complete without a wife and a mistress?*

"We'll file that under scathing. Or perhaps incendiary," Knightly remarked. He leaned back in his chair, a pose of deceptive ease.

The article was possibly disastrous. Yet he kept his calm because that is what he did and who he was, unlike Julianna, who worked herself up into such a froth over the slightest thing.

"I'd like to file it under inaccurate rubbish, which I presume it is?" she questioned sharply.

"To the contrary," Knightly replied easily. "I ought to congratulation *The Times* for finally getting their reporting correct."

"I am beside myself. Utterly beside myself," Julianna huffed. "This column is—well, it has me speechless with rage, and that is saying something, you must admit."

"No comment," Knightly said. Wisely, in his opinion.

"While I don't really care about Lady Lydia's feelings on the matter—" Julianna started, switching tactics.

"Which is perfectly clear given the columns you've submitted lately in spite of my explicit commands not to write about her."

"Do not distract, Knightly. This is about Annabelle. And you."

And that sparked his temper. He leaned forward, palms flat on his desk, eyes surely blazing.

"So you admit that it is none of your business, then?" he challenged.

"I beg your pardon?" He had flummoxed her, and now resisted the urge to crow in satisfaction. That's what she deserved for meddling in his personal affairs.

"It is between Annabelle and myself. Not you."

"So you admit there is something between you two," she replied, tilting her head inquisitively and thinking herself clever.

"Mind your own business, Julianna," he said, and allowed his irritation to reveal itself in his tone.

"I am employed by you to do precisely the opposite, thank you very much. My task is to mind everybody else's business."

"In that case, I excuse you from doing so in this instance," Knightly replied, pushed aside the unfortunate issue of *The London Times* and picked up the papers beneath. He started to read them in a not-so-subtle clue to Julianna that he was finished with this discussion.

Honestly, if she'd been a man, someone probably would have shot such a vexing, meddlesome creature by now.

Julianna placed her palms on his desk and leaned forward to speak to him in a low, menacing tone.

"Be a gentleman, Knightly. Have a care with her. She's fragile."

And that was not to be borne. Annabelle might have been a delicate flower, treated with the utmost care and handled only with kid gloves. But he was discovering that she was made of much sterner stuff, and treating her as such was a disservice to everyone. Bold Annabelle was something else entirely—

asking the questions no one had ever dared to voice to him, kissing him with a fervor that made him feel more powerful and *wanted* more than anything. Her kiss made him whistle as he walked down the streets.

He pitied those who didn't see that Annabelle.

"We must be talking about different Annabelles, then," Knightly told Julianna. "When I'd rather not discuss Annabelle at all."

"What should I tell her, when she sees that?" Julianna asked, pointing, witchlike, to *The Times.*

"Say whatever you like. Just remember that my personal business is just that—mine."

Julianna left in a huff, of course, and once relieved of her presence, he strolled over to the sideboard and poured himself a generous serving of brandy.

There were a long list of women and their feelings that would need to be soothed, thanks to that damned Man About Town, and a fortifying drink was certainly in order.

Lady Marsden probably wouldn't care, so long as he kept her secrets. He smirked—to no one in particular—because he knew why she had missed her second season, and Julianna did not. He ought to casually mention that to her, as payback for her meddling in his personal affairs.

Annabelle on the other hand . . . As he learned her, he knew that she had a heart that beat in overtime, and a capacity for feeling that verged on excessive. She rambled when she was nervous and possessed an extremely active and vibrant imagination. When he kissed her, he could feel her thinking, puzzling, wondering, and memorizing every second of it.

However, with some reassurance—that being a

firm command to enjoy it—she melted under his touch. Other women responded to him, but with Annabelle it felt like it mattered, and that made it feel . . . just *more*, really. When every touch of the lips counted, when every caress meant something, when every murmur or sigh was a pleasure unto itself . . .

What the devil had happened to him?

Knightly took a long swallow on the brandy and concentrated deeply on the burn. First, on his tongue. Then the back of his throat. Down, down, down to his gut.

When a man thought about some fleeting kiss with a woman the way he had just caught himself doing, it meant that . . . Well, besotted was the word that came to mind. Or worse—*beholden*. And it wasn't a fleeting kiss. It was one of those all-consuming, axis-altering kisses.

Besotted indeed. Bloody hell.

His mother appeared in the doorway just then, strolling in like some fiery-haired demon fairy. If he ever wondered what Julianna would be like in thirty years, he now knew.

Bloody hellfire and damnation. Mehitable, a man of gargantuan proportions who had been hired for the sole purpose of preventing such unscheduled appearances by irate readers, must have been drunk on the job. Or this was mutiny.

"What is the meaning of this?" she inquired, shaking a copy of *The London Times* at him.

Knightly downed the rest of his drink and returned to his desk.

"Mother, I have already had this conversation with Lady Roxbury. It might be a better use of your time to go speak with her, as I can tell you both are far more interested in discussing this than I am. I might also add that I am appalled to discover how many *Weekly* women have exposed themselves as readers of *The London Times*."

His mother sat in the chair before his desk.

"Utterly appalled," he repeated, and then returned to his work. Or tried to. He looked at the page but didn't manage to read a single word, try as he might.

"You do realize that Dear Annabelle is beloved by all of London," his mother said. "If it turns out that you were the man she was after . . ." Knightly stiffened, held his breath. Why did that thought paralyze him every time? His mother appeared not to notice and carried on.

" . . . Well, I daresay you'll have a mob of angry Londoners at your door." Was it wrong that he thought that spoke well of Annabelle's column and what a great story it would make?

"Mehitable will handle any angry mobs," he replied. After a stern talking-to about the admittance of angry females.

"For all you know, Mehitable may lead the mob," she challenged.

"No he won't. I pay his wages." Knightly stated this as simple fact. He just needed to remind Mehitable of that.

"Nevertheless," his mother persisted, "what are your intentions? Because if you throw over Dear Annabelle, with whom you obviously are infatuated—"

"Obviously?"

"I'm sorry. Are you in the habit of moonlit interludes with desirable young women and then kissing them—but not *liking* them? Especially when it seems you have an understanding regarding marriage with another woman. Have you inherited my talent for acting, after all?"

"Is this really any of your business?" he asked, growing angry now.

"What does that have to do with anything?" his mother asked, so genuinely perplexed by the concept of "minding one's own business" that he was struck speechless. She carried on in his silence: "At any rate, this story reminded me that I need to tell you something about your father. Before you make a mistake."

That got his attention. He set his papers aside.

"Your father loved us," she said plainly.

"I know that—" he began, but she waved him off.

"No, listen to me. He loved us. And he didn't love *them*, and they knew it. How do you think that boy felt growing up, always second in his father's attentions? Can you imagine it, Derek?"

He never had. Not once.

The heir, taking second place to his father's bastard child. He imagined the New Earl wanting to review his lessons, or asking after his father, who was never home. It began to dawn on Knightly what wretchedness the New Earl must have suffered, to be ignored, overlooked, second best. Knightly had always known he was loved.

"And Lady Harrowby was married but never had a husband, not really. But she *chose* that because your father told her about us before they were wed."

"Why did he marry her, anyway?" Knightly asked. If they were in love . . . why did they not make it official? So what if his mother was an actress? Wasn't half the fun of a title doing whatever you damn well pleased?

"Duty. Debts. Lack of courage at the crucial moment," she said, turning to look out the windows overlooking bustling Fleet Street. Did he detect tears? Did he detect more to the story—that her mother had asked his father *not* to marry someone else. Had she asked him to forget about duty and respectability and implored him to choose love instead?

His mother, now composed, turned back to face him. "They live in a world, Derek, where love doesn't matter."

He thought of Lady Lydia's plaintive question: *What if I wish for a love match?* He didn't have an answer for her, but he possessed a deeper understanding of the question now.

"I suppose it goes without saying that I wish you to have love," his mother carried on. "And if you still insist on some marriage for status and wealth, don't do it out of some notion to be like your father. It would be a dishonor to us both."

# Chapter 33

## A Misunderstanding with the Marquis

DOMESTIC INTELLIGENCE

*The total number of newspaper reporters arrested: 38*

*The total number of newspapers that have been shuttered: 4*

*Only* The London Weekly *seems immune. For now.*

*The London Times*

*White's Gentlemen's Club*
*St. James's Street*

**T**HERE was no point in refusing Marsden's request to join him for a drink at White's. They had business to discuss and it could happen here or there, sooner or later. That Marsden should wish to meet in a place that would display his rank and power was not lost upon Knightly. Clever, too, for White's would remind him of what he stood to gain—or lose.

I ought to belong here, Knightly thought as he strolled up the four short steps to the entrance to this exclusive haven.

The first thing he saw was the New Earl, seated

with a few gentlemen, card game in progress. The look in his eyes conveyed those taunting, menacing words: *Throw the bastard out. He doesn't belong here.*

Only now, Knightly saw beyond the obvious hatred in his glare to see hurt and confusion. When the New Earl leaned to whisper something scathing to his companion—all the while shooting daggers with his eyes—Knightly wondered what his relationship had been like with their father. Did they have the same long conversations? Did they share the same dry sense of humor? Did they go to the theatre together?

His mother had mentioned debts as a factor for the marriage. Had the countess's dowry paid for his own gentlemen's education? Had it provided the inheritance with which he purchased *The London Weekly*?

They were questions he'd never known to even ask. His mother had stormed in and delivered all this devastating information and then made an elegantly cutting exit, as befit one of London's best actresses.

The marquis had claimed a table in a dark corner of the club. He sat there, steely-eyed and seething. If he was supposed to be intimidated, Knightly thought, then the marquis ought to try harder. Or just not bother.

"I thought we had an understanding," Marsden began, without offering a drink. It was to be one of those conversations. "I thought I had been abundantly clear that I would steer the parliamentary Inquiry away from the notoriously unsavory reporting methods at your newspaper if you would marry my sister."

Knowing what he knew now—namely, the reasons Lady Lydia remained impossibly unwed—Knightly knew what a bad bargain it was. Not because she wasn't some pure ideal, but because her heart was otherwise engaged, and that would make for a cold marriage indeed. Certainly it wasn't good enough to violate truth number three: *Be beholden to no one.*

But that was information he had no intention of revealing. Yet.

"No date had been set," Knightly pointed out.

"Which is exactly why I am here," Marsden said. At least he was the sort of man who got quiet when enraged. None of that undignified blustering sported by lesser—though more amusing—men. "No wedding date has been set. Not even a proposal. And I hear that you enjoyed a significant, extended, private interlude with Miss Swift."

"You must be referring to the item that appeared in *The London Times* this morning. Surprising what information such a second-rate paper manages to uncover, isn't it?"

The mark hit home. Marsden visibly reddened. They now both knew that Knightly had learned he'd nearly bankrupted himself paying suppression fees to *The Times* and launched this Inquiry when his funds began to run out.

"I saw you. With Annabelle," Marsden said through gritted teeth.

Ah, now that was interesting. Not that they were spotted, for neither had made any effort at discretion—and why did they need to? Neither were haute ton, with reputations to maintain—but that Marsden gave a damn.

"I believe you are referring to Miss Swift," Knightly corrected.

"Devil take it, Knightly, we had an understanding," Marsden growled.

Knightly only shrugged, and said, "We did not agree upon a date by which I would propose. We did not agree upon a love match or some pretense of romance. We may have had an understanding, but there was no discussion of the terms."

"I assumed your word was that of a gentleman," Marsden said tightly.

"That was your first mistake, Marsden," Knightly said with a laugh—and a glance across the room at the New Earl. "We all know I'm no gentleman."

Marsden went silent. Was Marsden shocked that he had so directly referred to his bastardry when it was something he ought to be ashamed of?

In that silence, Knightly realized, deeply, that he was not a gentleman. He did not belong here, in White's. He missed Galloway's and its raucous company, the rustling sound of newspapers, and the scent of coffee and cigar smoke. He liked the ease one felt there. And the lack of angry glares launched in his direction.

"Pity, that," Marsden said thoughtfully, "because we gentlemen protect our own. And we actively suppress those who are . . . *not*."

The emphasis he placed on that little word, *not*, was remarkable. *Not* suddenly had the connection of rats, dung heaps, mud larks, and rotting corpses.

When Knightly replied, his voice was the drawl of a bored man. Between the glares from the New Earl (which were now, at this point, making it difficult to maintain a shred of that newly discovered empathy) and Marsden's overbearing manner and the restrained silence of this club, Knightly felt his chest tighten, as if a thousand-ton anvil pressed upon his chest, making breathing impossible.

He needed to walk and to get lost in the busy, meandering streets of London until night and silence descended upon the city. He needed the slap of cool air on his face. He needed to think about Lydia and Annabelle and *The London Weekly* and the family he'd never had. And to think about love.

He had no more time or patience for Lord Marsden and his bad bargains.

"Marsden, if you have something to tell me that I don't already know, I'd like to hear it. But the pretentious, heavy hand of the upper orders is not news. If it's not news, then I'm not interested."

"Oh, I have news for you, Knightly," Marsden said with a nefarious grin. "But I think I'll let you read it in the papers tomorrow. *The London Times*, in fact."

# Chapter 34

### Lovesick Female Driven to Desperate Measures

*DRAFT:*

*Dear Annabelle*
*   What is the proper way to conduct oneself after being discovered in a compromising position?*
*   Composed by Miss Annabelle Swift, unsolicited, on behalf of Mr. Derek Knightly.*

*Offices of* The London Weekly

**K**NIGHTLY must know that he was the Nodcock. No man as successful as he could be so obtuse. Annabelle allowed that all her sighs and blushes and stammers over the years were very missable. But they had kissed, Knightly and she. Twice.

Furthermore, the gossip columns had reported on it, thus mercifully offering concrete proof that such an exquisite event had actually happened and was not some wicked tease from her imagination.

And yet Knightly strolled into the weekly meeting with the same grin and drawling "ladies first" as he had for every other meeting since the dawn of time. He didn't act differently. He didn't give any indication that Something Momentous had occurred.

Annabelle scowled. Why was it all so hard, every step of the way?

A wink would have done wonders. A lift of one brow would have been a simple, unremarkable thing that spoke volumes to her. A knowing smile, perhaps? And really, what was the point of discretion now when *The London Times* printed up the details for all to see? Almost anybody in London now knew that:

1. At the charity ball benefiting the Society of Unfortunate Women, she and Knightly had enjoyed an extended, moonlit interlude, complete with a passionate kiss. Every Londoner was surely imagining the most wanton behavior on both their parts.

2. Knightly was one wicked lothario, dallying with an unmarriageable chit (Annabelle) while his very marriageable intended (Lady Marsden) languished in the ballroom.

Upon seeing her today, Owens had placed his hand on the small of her back and leaned in close to inquire about her extended moonlit interlude. Her response was a breathless "Nice" because she had been too flustered over his affection and concern. She gazed up to his warm brown eyes, searching for a reason why he would be so involved in the trials and tribulations of her little love life.

How to make heads or tales of any of it? A glimmer of anything remotely resembling acknowledgment might have gone a long way. Had Knightly nothing to say to her after that gossip rag? It was ungentlemanly to ignore it. Unsporting not to say something. Unless his silence was the answer she sought.

Sophie was chattering about weddings and the latest fashions; Eliza continued her reporting on the adventures of the Tattooed Duke, the previously unsuspecting subject of her writing, and now her husband.

Knightly warily turned his attentions to Julianna.

"Julianna, what salacious gossip might we find in your column this week?"

"I thought I might comment upon the Man About Town's recent column. Set the record straight, perhaps?" She asked this with a challenging lift of her brow.

"I don't know that there is much more to be said," Knightly replied, leaning against a table. Annabelle wanted to disagree strongly. There was plenty to be said—to her. Knightly added: "I'm certain any member of the aristocracy is engaged in much more scandalous activities that will be of significantly more interest to our readers."

In other words: don't talk about it. In other words: there was nothing to say. In other words: if we ignore it perhaps it will go away.

Julianna scowled. Annabelle did, too, for that matter. And then Knightly fixed his attentions upon her.

"Annabelle, what schemes do you have for us this week?"

It was on the tip of her tongue to say she would offer advice on how gentlemen ought to conduct themselves after passionately kissing women during moonlit interludes at a ball. Alas, Bold Annabelle had not progressed so far as to airing her personal business in public. Though she now entertained wicked and sassy retorts, she was not yet able to voice them.

Instead, she said, "I think it might be time for desperate measures."

"Are your efforts thus far unsuccessful?" Knightly asked with a lift of his brow. Was that a reference to their conversation or just a thing to do? And why did he have to be so impossibly handsome when he leaned?

"Oh, there have been some *small* successes," she replied, making every effort to sound haughty and dismissive. " Nothing grand enough to be *satisfying*."

Beside her, Julianna stifled a chortle, and Annabelle caught Owens's mouth hanging slack-jawed. These things made her rather proud of herself.

"What do you have in mind, Dear Annabelle?" Knightly was grinning, ever so slightly. She saw it in the upward tilt of the corner of his mouth, but mostly she saw it in his eyes.

"You'll see when you read my column," she said, with a little bit of sass, which was all bluster because she had no idea what desperate measures she would try.

"Not sooner?" Knightly asked casually. Oh, he had to know. He must! But she needed more certainty than a lift of his brow or an easily asked question in front of a room full of people.

Annabelle lifted her head higher and replied, "Quite a few of my readers have encouraged me to maintain an aura of mystery. And some even say that if the Nodcock cannot figure it out for himself, he doesn't deserve to know."

AFTER the meeting, the Writing Girls proceeded immediately to Gunther's for some ices. They parked Sophie's open-aired carriage in the shade of a tree, and with raspberry ices in hand proceeded with the important conversation.

"What desperate measures do you have in mind?" Sophie asked.

"Well, there are quite a few options," Annabelle said as she rummaged through her reticule and pulled out a packet of letters. "I have received dozens, but these are some of the more outrageous suggestions. This one says I ought to just print the truth in my column."

"Direct. But not exactly thrilling," Julianna replied.

"Unless you can be there when he reads it," Sophie said. "How fascinating it would be to watch his reaction! I wonder if he knows and would just coolly lift one brow and—"

"Correct a comma and carry on," Julianna added with a smirk.

"If he reads it, that is," Annabelle grumbled.

"You are not still vexed about that?" Eliza asked. "Because I'd wager he's poring over your every word these days." Annabelle hoped that was the case. If he wasn't wondering at this point, then he was more of a nodcock that she had thought.

"Perhaps. At any rate there are significantly more dramatic options than just telling him. For example, this one suggests I make a grand declaration at a ball."

"It's often so hard to hear in a ballroom," Sophie

said thoughtfully. "And if he's in the card room or the necessary when you give your big speech, it would be all for naught."

"With careful preparation, it could work," Julianna said. "It'd be terrifically entertaining."

"If I didn't perish of mortification first," Annabelle replied. She shuddered just thinking about speaking in public, let alone confessing the deep secrets of her heart to a crowd of strangers. "Here's another one: write a sonnet that confesses his identity and my love for him, commission a printing of one thousand flyers with the sonnet and toss them 'like leaves in the wind' from a hot-air balloon."

"That's an awful lot of effort," Eliza remarked. "But I know where you could get a hot-air balloon."

The other Writing Girls peered at her curiously and decided not to pursue that avenue of conversation.

"People have quite the flair for the dramatic," Julianna remarked, twisting a lock of hair around her finger. Eliza shrugged, reached over and selected a few of the pages from Annabelle.

"But a deplorable lack of consideration for logistics and costs," Sophie said. "Especially when they are not paying for it. Not that I blame them for it."

"If I'm to invest in this venture," Annabelle said, "I'd rather just buy more silk dresses and underthings. I certainly wouldn't spend it on printing sonnets or chartering hot-air balloons."

"Especially if you follow this reader's advice," Eliza said, "and run through the streets in broad daylight, wearing nothing but your unmentionables, proclaiming your love at the top of your voice." Sophie reached out for one, too.

"This one literally suggests shouting your love from the rooftops," she said with a laugh.

"I'll be carted off to Bedlam!" Annabelle exclaimed.

"It almost makes this one sound sane," Eliza said, looking up from the page in her hands. "Simply steal into his bedroom at the midnight hour."

"And then what?" Annabelle asked.

"Annabelle, please," Julianna said with a dose of exasperation in her voice. "Surely it's been covered in your novels and our conversations. If it hasn't been, then I am ashamed of our discussions and your reading material."

"Knightly will either ravish you or he will send you home directly," Sophie clarified.

"But when do I tell him? *What* do I tell him?" Annabelle asked, anxious. It was well and truly time for some sort of reckoning. If Knightly wasn't going to figure out that he was the Nodcock and *do something about it*, then she would make it abundantly clear so that he'd have no choice but to explain himself. Yet she wasn't sure how to make such a declaration.

"I can just see it now: 'Oh, good evening, Knightly! I just thought I'd drop by at this outrageously inappropriate hour to let you know that you are the Nodcock.'"

"There would be no room for ambiguity or misunderstanding," Julianna pointed out.

"Oh, he'll know he's the Nodcock the minute she falls off the windowsill onto his carpet," Sophie said. "Why else would she steal into his bedroom at the midnight hour?"

"We'll have to dress you in breeches," Eliza said, apropos of nothing.

"Why?" Annabelle asked, very nervous about the answer.

"For when you climb up a tree to the second-story window." Eliza said this so matter-of-factly that Annabelle was aghast.

"Are you mad?" she said. "Breeches! Climbing to a second-story window! Do you even know if there is a tree to climb?"

For goodness sakes, until recently the most daring thing she had done was lower her bodices or pretend a swoon. This was in another league entirely.

"Grand Gesture, Annabelle," Julianna reminded her. "Think of the great story this will make. Readers will devour it, and if nothing else, there is nothing Knightly loves like a stellar week of sales."

She was, alas, correct. But still . . . Annabelle was not convinced. Obstacles. She needed to present logical and insurmountable obstacles to this corkbrained scheme.

"I'm not sure of his address," she said.

"Number ten, Bruton Street. The red brick house," Julianna answered easily.

"Nor do I have breeches," Annabelle pointed out.

"I do," Sophie said. "They were Brandon's back in the day. Of course you may borrow them."

"You're too kind. But I have no idea how to climb a tree or a wall," she said with some desperation.

"It's easy, I can show you," Eliza said with a mischievous smile.

And that was how Annabelle came to be perched precariously on the windowsill of Knightly's bedroom. In breeches. In the midnight hour.

# Chapter 35

## Annabelle, Out on a Limb

**DEAR ANNABELLE**

*On behalf of your readers, I do declare it is time
you employ drastic measures.*

Penelope from Piccadilly
The London Times

**A**NNABELLE generally believed in focusing upon
the positive things in life. Thus, as she dangled precariously in the tree outside of Knightly's house, she
thought, At least I'm not in a hot-air balloon. As per
Eliza's tree-climbing instructions, she kept hold of
one branch at all times and thanked her lucky stars
her friend advised her to wear gloves. Her friend
did not mention this activity would ruin said gloves.
But at least she would get a new pair. A small consolation.

That is, if she survived.

As Annabelle increased her distance from the
ground, she had second thoughts. Did love really
require grand gestures? Wasn't true love to be found
in the little things, like holding one's hand or sit-

ting comfortably around a gentle fire? Inside. On the ground.

When it came time to ease off the rough branch and onto the stone windowsill, Annabelle saw new merit in the suggestion of dashing through the crowded city streets clad in nothing but her unmentionables. Surely that was a much less perilous activity.

She finally reached the window of what she hoped was Knightly's bedchamber. Although, a small part of her hoped she tumbled into an empty room and could slink away and pretend this whole thing never happened.

She held onto a branch and with one hand reached out precariously to open the window. One awful truth was clear:

The window was locked.

"Oh no," she muttered. "Oh no, no, no, no, no."

An unfortunate creaking sound emerged from the branch. The kind of creaking sound before the whole limb threatened to break off and plummet to the ground.

"No," Annabelle told it. "Stay."

She felt it sag under her weight. Awkwardly, she adjusted her position to rely more heavily on the windowsill.

Some bits of gravel and brick broke off, falling ominously to the ground.

Desperately and carefully, she tried to open the window again. It was large, heavy, and very much locked.

She really ought to have run through the streets in her unmentionables instead.

"Okay, Annabelle, you have three options," she

said. Yes, she was now speaking aloud to herself. If she survived this, then she'd go straight to Bedlam and check herself in for the safety of herself and tree branches everywhere.

*Option the first:* attempt to climb down and hopefully pretend nothing ever happened. And never ever complain about a lack of romance or grand gestures again. At the moment both seemed vastly overrated, and it was her noble duty to warn every other young, romantic woman that she ought to relinquish such foolish notions.

*Option the second:* Holler for help. Because when one was in such a mortifying position, drawing the attention of the entire neighborhood was just the thing. Option the second was quickly dismissed.

*Option the third:* knock on the window. And pray that a very blind and mute servant assisted her entry and subsequent exit from the house so no one would be any wiser.

The sound of wood splitting rent through the night air. The branch suffered some fractures. Annabelle's heart missed a few beats.

*Option the fourth:* fall to her death in Knightly's garden. It would make a dreadful mess, and be terribly awkward for him, she presumed. She did so hate to inconvenience people . . . However, she would be dead and presumably no longer plagued by such worries.

Annabelle instead knocked on the window glass. And waited. She knocked again.

Somewhere nearby a cat mewled. A dark cloud passed over the cool, bright moon. A cool breeze rustled the leaves on the tree.

This was his bedroom window, was it not? It had

been a calculated guess based upon Julianna's visit to Lady Pettigrew's home just two doors down.

"Oh blast," Annabelle muttered.

The tree branch cracked and creaked again.

"Curses," she swore. "Gosh darn it to heck."

Annabelle knocked on the window again. And finally, oh finally, Knightly opened the window. She had never been so happy to see him. She had also never wished to see him less.

"Annabelle?" He rubbed his eyes as if he could not believe that she was perilously clinging to his windowsill and a tree branch.

"Hello," she said. *Hello? Oh for Lord's sake.* She was trapped on his windowsill, clinging desperately for her life, in the middle of the night, so *Hello* probably wasn't the worst thing she could have said. She ought to have gone with *Help* instead.

"What the devil are you doing?" he asked. Rightfully so. But truly, not the best time.

"Um, a grand romantic gesture?" she offered. He lifted one brow and didn't say a word. He was going to let her ramble out an explanation, drat the man. Well in that case she would give the only reason he would accept. "This is actually research for my column. For *The Weekly*."

"I know where you work, Annabelle."

"One of my readers suggested it . . ." Her mouth went dry when she saw that he was not completely attired. He wore breeches. And a shirt that was carelessly thrown on and not one button done up. Not one. His bare chest was exposed. His hard bare chest. It was very flat, except for all the planes and ridges of his muscles. She thought about tracing her fingers along . . . feeling him . . .

And it would be the last thing she ever did. Falling to her death because she let go of her tree branch in order to caress Knightly's bare chest.

"I recognize that this is an unexpected and increasingly awkward situation," Annabelle said. "I considered climbing down and pretending nothing ever happened, but the branch is beginning to break—I'm terribly sorry and you can take it out of my wages."

She paused for breath and to consider the cost of one, lone tree branch. "The fact of the matter is that I'd be much obliged if you'd help me in. It turns out that given the choice, I'd rather die of embarrassment instead of falling and breaking my neck."

"Come inside, Annabelle. But you have some explaining to do."

Knightly held out his hand. She hesitated. The prospect of explaining to him that he was the Nodcock, that she had involved all of *The Weekly*'s readers in a scheme to seduce him, and that she risked her neck to do so, all while he wore naught but fitted breeches and an open shirt was just . . . unfathomable, impossible, and utterly terrifying.

She really ought to have run through the streets in her unmentionables. This was London, no one would have blinked twice.

But the branch cracked further, and a shriek might have escaped her.

She reached for his hand.

ANNABELLE tumbled into his arms, warm and luscious, tempting and maddening.

She was a tangle of long, slender limbs and smooth, alluring curves. Her soft curls brushed against his cheek and he inhaled the scent of her, like roses. He remembered this from the day she had tumbled into his arms during that minor carriage accident. He wanted her then. He wanted her now.

"What are you doing here, Annabelle?" The question had to be asked, even though he wasn't sure he wanted to hear the answer. He reluctantly released his hold on her and took a step back.

She bit her lip. Gazed up at him. Heaved such a sigh, as if so disappointed in the world, her fate, and him. He felt a dull ache in his chest. He didn't want to hurt her or let her down.

"Do you really not know?" she asked, forming each word slowly.

"Know what, Annabelle?" This truth was too important to just be assumed. Too much rested upon it to leave it an understanding. She had to say it aloud.

She mumbled something almost unintelligible.

"I am *a* nodcock or *the* Nodcock?" he clarified. It was a minor but crucial distinction.

"The one and only," Annabelle said softly.

"I am the Nodcock," he repeated, and she nodded her head slowly. *Yes.* He exhaled, all suspicions confirmed and all fears realized. After *years* in which she adored him from afar, while he didn't notice her, it had come to this.

Knightly couldn't think of all the profound implications of this simple, devastating fact—he was the Infamous Nodcock, he was Annabelle's heart's desire and had been for quite some time. He could only concentrate on the facts before him.

Annabelle, standing in a ray of moonlight falling into his bedroom. After midnight. In breeches.

"And you thought the best way to inform me

of this was to climb in my second-story bedroom window in the dead of the night?"

"Well if you had noticed me sooner, I wouldn't have had to resort to such desperate measures," she said, rebuking him.

"You are saying I caused this . . . this . . ." He raked his fingers through his hair and still couldn't think. He was the Nodcock. She had said so. All the sighs, faints, lowered bodices, and affectionate touches had been for him. She had literally and figuratively gone out on a limb to reveal her feelings to him.

And now he was expected to show his.

He felt desire. And a million other things he couldn't make sense of.

"I'll just be on my way, then," she said, stepping across the carpet toward the bedroom door.

"That's all?" he asked. She had come all this way only to leave?

"They said you would either ravish me or send me home. If *this* is ravishment, then it has been vastly overrated," she said. He choked on shock, and mirth.

"Annabelle," he said, because something needed to be said. Volumes needed to be said. But he had nothing to follow it up with. He was at a loss for words. He noticed that the few burning candles in the room added a soft, warm, inviting glow to her skin. But it didn't seem the thing to say.

"My audacity has left you speechless," Annabelle said, punctuated by another one of those sighs. Like the world had met her low expectations.

But that was beside the point at the moment.

"Your audacity?" His jaw dropped open. The fool woman had nearly fallen to her death at his doorstep. From what he gathered, she had escaped her bedchamber in Bloomsbury, crossed London alone in the middle of the night, and then proceeded to climb the tree in his garden and break into his bedroom. What insanity or desperation propelled her, he had no wish to know, though he had a sinking feeling he knew.

All that talk of ignorant nodcocks and desperate measures. He had invited this.

"Audacity, I suppose, is one way to describe it," he said, after taking a deep breath and exhaling slowly. "I was thinking that was a bloody stupid thing to do. Do you have any idea how dangerous that stunt was?"

Knightly caught himself pacing and running his fingers through his hair as if he were actually about to tear his own hair out with frustration.

She could have been hurt. She could have died, twice or thrice over. This forced him to consider a world without Annabelle—his heart stopped for a moment and resumed with the sound of her voice. *A world without Annabelle . . .* It would be bleak and lonely and cold. It was sadly lacking in a young woman's fearless attempts to come out of her shell.

He did not want to know a world without Annabelle.

"It did cross my mind, yes," she replied. "However, it seemed preferable to a hot-air balloon ride or running through the streets in an advanced state of undress."

Knightly stopped pacing to stare at her.

"What does that have to do with anything? No, do not tell me." He shook his head. " I don't want to know."

"Suggestions from readers as to how I might attract the attentions of the Nodcock," she explained in a very small voice.

"I am the Nodcock," Knightly said, needing to repeat the words again. Eventually, the truth would seem real, make sense and take hold.

"Am I not in your bedroom in the middle of the night after risking my life?" Aye, she was. And standing in a puddle of moonlight. Risking her virtue, too.

She had mentioned ravishment, throwing the word out like a lure. She didn't need to. The sight of Annabelle in his bedroom was enough. Annabelle in his bedroom dressed so that all her curves taunted him was further temptation. Annabelle, in so many words saying she wanted him, nearly undid him.

"By some miracle you are here, yes, and not in a mangled heap in my garden," he said, because the thought of a world without Annabelle made him feel as if he couldn't breathe.

"I thought it would make a good story for *The Weekly*," she explained.

"Did you not think of how it could have gone wrong?" he said, voice rising. It was fear of having almost lost her, of still possibly losing her. That decision he had avoided was now here in his bedroom saying words like "ravishment" with her plump lips he wanted to feel everywhere on his body.

Would he choose her, or belonging?

"Of course I considered that! When I was stranded on that branch and your windowsill, I thought about it extensively. But I wouldn't have been there if Julianna and Eliza had not assured me it would be perfectly fine."

"Oh, those two. Those two are trouble. And the

breeches," Knightly said, taking a long, rich look at her legs clad in the fitted kerseymere breeches that clung to her hips and thighs in such a sinful way.

He should not look.

He could barely wrench his gaze away. God, he wanted to strip them off her, to reveal acres of pale skin, bathed in moonlight.

"I'm not sure if your breeches show sense, given your tree climbing escapades or even more madness. What if someone had seen you?" he asked. In the back of his mind he thought that none of this really mattered—she was safe, no one had seen her. But something momentous was going to happen. He and Annabelle were going to make love. There was no avoiding it, really. It had been inevitable, he supposed. He wanted to know her, intimately, more than he'd ever wanted anything.

*Anything.*

And he needed a moment to process that everything was about to change.

"Miss Overlooked Swift, remember? Spinster Aunt from Bloomsbury! So what if I was spotted? What do I have to lose?" There was a note of anguish in her voice, but defiance in her stance. "No one ever *sees* me, Knightly. Least of all you. Which is why I have to do utterly mad and dangerous things to get attention. And now here I am and my intentions are clear. What do you have to say about that?"

He had seen her—or started to, these past few weeks. He'd been driven to distraction by her—but just these past few days. He thought of all the years they met every week when she sighed when he walked into the room, and he had thought nothing of it. Never even noticed.

Of course she had to climb a tree and knock on his bedroom window to get his damned attention. She had risked her life and heart for him.

"I am the Nodcock," he said. Again.

"I'm dreadfully sorry about the name," she said, smiling sheepishly.

"I shan't forgive you for that," he said sharply. Good God, if anyone knew he'd never live it down.

"I wouldn't either," she replied with a shrug. But they both knew her heart was so damn big and loving she would forgive almost anyone anything. Even a bastard like him.

"I suspected as much," Knightly added. "I was thrown off by Owens and Marsden. And I suppose I didn't want to see. But I suspected."

"And yet you let me take it this far?" she asked, horrified. Understandably so.

"Last week you were only fainting in my arms, Annabelle. And now you're risking life and limb to break into my bedchamber in the middle of the night? How was I supposed to know you would go to such lengths?"

If he had seen this coming . . . If he had known that she would resort to this . . . What would he have done? He groaned when his brain supplied the idiotic suggestion of lining the ground with feather mattresses in case she fell.

The truth was, he didn't know what he would have done. The sight of Annabelle in breeches and a thin white linen shirt didn't exactly facilitate rational thought either.

"You let me throw myself at you when you knew!" And then Annabelle folded her arms across her chest and stomped her foot. Bloody adorable.

"Suspected," he clarified. "I suspected but I was not certain. I did not have the facts. And I operate on facts."

"You suggested I give up the ruse," Annabelle pointed out, and it sounded like an accusation. It sounded like he had lured her here. She stepped closer to him. He swallowed, hard. "You asked if I wanted satisfaction," she whispered.

"Be careful what you ask for, Annabelle," he warned.

She took another step in his direction. If she came any closer, he could not be held responsible. A man could only endure so much temptation. As it was, his self-restraint was already straining under the pressure.

He wanted to claim her mouth, sink his fingers in her hair, strip off those breeches. He wanted to feel her skin, hot and bare, underneath his. He wanted to see if one of Annabelle's infamous blushes went beyond her cheeks. He wanted to bury himself inside her. He wanted to know her, possess her, make love to her so thoroughly it would be impossible to move.

"Well, I have given up the ruse," Annabelle said plainly.

There were reasons, good reasons, why all those things he wanted should not happen. He could not think of one now. Not one.

"You want satisfaction, Annabelle?" He looked down at her face tilted up to his. Her eyes were large, searching. Her lips were plump, red, and slightly parted.

"I think so," she replied, revealing that devastating innocence of hers. She was offering that to him, along with her trust and her faith. That was why Annabelle scared him, and why he'd been reluctant to see the truth.

With Annabelle, it would matter.

With Annabelle, there would be no turning back. There would be no marriage in the aristocracy, there would be no parity with the New Earl. He still wanted these things. But in this moment he wanted Annabelle more.

When Knightly made a decision, it was swift and sure and he followed through without looking back. On the spot, in the moment, he chose Annabelle.

His life's ambition, tossed out the window in exchange for the chance to lose himself in her kiss, her touch, her sighs. That's how much he wanted her.

"Oh, you do want satisfaction, Annabelle, you do," he promised. His voice was rough. "I'll show you."

He did not start with a kiss. She had kept him in suspense, wanting, waiting, and teasing for weeks. Tonight she would suffer the same . . . though he was damn sure she was going to revel in every second of it. He'd make sure of that.

Her hair was pulled into a tight bun, and he began by removing the hairpins holding those curls back. A mass of thick blond curls tumbled down around her shoulders. Annabelle, undone.

His breath hitched. He had known Annabelle was pretty. But with her hair down she was beautiful. Like a goddess. Like it was impossible that he should not have noticed her all these years . . .

Well, he was going to discover her now. He was going to give her years worth of attention, in one night.

She gazed up at him. It pulled hard at his heart.

No one had ever looked at him like that. She was nervous, and she was putting herself in his care. She had literally gone out on a limb for him when no one else ever had. And she stood before him, waiting . . .

Then Annabelle licked her lip; a nervous gesture that he found unbelievably erotic. She would stay the night and, he thought wickedly, she would like it.

"Annabelle," he said, clasping her cheeks in his palms. There were all these things he should say. All these feelings he didn't have the words for. The woman left him speechless and nearly breathless. "Annabelle."

She tasted like sweetness and trouble. A marvelous combination. She responded hesitantly at first and then he could feel her reservations and nerves calm and fade. He didn't know he could do that with a kiss. Was he drunk on that power? Or just drunk on Annabelle?

They kissed in the moonlight, until he could stand it no longer—a minute, maybe two. He was desperate to know her. How soft was her skin? How did she sound when he pleasured her? How did she taste, everywhere? How did it feel to be inside her?

Knightly needed to know. Knightly sought answers.

One could not make proper love to a woman while she was dressed as a boy. He tugged at the shirt, pulling it from her breeches and above her head. Buttons seemed to have gone flying; he heard them skittering across the floor.

Annabelle folded her arms over her chest.

"Oh no, my dear Annabelle," he murmured. "I need to see you."

Truly, he needed to. Like he needed air. He needed

to know how the real vision of Annabelle compared to the one he had conjured up, late at night when he was alone. He knew this would far surpass anything he'd imagined.

Yet in the far recesses of his mind, Knightly was aware that this was likely her first time. She'd be shy and uncertain and would need an extra gentle touch.

To even things out, he took off his own shirt, dropping it carelessly on the floor.

Her eyes widened as her gaze roamed over his naked chest. Perhaps that didn't put her at ease. Knightly couldn't help it; he grinned. Then he tugged her closer and kissed her some more. Her arms stole around him, tentatively to start.

Slow, he reminded himself, *slow.* He wanted this to be perfect for her. And her hesitant touch set him on fire. Something about being where no man had been before. If he did one thing in his life, it would be to make sure that this moment had been worth waiting for, for her.

When he could take it no longer, he guided Annabelle to the bed; he needed to feel her utterly naked, beneath him. He needed to make love to her. Needed to like he'd been blind, and now had the gift of sight and never wanted to close his eyes again.

WHEN Annabelle had thought about this night, in all honesty, this was the part she had thought about most of all. Never mind that it was her first time and her knowledge was limited to the occasionally illuminating conversations of her fellow Writing Girls. She knew what was supposed to happen. She had wondered what it'd be like.

She hadn't known. Dear Lord, she hadn't known. To feel this close to someone and to feel this wanted was to really know, for a moment, how cold and lonely she had been. Then Knightly proceeded to chase that feeling away every time he uttered her name in a husky voice, looked at her with undisguised craving. That was to say nothing of his kiss, which set her body and soul afire, and his touch, which stoked that fire.

Knightly lead her to his bed and together they tumbled down to the feather mattress. His bare skin was hot against her bare skin. She loved it. Loved the possessive feeling of his weight on hers. His fingers threaded through her own. It was the sweetest thing that he should still hold her hand in a moment like this when they were naked and tangled together. She didn't know quite where she ended and he began.

"I can feel you smiling as we kiss," he murmured, and she laughed softly. Knightly's mouth nibbled oh so gently on her earlobe and it sent shivers down her spine.

"I wanted . . ." she whispered, but then gave up. She meant to tell him how she had wanted him, wanted this . . . But Knightly's palm closed over her breast, gently caressing and holding. He shifted his weight and her protest became a gasp of shock and then of pleasure when his mouth closed around the dusky, sensitive peak.

Knightly did the same on the other side. Annabelle gasped, and Annabelle sighed, and Annabelle took the lesson she had learned from practicing fainting and just *let go*. Those sighs turned into murmurs of pleasure and she writhed beneath him.

It was exquisite what he did to her with his mouth . . . leaving a trail of hot, scorching kisses from her breasts down to her belly, across to the indentation of her waist and lower still. The stubble on his cheeks was a wicked contrast to the softness of her own skin.

And then Knightly kissed her *there*. This she had certainly never imagined . . . didn't even know . . . He licked the bud of her sex, slowly back and forth at first. Breathing suddenly became impossible. And then slow leisurely circles around and around as a particular heat intensified, and with it a feeling of increasing pressure.

Annabelle gripped the bedsheets in her palms. She couldn't breathe. She felt like she was on fire. Like she might explode. The pleasure was so deep, so intense, so overwhelming, she simply couldn't fight it. So she didn't. She let go, cried out from the joyful release and surrendered.

She had risked her life for this. Risked rejection and mortification at the hands of the man she loved more than anything. It had been worth the risk. So very absolutely worth it.

"Annabelle," Knightly said, his voice rough with desire. "I want you."

She fixed her gaze upon Knightly. His dark hair fell rakishly down before his blue, blue eyes. How she had ached to hear those words from his lips. She had longed to see him thus: desperate for her.

She grinned wickedly—surely she now deserved to grin wickedly—and kissed him. It was now his turn to sigh.

"Annabelle, I need you," he murmured. She felt his arousal, warm and hard, pressing at the entrance between her legs. She arched her back, tilted her hips, intrigued by the sensation of it. Knightly groaned, then claimed her mouth for another kiss. She felt the heat surging again. Felt the sparks. Felt like she wanted more.

"Tell me to stop," he gasped. She wrapped her arms around him, entwined her legs with his. She couldn't get close enough to him. There had to be more. They had to be closer. She wanted more.

"I want to be yours," she whispered. "I want you."

When Annabelle whispered those words, there was no going back. Even if Knightly had wanted to stop, not even the devil and all the angels in heaven could make him. He entered her, slowly, because he didn't want to hurt her and because he did not want to miss a second of this. This one moment, this once.

She was warm and wet and ready for him. He pushed ahead until he was fully inside of her. Until there was no going back. Until he and Annabelle, at long last, were one.

"Oh, God, Annabelle," he rasped, and then he thrust gently. She gasped with pleasure. He thrust again, harder, and she moaned with desire. And then again and again. He lost himself in the rhythm, in the scent of her and the sound of her soft cries of pleasure. Lost himself fully in the taste of her skin and surrendered to the overwhelming need to love her completely, to possess her entirely. He cried out, reaching his climax. She did too. He heard her cries of pleasure and felt her contract around him. He lost himself in this moment in which he noticed Annabelle, all of her.

# Chapter 36

## The Morning After

PARLIAMENTARY INTELLIGENCE
*There are rumors that Lord Marsden's Inquiry is
about to get worse—much worse.*
    *The London Weekly*

**A**NNABELLE awoke in Knightly's embrace. He held
her close and her head rested on his bare chest. She
heard his heartbeat, strong and steady. She held
him, too, with one of her arms flung over his chest
as if to say *mine*.

She thought she might have been having an extremely vivid dream in which she could experience
the scent of him and the glorious sensation of his
bare skin against her bare skin. But it was real.

This was real.

The world must have altered its course sometime
in the night. Perhaps it started spinning in the other
direction or started to orbit the moon instead of the
sun. The world as Annabelle had known it ceased
to exist.

Good riddance, she thought.

And to this wonderful new world, she practically purred good morning.

She didn't often feel contentment. Usually she woke up slightly disappointed to open her eyes to her attic bedroom and to the chores and drudgery of the day that awaited her. But she summoned her hope and sunny disposition and dared to dream perhaps that day would be different.

The word, *contentment*, now had a new definition, and it was Knightly's arms around her. It was this feeling of nothing between them, not even so much as a chemise or a bedsheet.

Or perhaps, Annabelle thought with a smile as she happily drifted from deep sleep to fully awake, perhaps this was joy. To waken in the arms of the man you loved. What could possibly be better than that?

Hmm . . . She smiled bashfully and blushed. They had made love. She'd had no idea. None at all. He'd teased and seduced New Annabelle to heights Old Annabelle never could have imagined.

Annabelle sighed, and this time it was a sigh of absolute and utter pleasure.

"Good morning," a man's voice greeted her. That never happened in her old world. And it was Knightly's voice, still rough from sleep.

"Good morning," she replied. It was a good morning indeed. She stretched and yawned and nestled closer to him. She loved him, and they had made love. Her heart had always belonged to him, and now the rest of her did, too.

"You are trouble, Annabelle," he said, turning on his side to gaze down at her. He brushed her hair out of her eyes, away from her face. Her hair was surely in a state. But she didn't care, not when he was looking at her like that.

"No one's ever said that to me before," she replied. "I like it. I probably shouldn't but I do."

"Good," he practically growled. But he grinned, too, and claimed her mouth for another kiss. He clasped her breast and she arched her back, pressing herself closer to him, to encourage him to that again, and more.

"You are absolutely trouble," he murmured as he feathered kisses along her neck. "For the first time in history, I will be late to the office."

"At least you don't have to worry about losing your position," Annabelle said, and wrapped her arms around him and pulled him even closer.

"And I have a very good reason for being late," he murmured as he rolled atop her. She parted her legs and felt him straining against her, ready. Oh so ready.

They made love again, trading in the cool glow from the moon for the softness of morning light.

"Annabelle," he whispered, holding her close after they had both cried out in pleasure and lay for a while in each other's arms. "Oh Annabelle."

It was inevitable that reality would intrude. It took the precise form of Knightly's valet, who discreetly entered the bedchamber with a tray of steaming black coffee and a thick stack of newspapers, which he set down on the bedside table before disappearing into what must have been the closet. Not once did he seem to register Annabelle's presence in his master's bed. Naked. Covered only by a bedsheet.

"I would feel better if your valet seemed to find this unusual," Annabelle remarked.

"Part of his job is to maintain an inscrutable expression at all times. At any rate, rest assured that I do not often have women sneaking into my bedroom in the middle of the night."

"I hope you don't mind I did that," Annabelle said bashfully, and Knightly laughed. She loved his laugh. Couldn't believe she was in bed, naked, with Knightly. And they were laughing. Dreams she hadn't known to dream were now coming true.

"Oh, Annabelle," he said, still laughing but pausing long enough to drop a kiss on her nose. "Oh, Annabelle."

"I'll take that as a no, you don't mind," she said with a touch of laughter.

"Good," he said . . . but all trace of laughter was gone from his voice. She peered over his shoulder at the newspaper he picked up and recognized the large masthead of a certain rival paper.

"*The London Times*, Knightly?" she said. She supposed he already knew every word of *The London Weekly*.

"Hell and damnation," he swore.

"What is it?" she asked, peering over his shoulder. She read the headline: THE LONDON WEEKLY UNDER INVESTIGATION. "Oh. That's not good," she said, which may have been the biggest understatement of 1825.

He scanned the lines quickly.

"I have to go," he said, tossing the paper aside, right into Annabelle's lap. He rubbed his eyes and the stubble on his jaw. She saw him glance around the room, bewildered. Worse, she saw that any lovely magical interlude they had shared was over. Knightly might still have been right next to her in his own bed, but in his head he was already at *The Weekly*.

He located his breeches and pulled them on before strolling off toward what she presumed was a dressing room of some sort. When he emerged a few moments later, he was dressed and groomed and looking like the Knightly she had known for years. Perfect, aloof, commanding, and ruthless.

"Stay as long as you'd like, the servants will take care of you," he said, quickly dropping a kiss on her mouth. Her lips were still parted and wanting when he pulled away and headed to the door.

He paused for a second with his hand on the doorknob and glanced at her over his shoulder. His blue eyes focused on her for a moment, as if committing the sight to memory. As if he wouldn't see it again.

"Damn," he said softly.

The door clicked softly shut behind him. Like that, he was gone.

What did *that* mean? She pulled the sheets up higher, as if to comfort herself and ward off the growing cold, which had nothing to do with the temperature of the air, only an unfortunate feeling inside. When Knightly left, it was like the sun stopped shining.

And now he was gone and she was still naked in his bed, alone.

"This is awkward," she muttered to herself. Being a Good Girl her entire life meant that she had never even contemplated what she might do if she found herself naked and alone in a gentleman's bedchamber in broad daylight.

Her first thought was to put some clothes on. Yet the only clothing she had with her was better fit for a lad and in a wrinkled heap on the floor on the far side of the room.

It was one thing for a woman to dress as a boy with the darkness of night to aid her. It was quite another for her to stroll through the streets of Mayfair during midday. Julianna had done it once . . . but Annabelle did not possess Julianna's brisk, determined stride.

Plus, she thought her shirt might have been divested of a few buttons.

Even more perilous than walking through the streets of London at midday in such a state was returning to the Swift household. By now they must have discovered that she was missing, if only because breakfast wasn't set out or fires weren't lit or the children weren't woken at precisely six in the morning.

Annabelle glanced at the clock; it was eleven. Eleven in the morning!

"Oh, dear," she said to herself. The raptures of pleasure and love she'd been basking in were now ebbing, replaced with panic.

She should know what to do. She was Dear Annabelle. She always knew what to do. Matters of practicality were her strong suit. It was in the romance department that she was an utter nitwit. In her head, she positioned her situation as a letter to Dear Annabelle, with half a mind to submit it to Knightly.

*Dear Annabelle?*
   *A "gentleman" left me stranded and naked in his bed. What to do?*
   *Mortified in Mayfair.*

If only Knightly hadn't dashed off, leaving her like this!

What had she expected? If there was one thing known about Knightly, one carved-in-stone fact, it was that *The London Weekly* came first and last. He spent so much of his time in the office that the Writing Girls had fiercely debated whether she should climb into his bedroom or drop in to *The Weekly* offices. They only settled on his bedchamber because Mayfair would be safer than Fleet Street at such an hour.

She should not take it personally that he had run out, leaving her naked in his bed with no clothes. It was just how he was.

Unless he meant to strand her here, awaiting his return, like some obliging mistress? While there were worse things than laying about in bed all day, with Knightly's scent still on the pillows, she knew she could not wait for him. For one thing, it seemed undignified. For another, for all she knew it could be days before he returned.

What to do, oh what to do?

She pulled the silk bell cord. And waited. Pulled the sheet up higher and waited until a moment later when an older woman opened the door and behind her a maid with a tray.

"Mr. Knightly told us to take care of you, so we'll do just that. I'm Mrs. Featherstone, the housekeeper."

The women acted thoroughly unsurprised to

find a naked woman in his bed. Annabelle scowled. She didn't think he'd been a monk, but why didn't anyone find it at all remarkable?

She considered asking, but decided she did not want the answer. Instead, she requested assistance in sending a note to Sophie.

# Chapter 37

### Quest for Rogue's Heart Leads to Disaster

FASHIONABLE INTELLIGENCE BY A LADY OF DISTINCTION
*Dear Annabelle has launched a craze for feigning
faints and tantalizingly low bodices among the ton's
debutantes. Mothers and determined bachelors are
afraid of what she will do next.*

The London Weekly

**S**OPHIE came to her rescue and arrived shortly
with a dress, stockings, a bonnet, and all the other
items necessary for her to appear in public. It was
lovely that she did not have to explain why such a
favor was required.

"I trust the evening was successful," Sophie inquired after they were comfortably ensconced in
her carriage.

"Oh yes," Annabelle said. At the thought of it,
that warm glow returned. Her cheeks inflamed, as
they were wont to do, when images from the night
before flashed in her mind. But then she recalled
Knightly's abrupt exit. "But this morning . . ." How
to explain this morning?

"I trust you both saw the news. *The London Weekly*

under attack," Sophie said softly. "Did you read the article?"

She had done so while nibbling toast and drinking tea. Mrs. Featherstone had given her one of Knightly's shirts to wear, and she'd been loath to take it off when Sophie arrived with more suitable public attire.

"It's rather bad, isn't it?" Annabelle asked. *The London Times* had reported that Marsden's Inquiry would be expanding to review all newspapers, starting first and foremost with *The London Weekly*. The newspaper's owner and editor would be called to testify. He might be charged with libel. He would almost certainly find himself in prison.

"He might lose the paper, Annabelle." Sophie said this softly, her expression woeful.

"He owns it. How can they take it away?" she asked. More to the point, *The London Weekly* belonged to Knightly in a way that went beyond mere possession. Like it was his heart, or his soul.

"Well, the paper might lose him if the Inquiry determines that we broke the law with our reporting methods. Just think of Owens and Eliza . . ." Sophie said, wincing.

The devil only knew what Owens had done for stories: he'd posed as a Bow Street Runner, a guard at Windsor Castle, a footman at the Duke of Kent's residence. Those were the exploits they knew of.

Eliza had been disguised for weeks as a housemaid in the Duke of Wycliff's household, exposing his most intimate secrets each week (before he married her, that is).

"They couldn't possibly send a duchess to the tower." Annabelle's heart clenched, imagining such an awful fate for people whom she loved so dearly. They hadn't really done anything wrong. No one had been hurt.

"It's unlikely they would go after Eliza. Really, Marsden is just out for Knightly. Rest assured, Brandon is working tirelessly behind the scenes, and even Roxbury and Wycliff have deigned to show their faces at the House of Lords for the first time. But Marsden is furious."

"Why? What has Knightly ever done to him?" Marsden, who had sent her pink roses. Marsden, who had coined the phrase "the Nodcock." Marsden, who had been one of the few gentlemen to ever pay attention to her. She felt betrayed for thinking him kind, a friend. She felt like a traitor to Knightly for her friendliness toward Marsden. She also felt like a fool.

"Marsden is livid because it seems Knightly and his fortune were supposed to marry his sister— whom no one else will have," Sophie said, and with an apologetic smile added, "Then Knightly was seen with you . . ."

"Oh," Annabelle said in small voice, thinking of their kiss in the moonlight at the charity ball. The moment when she really, truly fell in love with Knightly as he was, not Knightly of her dreams. She had thought that hour enchanted, and never considered that such destruction would be left in its wake.

Knightly had been courting Lady Lydia and was her only marital prospect, thanks to all those rumors and the missing second season. Was she now doomed to a life of spinsterhood, because of her? Knightly had been courting her, too, in order to protect his beloved newspaper. Was he doomed to lose the thing he loved most in the world?

It trying to obtain her own happiness, it seemed she ruined the lives of two innocent people.

"Oh no," she whispered as she all too clearly saw how this was her fault. All of it—Marsden's fury, Knightly's fight for *The Weekly*, Lady Lydia's impending spinsterhood. If she hadn't caught his eye and glanced over her shoulder, as per the suggestion of some stranger, when she strolled onto the terrace . . .

If she hadn't fainted into his arms, or left that shawl behind, or lowered the bodice on each dress she owned in a hope to catch his eye, and then his heart . . .

*If she hadn't thrown herself at him week after week . . .*

If Knightly had never noticed her, he would have married Lady Lydia and everything would be fine. There wouldn't be an inquiry or a trial or the threat of prison. He wouldn't be faced with the loss of the thing he loved most of all.

But she had grown selfish and desperate in her loneliness. She had tried tricks and schemes to turn his head. She had forced him to catch her when she fainted. She had climbed a tree and tumbled into his bedroom in the middle of the night.

It had never occurred to Annabelle that she was distracting him from something else or someone else.

She had only wanted his love. Now it seemed that she'd ruined his life in her quest for it.

"What do I do?" she asked. She had to fix this, somehow. Because this disaster was her fault and because she loved him, she had to make this right.

"Wait and see, I suppose . . ." Sophie said with a little shrug.

"No, I must fix this," Annabelle vowed. She would. No matter what it cost her.

# **Chapter 38**

### *The London Weekly* Courts Scandal

FASHIONABLE INTELLIGENCE BY A LADY OF DISTINCTION
*The matrons of the ton are united in their fury against
the vice of gossip in the press and have pledged their
support to Lord Marsden's efforts to promote a "decent
and honorable" newspaper industry. That is, until
they must go without their scandal sheets.*

> *The London Weekly*

*Galloway's Coffeehouse*

**I**T had been one hell of a day and one hell of a night.
Darkness came and went; Knightly noted its arrival
and passing from his desk.

He barely slept, barely ate, barely drank.

Barely even thought of Annabelle.

Oh, she was there, in a way—somehow her scent
had clung to his skin. When his attention faltered
and his gaze drifted to the clock, Knightly thought,
At this hour last night, Annabelle was clinging to
my windowsill for dear life. At this time last night
Annabelle was climaxing in my arms, from my
touch.

And truth be told, he even thought, At this time yesterday, I was blissfully unaware . . .

He had been blissfully unaware that Dear Annabelle was intent upon seducing him. Didn't know that Annabelle loved him. Hadn't claimed her in the most irrevocable way. He didn't have to do anything about it. But now there was no question that something must be done about Annabelle. But he couldn't think about it. He did not have the time to puzzle it out. Not tonight, of all nights, when he had few precious hours to respond to the direct attack to his beloved newspaper.

Knightly and Owens had taken the unprecedented action of stopping the presses so they might rewrite, reset, and reprint a new edition of *The London Weekly* that included a letter from the editor responding to the attack.

They ended up rewriting nearly the entire issue.

"This isn't working," Owens had muttered, staring down at the draft of a letter from the editor on the table between them. Dusk was settling over the city, and they'd been working ceaselessly since first light.

"You're right," Knightly reluctantly agreed. The front-page story just wasn't hitting the right notes of outrage, defiance, and humor. Instead it came across like a boorish lecture on the importance of a free press.

Knightly rubbed his jaw. He had left Annabelle hours ago . . . Was she still in his bed? What would it be like to come home, knowing Annabelle awaited him?

He refused to consider it. Instead, he strolled across the room and poured a brandy for himself and Owens.

"You know, Owens, we should show them what a government approved paper reads like."

"You mean cut out all the good bits?" Owens retorted.

"Basically. And then we rewrite this first page article to explain. You know, 'The London Weekly gives its readers exactly what they want. You asked for this piece of rubbish edition of the paper. And the readers who didn't want this know why they should be riled up, and who they should direct their anger at. Enjoy.'"

"I like it," Owens said with a grin. "One hell of a statement. But we won't have time to rewrite and reset the type for the whole issue."

"Black it out. Cross it out. That way there's no change in the pages just black lines showing what they're missing," Knightly said, and then he thought about it more and got excited. "Can you just see it? Most of the paper will be blacked out."

"Genius. There will be hell to pay for this," Owens said. But he was grinning, and Knightly knew he was imagining this utterly defiant edition of the paper with those taunting black lines.

"Publish and be damned," Knightly said, raising his glass in cheers.

It was one hell of a gamble. Give 'em all exactly what they ask for, sit back and watch them howl. Marsden might be on a personal quest against him, but he was going to make this into a public spectacle. Which is why, exhausted as he was after working for twenty-four straight hours, he went not home to his bed, but to the coffeehouse. To Galloway's. His club.

He wanted to watch readers react. Wanted to see what he left a beautiful woman in bed for.

He would go to her. Even though he didn't know quite what to say. The irony that he, a professional master of words, did not know the right ones for this occasion. She loved him. He made love to her.

A proposal of marriage wouldn't be remiss, but . . . what about love matches and half brothers who refused to acknowledge him? What about hopes and plans he'd long possessed, and what about his impending imprisonment? They would arrest him, surely. Especially after the stunt he pulled with this new issue.

Knightly sipped his coffee, flipped through the pages of *The London Weekly*, and more often than not glanced at the other patrons around the room.

He noted with no small amount of satisfaction that most of the blokes in the coffeehouse were reading his newspaper. Some laughed. Some had their brows knit into deep lines as they tried to puzzle out what the damned articles said. Or maybe they were realizing the stranglehold on news that the government was attempting. More than stamp taxes, or window taxes.

Knightly was reminded, then, that this wasn't just a personal battle between Marsden and himself, nor was *The Weekly* just his darling pet. It was the newspaper that was written for the people he grew up with—tradesmen and actors, barristers and shopkeepers. And it was the paper for the people he aspired to associate with. It was, like himself, a mix of high and low. He was not one or the other, no matter what his aspirations might be.

As per their usual routine, Drummond and Gage ambled in and took seats at Knightly's table near the window. They also looked worse for wear, Gage especially, probably after a long night at the theatre and an even longer night at some demimonde soiree. Those routs were much less decorous, Knightly had to say, and thus much more fun than ton parties.

Gage held his head in his hands and groaned. One could practically smell the alcohol emanating from his pores.

Drummond took the paper and wordlessly flipped through quickly until hitting a certain page. Knightly watched, slack-jawed in something akin to horror. All those hours, all the careful deletions, the presses stopped and restarted, a staff on the verge of mutiny, all on a day he could have spent in bed with a beautiful, loving woman . . . and the man went straight to Dear Annabelle.

It was his turn to groan.

"Dear Annabelle," Drummond said with a sigh. "How fares your quest for love?"

Knightly rubbed his stubbled jaw. He leaned back in his chair. This was going to be interesting.

Drummond grinned at Annabelle's words on the page and then laughed at something she'd written. Knightly remembered editing it in an advanced state of frustration. The exact words hadn't stuck with him; just a feeling of confusion, wanting, refusal to engage.

"What's so funny?" he asked.

"She fainted into his arms!" Drummond said with unabashed amusement. "Listen to this," he said, as he read aloud from the paper: " 'Quite a few letters arrived my way, written in a matronly handwriting from Mayfair addresses, encouraging me to feign a swoon in the particular gentleman's arms. I am given to understand that this maneuver plays to a man's chivalrous instincts—to start. But then to hold a comely young maiden in his arms is supposed to arouse his baser inclinations as well.'"

"That's funny," Gage muttered, managing to lift his head from his hands, but only for a moment. Green. The man was positively green.

"This girl . . ." Drummond said, shaking his head and grinning. "I say, I am in love and have never even met the chit."

Knightly fought to keep a scowl off his face.

Annabelle was *his*.

In the only way that mattered.

Memories of that night crashed over him, like waves on a beach.

Annabelle in the moonlight—desperately hanging on outside of his window. He'd heard the phrase "having one's heart in the throat," but hadn't understood it until that moment. He almost lost her, far too soon.

Annabelle in breeches, showing off her long slender legs. Later in the night, she wrapped those legs around him as he buried himself deep inside her. Knightly closed his eyes . . .

Annabelle in nothing. Her skin, oh God, her skin was milky white and pure, and so soft. A soft pink blush, everywhere. Her mouth, her kiss, her tentative touch growing more bold as he showed her dizzying heights of pleasure.

He could still feel her, still taste her. He still craved her.

His lungs felt tight, like he couldn't breathe. It wasn't because of the smoky haze in the coffeehouse either.

He still desired her, still wanted her, and still needed more of her. And yet—how badly? How much? What price was he willing to pay for Annabelle in his bed?

Drummond chuckled and muttered, "Baser inclinations. God, I'd love to show her—"

Before he even knew what he was doing, Knightly had leapt across the table and grabbed a fistful of Drummond's cravat.

Coffee spilled across the table, pouring over the edge. The ceramic mug cracked in pieces as it hit the hardwood floor.

Drummond's face took on a shade of crimson.

"Oi! Some of us are sorely feeling the aftereffects of alcohol," Gage muttered, but no one paid him any mind.

"I strongly suggest you do *not* finish that sentence," Knightly said. There was a lethal tone to his voice he didn't recognize.

"Really?" Drummond asked. Since he managed to imbue the word with some sarcasm, Knightly determined that he still had too much air, so he twisted the bunch of fabric in his fist until Drummond was gasping for breath.

"Really," Knightly drawled. Then he let go, took a seat and waved for another coffee.

"You're the Nodcock, aren't you?" Drummond said.

"Bugger off," Knightly told him. It was the wrong thing to say. It only encouraged him. Even Gage lifted his head.

"How did it feel to have Dear Annabelle faint into your embrace?" Drummond inquired. "Were your baser inclinations aroused?"

Gage snorted, laughed, and then groaned.

"Really?" Knightly replied, lifting one brow for emphasis.

"Really. How have you missed her all these years?" Drummond propped his head on his palm, elbow on the table. Beside him, Gage laid his head on the table in defeat.

"What's wrong with him?" Knightly asked, looking warily at their supremely ill friend.

"Some people think it's a good idea to accept a wager to see if one can drink an entire bottle of brandy in one evening," Drummond explained witheringly.

"I won," Gage grumbled.

"But at what cost?" Knightly mused.

"But let's not discuss Gage's idiocy, as that is expected of him," Drummond said with a dismissive wave of his hand. "I'm more interested in your idiocy, Knightly. How have you missed Annabelle all these years? Is she actually not that pretty?"

"She's pretty," he said tightly. By pretty he meant soul-wrenchingly beautiful, the kind of gorgeous that brought a man to his knees. Actually did, last night.

"Pretty? And you only just noticed this . . ." Drummond pointedly let his voice trail off. " . . . yesterday . . . a week ago . . . a month ago?"

When she started trying to make him notice. When he informally betrothed himself to a perfectly fine woman who possessed no traits that attracted him, other than her high society connections. When it was too late for him.

Aye, he noticed Annabelle not in all the *years* when he could have, but waited until it was absolutely and completely inconvenient to do so. No wonder she called him the Nodcock.

"I take it you've noticed her now, Nodcock," Drummond remarked.

Knightly lunged across the table once more, once again tugging hard on Drummond's cravat, by now a limp and wrinkled scrap of fabric.

"Have mercy on a man," Gage pleaded. "Please. For the love of Annabelle."

"This is serious, is it?" Drummond asked after Knightly released him—but not without a threatening look.

"It's none of your damned business," Knightly said. And still—still!—Drummond blithely carried on, provoking him more with each word he uttered. That was the problem with longstanding friends— they felt utterly free to go too far and to enjoy every step they took over the line.

"*Au contraire, mon frère,*" Drummond declared. "Annabelle's business is all of London's business. If you do not do right by this chit, I will come for you—if you are the Nodcock, that is, and not some desperate pretender—and I will bring the mob. And then I will go and console Annabelle myself. Nakedly."

This time Knightly swung at him; his fist connectedly solidly with Drummond's jaw. Satisfied his point had been made, Knightly quit the coffeehouse.

# Chapter 39

### An Offer She Can Refuse

#### DEAR ANNABELLE

*Attentions are one thing, affections are quite another.
True love cannot be sparked by parlor tricks. A lower
bodice will catch a man's gaze, but it will not make
him care. A forgotten shawl may afford a moment
alone, but it will not lead to love . . . and if it did,
would that be fair? This author thinks not and en-
courages all—particularly Scandalously in Love—to
hold out for true love.*

> The London Weekly

**K**NIGHTLY arrived at the Swift household later
that afternoon, after a nightmare-plagued sleep in
which Annabelle fell from that branch and he hadn't
caught her in time.

A maid answered the door. That wicked sister-
of-law of hers made the most snide and horrid comments when he stepped into the drawing room.
This time, children were present. Plump little faces
looked up at him from their books and games with
sullen expressions. They did not seem pleasant.

Her brother reluctantly took his damned issue of

*The London Times* and the rest of the family into another room, only at Knightly's request that he and Annabelle might have some privacy.

The man did not seem the slightest bit curious why his unmarried sister might wish to have a private audience with a gentleman. Really, he ought to have pulled him aside to ask his intentions. That he did not was a black mark in Knightly's book, even though it was to his own benefit.

He needed to take her away from this house, the awful relatives and uncomfortable furniture. He would install her in his town house. They'd make love each night. And during the day she'd easily be able to walk to the Mayfair homes of the other Writing Girls and the shops on Bond Street. She'd want for nothing.

Maybe he'd even marry her. The thought crossed his mind, and for the first time his heart didn't rebel.

Knightly was glad he'd brought flowers. Pink roses. She seemed like a pink roses kind of woman. She had told him that, at any rate. He'd waffled because Marsden had sent them to her. Knightly had no idea that the purchase of flowers for a woman was so fraught with peril.

"Annabelle," he said once they were alone. "Annabelle," he said, with urgency and lust and fear and restraint.

"Good afternoon, Derek," she said softly.

She smiled faintly, with just a slight curve to her lips. Her eyes seemed more gray than blue—he noticed those subtle distinctions now. Something was wrong. He knew it, because he knew her now.

"I'm sorry I didn't come sooner," he said.

"That's all right. You had quite a lot to do with

the paper. I understand," she said softly. Annabelle
was always so understanding and generous. In this
situation, any other woman would be hollering
at him like a banshee. But Annabelle knew what
this meant to him and let him have his moment.
It was admirable of her—or was it too nobly self-
sacrificing?

"I brought you flowers," he said, reduced to stating the bloody obvious. Good God, what did this
woman do to him? He mastered tense negotiations,
dealt with irate readers, and conducted interviews
and interrogations eliciting all manner of incriminating confessions.

"Thank you," she said softly. She took the bouquet and inhaled deeply with her eyes closed, the
pink buds casting a pink glow over her skin.

When she opened her eyes, they were still more
gray than blue, more haunted than happy.

He exhaled impatiently, annoyed with himself.
He should just treat this like a business negotiation
in which the goal was to achieve a mutually satisfying outcome.

Yet he was dealing with a woman, with Annabelle
. . . A confession of his feelings was in order, which
was a problem because he didn't know how to make
sense enough to explain them. Hoping she'd favor
disorganized honesty rather than artfully arranged
sentiments, he plowed ahead.

"Annabelle, about the other night . . ." he said,
clasping her hands. "I can't stop thinking about it.
About you. Now that I finally see you, I never want
to close my eyes. I want to know you."

"Oh, Knightly," she whispered. Those haunted
gray eyes were now slicked over with tears. Her eye-

lashes were dark, damp. Where those tears of joy? A man could hope, but he could not be sure.

Knightly felt as if he were thrust upon the stage on opening night, to perform in a play he had never watched or read. He didn't have a flair for the dramatic, or an ability to improvise.

He stated facts. That was all. He would state them now.

"I want you to live with me, Annabelle. And I want to save you from this awful household. You'll stay with me and spend your days with the Writing Girls and writing your advice column and we'll spend long nights together.

"That does sound lovely," she said, and he heard the *however* that was yet unspoken. And then she sighed—a sigh so laden with feeling that even he felt it deep in his bones. It was a sigh containing heartache, whispering of a cruel, cruel world, and suggestive of utter, unrelenting sadness.

She used to sigh with happiness when he walked into the room. Bewildered, he wondered when that had changed, and why.

"But I cannot." She said the words flatly.

She said no.

Annabelle said no.

For a second Knightly's heart stopped beating. Blood stopped circulating, air ceased to flow. He would have sworn that the earth stopped spinning. Even though he stood on firm ground, the sensation of falling stole over him. In this epic fall, he reached out for Annabelle but she pulled back her hand and turned away.

He stiffened all over, bit down hard. He had felt this before, years before, when he was thrown out of his own father's funeral. *Throw the bastard out. He doesn't belong here.* This feeling was a desperate, driving need to belong. It was abandonment and rejection from the one he needed approval from.

At this moment it was all the more devastating because he'd never expected it—she was Dear Annabelle intent on wooing him, the Nodcock. All of London knew this. All of London had cheered her on. This was her moment, and she refused it.

He had thought she'd throw herself into his arms and kiss him with love and gratitude. He never thought she would say no.

Worse, worse, a thousand times worse, he realized in this moment that he *wanted* her to say yes.

"Cannot or will not?" he asked sharply. His chest was tight. Breathing was impossible.

"I forced your hand, and that wasn't right," she explained in an anguished voice. "And now with this awful business at *The Weekly* . . ."

"Leave the paper out of this, Annabelle," he said roughly. He didn't want any favors or her idea of better judgment. His temper flared, and he didn't try all that hard to restrain the anger. He stepped closer to her, looming above her. There was no anguish in his voice when he said, "You made me notice you. You made me see, and now I can't stop thinking of you."

"I didn't realize the consequences!" she cried, stepping back. "And you *say* forget the paper, but you can't really mean it. I know you, Knightly. I know you better than anyone."

They were both thinking of how he'd rushed out and left her alone in the morning after making love to her. He had not forgotten the paper. It had been at the forefront of his mind even as a beautiful, naked woman who loved him was in his bed. After risking her life and her reputation and her everything to get there.

These facts revealed a brutal and unflattering truth.

"Knightly, you ought to marry Lady Lydia and have your newspaper and forget about me." She said this in such a small, pitiful voice. But he couldn't feel pity, not now.

Not when he only discovered what he'd lost as it was slipping away.

Like he hadn't appreciated sunlight until a month of gray skies and rain, he had the feeling a long, dark winter was only just beginning.

He was angry, and though it was petty and cruel, he needed her to know that.

"I can't stop thinking about you, Annabelle. You wanted my attentions, and now you have them and you're throwing it back in my face."

"I'm so sorry," she said. A few tears streamed down her cheeks. He wanted to kiss those tears away. Wanted to take her in his arms and hold her. They probably both wanted that. But she wouldn't allow it now, would she?

"That makes two of us," he said. With those parting words, he left.

# Chapter 40

## Woman Drowns in Own Tears (Almost)

*If you love something, set it free.*
**Some heartless and unfeeling person**

*Annabelle's attic bedroom*

**A**NNABELLE sat at her little writing desk, tears sliding forlornly down her cheeks. To her left, a bouquet of dead and dried pink roses. To her right, a fresh bouquet all luscious and fragrant. Before her was a sheet of paper and her writing things. She intended a reply to Lady Marsden. And she owed an explanation to London.

But her heart was too broken for her brain to even contemplate words and sentences.

Relinquishing Knightly and releasing him from any obligation to her was the right thing to do. She was certain of it.

But God, oh God, it hurt. Hurt like when they buried her parents, but worse, because Knightly was still living and breathing in the world. Probably hating her, too, which was not the passion she'd been trying to incite in him.

She could still vividly recall what it felt like to be held in his arms. She could still taste his kiss, and her body remembered what it was like to have him inside of her. To be wanted and possessed by him. It was . . . it was a kind of glory that could never be replaced. It was why she had refused Mr. Nathan Smythe from the bakery up the road. She had waited for this and it had been worth it.

Yet she refused him.

She was mad, utterly mad.

No, she was a Good Girl. She was Annabelle who always did the right thing, and who always put others before herself. Old Annabelle or New Annabelle, it was all the same. Her own happiness was the least of her concerns, especially when it came to what was right. Or what was best for Knightly.

She knew the truth: she had teased and tugged his affections from him. Could they ever be happy knowing that she conjured up love like a wicked sorceress? Could they ever be happy knowing that he had sacrificed his life's ambition of conquering the haute ton for marriage to a Spinster Auntie of no consequence?

Annabelle did not believe happiness was possible under such circumstances. She wanted true happiness.

Much as she loved him, she still loved and cherished herself, too. If she cared any less, she would have accepted his paltry offer. She would have sacrificed her body and soul to be his lover. She would be his little mistress who penned the cute advice column until he tired of her or found a duke's sister or an earl's daughter to marry.

So parted they must be, however much it might hurt. Dear God, this hurt.

She'd made him notice her. But she didn't make him love her.

# Chapter 41

**Breaking News: the Nodcock Finally Falls in Love**

*Dear Annabelle,*

*We, the undersigned, think the Nodcock does not deserve you. Nevertheless, we wish that he would come to his senses and love you.*

*Penelope from Piccadilly (and two hundred additional signatures)*

**S**HE made him want her.

She giveth and she taketh away. He wanteth.

He didn't know . . . didn't know . . . until it was gone, all gone.

Last night the wind had blown, knocking a branch against the glass and rattling the windowpanes. The alacrity with which he dashed out of bed and leapt to the window was mortifying when it was all too clear that Annabelle wasn't there, awaiting his rescue. It was just the wind, and he'd suffered from an extreme case of wishful thinking.

He drank, as a man is wont to do when confronted with his innermost emotions, particularly ones pertaining to the heart.

He threw himself into work but found no joy in it, not even when *The Weekly*'s rebellious version outsold all others. Another sales record had been reached. His mantra, *scandal equals sales*, had once again proven to be gold, pure gold. The milestone passed, uncelebrated.

There were rumors he would be arrested. He didn't give a damn.

When it came time for the weekly writers' meeting, Knightly strolled in, taught and tense and determined to show no emotion.

"Ladies first," he said with what he hoped was a good approximation of a grin. He glanced around the room, fighting and losing the battle of where his focus would reside. His gaze landed on Annabelle.

She wore one of the Old Annabelle dresses, a drab frock in a particularly dull shade of grayish brown. The cut and fit of the dress did her no favors. He could say that now because he knew the long, lithe legs hidden under those skirts. He knew the gentle taper of her waist, the flare of her hips, and the perfect swells of her breasts.

It was all hidden away behind a sackcloth disguised as a dress.

The sight of her still took his breath away. He felt a hot, tortured flare of longing.

He saw her shoulders roll forward as she clasped her hands in her lap. Her eyes were downcast. It was the posture of Overlooked Annabelle.

She no longer wanted him to notice her, did she?

Yet she sighed when he walked in; his every nerve was attuned for this one small indication that she still cared. It was vitally important that she still cared.

The meeting progressed. Knightly acted as if nothing had ever occurred between him and Annabelle. His pride was on the line here, his reputation amongst his staff. He was Mr. London Weekly Knightly—cool, reserved, ruthless, and inscrutable. He would be damned, *damned*, if they knew he had been laid low by a woman.

However, he could not ignore her. After the other Writing Girls had mentioned their stories for the week, he turned to Annabelle and fixed her with the Knightly stare. She shrank back a little more. His head lifted higher.

"Dear Annabelle, what's the latest from your column?" He fought to keep any emotion from his voice. His anger, though, started to fade with every glance of her blue eyes.

"I don't think I've written about etiquette enough recently, particularly the proper use of fish knives," she said.

The room fell silent. Nervous glances were exchanged.

"Bugger etiquette and the cutlery. What happened with the Nodcock?" This came from Grenville, of all people. Grumpy old, Parliament-obsessed *Grenville*.

Every head swiveled in the direction of *The London Weekly*'s resident grouch. Julianna's jaw dropped open. Alistair coolly lifted one brow. Sophie and Eliza were grinning, and Owens looked up from his notes, shocked.

"What? I'm the only person here who read Annabelle's Adventures in Love?" Grenville asked gruffly. "Anyone who claims not to have done so is a liar."

"We're all agog that you are interested in something other than . . . Parliament. Something . . . human," Julianna sputtered.

"I'm not dead, am I? I can appreciate Annabelle's low-cut bodices as much as the next bloke." One of the ladies gasped.

"Grenville," Knightly said in a warning tone. She was not to be spoken of thusly, not in his presence.

"I liked New Annabelle and her crazy schemes," Owens said affectionately. He smiled at her, but she didn't see it, as her gaze was studiously fixed upon the tabletop. "She's got that mixture of sweetness and wickedness, if that makes sense. She's funny."

"She wore much better dresses," Alistair added, and he glanced at the grayish brown gown with a wince.

"I'm right here," Annabelle said. But she was Overlookable Annabelle today so her voice lacked any force or volume, and she didn't carry herself in a way that compelled one's attention. It was remarkable to witness. In fact, it was all too clear now how she had escaped his noticed all those years. From the softness of her voice to the quickly averted gazes, Annabelle hadn't made herself known.

"I for one want a conclusion to the story," Grenville said. "Even if it turns out the Nodcock is just that. Or worse."

Knightly bit his tongue. The fellow writers heartily agreed, yet they all carefully avoided looking in his direction.

"The story is over," Annabelle said, this time with a little more force.

All heads swiveled to look at *him*—not her, but him!

At that moment a horrifying truth became clear:

every single one of them had known of Annabelle's infatuation with him, and had for years.

All those weeks when Annabelle had sighed and he'd carried on, utterly oblivious, they had known.

All those weeks when Annabelle tried her "crazy schemes," they had been waiting and watching for him to finally, *finally* notice her.

He truly was the last person in London to know. He deserved this torture of having glimpsed her, and lost her.

"It ought to have a happy ending." This came from Owens, to his surprise. What the devil did a rough and brash young reporter care about happy endings? But even Knightly couldn't miss the affectionate glance that Owens gave Annabelle. It seemed New Annabelle had earned his affections, too.

"Happy endings equals sales?" Julianna offered.

"It's up to Annabelle, is it not?" Knightly challenged.

"Only a nodcock would think that," Grenville stated, punctuated with a *harrumph.* Heads nodded all around.

Knightly glanced at Annabelle looking all wistful and forlorn and heartsick and wearing the most god-awful gown he'd ever laid eyes upon. Old Annabelle was present today: quiet and shy and desperately trying to be overlooked.

Oh, but he knew a different version of Annabelle, who climbed trees at midnight and kissed him like every kiss meant something beautiful and something true, like it was the first time and the last time all at once. That New Annabelle had wrapped her lithe legs around him as he buried himself in her.

She went out on a limb for him, in more ways than one.

New Annabelle had transfixed him, bewitched him.

But she couldn't quite shake Old Annabelle, could she? But was that such a bad thing?

She impressed him with the way she walked steadily and kindly through life, even though more often than not the world didn't spare a second thought for her. He finally saw that Annabelle gave, gave, gave, and asked for nothing in return. She offered thoughtful advice to complete strangers, minded those brats, and slaved away at domestic drudgery.

Annabelle, who could contain oceans of emotion in a little sigh. Who had every reason to be bitter, yet imbued everything with such sweetness and hope.

Annabelle, so often overlooked.

Oh, he saw her now. Did he ever.

Suddenly, he couldn't breathe. The truth hit hard like that.

That was one amazing woman, sitting there, making herself invisible. She was kind, beautiful, generous, daring, and funny. She possessed the courage to ask for help and to share her triumphs and embarrassments with the whole city. She possessed the strength to do the right thing even when it was the hard thing. He could see that now.

At that moment Knightly fell completely in love with Annabelle.

# Chapter 42

## What Would Dear Annabelle Do?

OVERHEARD
> *When I find myself in times of trouble, I ask,*
> *"What would Annabelle do?"*
> *Overheard in a coffeehouse*

*Galloway's Coffeehouse*

**K**NIGHTLY loved her. The thought would not leave, but he didn't exactly wish it away either. The question of his intentions regarding this newly discovered love was another matter entirely.

"You ought to brace yourself for the mob, Knightly," Drummond said grimly. According to Drummond, hurting Annabelle was a crime punishable by a slow and painful death by medieval torture instruments.

Knightly didn't want to hurt her, he wanted to love her.

"When did the whole damn world fall in love with Annabelle?" he wondered aloud. How did he miss this?

"I ought to plant you a facer for even asking that

question," Drummond said. "She's a bloody delightful chit and she writes for your paper. How did you not see this unfolding?"

"You ought to have seen it before anyone else," Gage said. "Do you even edit the paper or just lord over it?" he, smirking.

"Until just recently she wasn't exactly clamoring for my attention and I had my sights set elsewhere," Knightly answered. He knew now that she hadn't let him see her. It was fascinating the way she could blend into the background at will, and even more amazing that she had launched herself into the spotlight.

"Now that's a different matter. More interesting," Drummond mused, sipping his coffee and staring pointedly at Knightly.

"By interesting he means feel free to elaborate," Gage explained.

"Annabelle inconveniences everything I had planned for myself," Knightly confessed. "I was going to marry some aristocratic woman and take my place in society. I had even contracted an informal betrothal. An understanding, at any rate. Everything was just in reach. But I did not plan for Annabelle."

"Change your plans," Gage said with a shrug.

"This is not a matter of what to do on a Tuesday evening, Gage," Knightly retorted. "One does not give up lifelong plans on a whim."

"Are you calling Annabelle a whim?" Drummond challenged, as he deliberately rolled up the sleeves of his shirt and folded his hand into a fist.

"Look, you can drop the Protector and Defender

of Annabelle act," Knightly retorted. That was his job. Or it ought to be.

"I don't think I can. Not while you're still acting like a nodcock," Drummond said with a smirk. Knightly fought the urge to wipe the smug look right off his face in a violent manner.

"I'll never forgive her for that name," he muttered instead.

"I love it," Gage said, grinning. "Nodcock."

"At any rate, Annabelle no longer wants me," Knightly said plainly. Drummond's reply was awfully succinct.

"Bullshit," he said.

"No, really. She told me to marry Lady Marsden to save the paper. After all she did to get my attentions, and she just drops me at the slightest obstacle."

"You're in love with her, aren't you?" Drummond questioned. His expression warned Knightly to answer carefully.

Knightly shrugged and sipped his coffee. It was tantamount to a confession.

"It's about time," Gage said. "Nodcock."

"What am I to do while she has these stupid ideas of noble self-sacrifice?" Knightly asked. If they were such geniuses, let them figure it out. His only idea was to have a reasonable, logical conversation with Annabelle where he would present the facts: they loved each other, they should marry, and it would be pleasing to them both. However, even he knew more romance and more theatrics were needed.

*Drama is for the page.*

Not anymore.

"Funny you should ask that," Drummond began

grandly. "Because lately, when I find myself in a quandary, I merely ask myself, 'What would Annabelle do?' I find it's really the only guiding principle I need."

"Hmm," Knightly said. He took another sip of his coffee.

What would Annabelle do?

More to the point, what *did* Annabelle do when she wanted to attract his affections?

Knightly's lips tugged into a slight smile before breaking into a full grin—because she had left very detailed and explicit directions. She lowered her bodice. Tried sultry glances. Left something behind. Employed a rival. Fainted into his arms. Climbed into his window at midnight.

Annabelle, in her infinite faith in the universe and unshakable optimism, would *try* no matter how risky or scary. She literally would go out on a limb for those she loved.

Suddenly, his course of action was clear. He was going to win Annabelle's affections back. And he was going to employ all the tricks she had.

# Chapter 43

**Fashion Alert from *The London Weekly***

FASHIONABLE INTELLIGENCE BY A LADY OF DISTINCTION
*Particularly emotional maidens have taken to wearing pink roses pinned to their (decidedly low) bodices in support of Dear Annabelle's heartache over the Nodcock. One hopes that he finds a way to make amends.*
    The London Weekly

*Offices of* The London Weekly

**A**NNABELLE could not stop staring at Knightly. That was nothing new. What was new, however, was that he was not wearing a cravat, nor was his shirt done up all the way to his neck as it ought to be. In spite of fashion and respectability, he wore his shirt open, exposing a vee of his chest.

It was distracting, to say the least.

She had kissed him there, pressing her lips to his hot skin, tasting him. She remembered as if it was only last night. Funny how the memory brought back all those sensations. She had tried so hard to put those thoughts aside, at morning, at night, during the day, in meetings. Anytime, really.

She had done the right thing in refusing him. She knew this in her heart and her mind. But her body craved him nonetheless.

"Did you see that Knightly did not wear his cravat today?" Julianna asked as they strolled through *The Weekly*'s offices on their way outside.

"Is it a new fashion, Sophie?" Eliza inquired of their fashion-forward friend.

"Not that I'm aware of. And not one that my husband would ever follow, however enticing it may be," Sophie replied. "Not that I am enticed by Knightly."

"Annabelle, surely you must have noticed," Julianna said. All three paused and turned to peer at her. She fought valiantly to keep the blush from betraying her.

Of course she had noticed. She had been riveted. If she were faced with a firing squad that had been instructed to hold its fire only *if* she could relate one item of discussion from that meeting, she would meet her death thinking only of the small amount of Knightly's exposed skin that she had once kissed and caressed during the most glorious night of her entire life.

But Annabelle did not say anything of the kind. It hurt too much to dwell upon it, and she couldn't fathom speaking of it. Plus, they stood near the open doorway to Knightly's office where he sat at his desk, writing. A lock of dark hair fell into his eyes. She folded her hands in her skirts to restrain herself from strolling in and brushing it aside.

He might look up, tug her into his lap, lower his mouth to hers . . .

"Annabelle?" Sophie said curiously. "Are you all right?"

"I'm sure he was merely warm," Annabelle replied. "Or perhaps the cloth had come undone and his valet was not present to attend to him."

Jenkins, his valet, who was paid to be inscrutable. Oh, must she know all these details about him? She had collected them carefully over the years, and months and weeks and days, never knowing how the knowledge would torture her.

KNIGHTLY had overheard them, and he dropped his head into his hands. He resisted the urge to pound his head against the desktop.

"Oh, Annabelle," he muttered. The sweet girl was utterly oblivious to his scheme—thus far. For the first time he had a hint of what Annabelle must have felt every time she sighed or blushed and he didn't notice: utter frustration. Enormous, enraging, frustration. Wanting to howl frustration. She was amazing, that Annabelle.

With a weary sigh of his own, Knightly reached into the top drawer of his desk, where he kept among other things—a loaded pistol, a flask of brandy, pens, important papers, and a list of every trick she had employed in order to gain his attention and affection.

He crossed *Lowered bodice—or the male approximation* off the list.

# Chapter 44

## Gentleman Shows Shocking Disregard for Attire

THE MAN ABOUT TOWN
*It seems that Mr. Knightly's courtship of Lady Marsden has concluded—without a betrothal announcement.*
The London Times

*Offices of* The London Weekly

THE following week, Annabelle dragged her heart-broken and forlorn self to the regular gathering of writers because really, she thought, she did not suffer enough.

Blanche had been especially keen on haranguing her lately, for the parlor wasn't dusted thoroughly, she said, or she couldn't see her reflection in the silver. Fleur had become exceptionally moody, prone to fits and sulks that left the entire household walking on eggshells. Watson and Mason were constantly at odds, which meant a racket the entire household had to endure, compounded by Blanche's fishwife shrieks requesting silence. Brother Thomas continued to read *The London Times.*

Annabelle sought refuge in her attic bedroom,

where she was faced with letters from readers livid at her handling of "the Nodcock situation." She read them all and desperately wished to explain that it was all a misunderstanding. That she had made a noble sacrifice. That they were hurting her feelings, and to what end?

She had been overlooked before but she had never been so cruelly criticized.

*You made a mistake and you will rue the day you threw his proposal into his face,* wrote Harriet from Hampstead Heath.

*You're a cruel, heartless woman. How do I cancel my subscription?* wrote Angry in Amersham.

*My sympathies had been with you and now they are with the Nodcock, you wanton hussy,* wrote some coward who hadn't dared sign a name.

Had she made a mistake? She thought about it and shed copious amounts of hot, salty tears and thought some more (and in all honesty wept more, too). In the end she concluded that she had done the right thing, despite the furious letters. It was love under false pretenses—if at all—and it wasn't acceptable.

She had waited far too long to settle for anything less than true, eternal love.

The Writing Girls had discussed it over a strong pot of black tea and ginger biscuits.

"I think you might be absolutely mad," Julianna had told her. "But that is always what they say of the most courageous."

"I think she is very wise and noble in her actions," Sophie said. "Especially as she was so swept up in the throes of passion."

"You did the right thing, Annabelle," Eliza said, patting her hand consolingly. "He'll come around."

"And if not . . . ?" Annabelle asked. She tried to lift one brow and couldn't manage it. She'd taken to practicing that in front of the mirror and had about as much luck as she did with the sultry gazes. Which is to say, no luck at all. Curses.

They hadn't a reply for that, which was not reassuring in the slightest.

*Would it really be the end of the world if Knightly never truly loved her?*

Yes, she concluded. It was one thing to be a Spinster Auntie to Wretched Relatives, but to do so after knowing, for one night, the most exquisite and glorious passions and the heart-stopping, breathtaking, soul-shattering touch of a devastatingly handsome man? Returning to the dull lonely life of Old Annabelle was unbearable.

Nevertheless, Annabelle endured, because that is what Annabelle did.

Thus she attended meetings even as they were now a particular kind of torture because of the pleasure she had known and forgone.

There was never any thought of giving up her writing, though. Other people's problems distracted her from her own. And it felt good to help other people use the right fork, address a countess properly, find new uses for vinegar, or solve a spat between sisters. With her writing, she made other people happier, and someone ought to be happy, if it wouldn't be her.

The writers had all gathered, waiting. Knightly always made it a point to arrive last. Outside, wind rattled the windowpanes. There was a low rumble of thunder in the distance. The air was positively electric.

Knightly strolled in.

"Ladies first," he said with a grin. She didn't sigh because she was distracted by something particularly wicked in his grin today. She saw a certain light in his eyes. It went without saying she knew all the sparks and dimensions of Knightly's gaze.

Annabelle sat up straighter.

A meeting progressed in which nothing remarkable happened, or so Annabelle assumed. Her attention had been drawn to the exposed vee of Knightly's chest. Once again he was eschewing fashion and modesty and not wearing a cravat. How positively scandalous.

It put her in mind of that night. That one glorious night. She clasped her hands in her lap.

About halfway through the meeting he slowly shrugged out of his jacket. That night he'd allowed his shirt to slide off his shoulders, down his muscled arms and falling to the floor, exposing the broad expanse of his chest. Today he set the jacket on the chair and carried on with the meeting wearing nothing but his shirtsleeves and a waistcoat that highlighted how his chest tapered from his broad shoulders to his waist . . . and lower.

Annabelle's cheeks flamed at her wicked thoughts of Knightly, naked. She bit her lip, hard.

Of course he took his jacket off, she thought; the temperature seemed to have spiked ten degrees. Yet when she glanced around, no one else seemed bothered. Sophie even pulled her shawl tighter around her. She ought to see a doctor about that, for she herself was just about burning up.

Knightly stretched his arms, and she could have sworn she saw the ripple of muscles under the thin white linen of his shirt. Her mouth went dry. She was suddenly parched.

She missed him. Oh, did she ever. She missed his voice and his smile and discovering the real Mr. Knightly. She missed his touch and a whole lot of very unladylike things.

Knightly rolled up the sleeves on his shirt, exposing his forearms. Good Lord, she was now all agog over his arms. Who was the Nodcock now? But those arms had held her—no one else ever held her. Those arms had pulled her close and made her feel loved and cherished, if only for one night. She decided then and there that Knightly would be the only man to know her thus. No matter what happened, there would be no one else.

The heat increased, her skin felt feverish. She was certain her cheeks were pink and that everyone would know she was thinking such wanton thoughts.

Perhaps she did make a mistake. Perhaps she had been too picky and particular about the exact proper circumstances in which love ought to happen. It was a wild thing, wasn't it? Who was she to impose all the rules and strictures on love?

The meeting concluded and Knightly walked out. She felt the loss intensely as she watched his retreating form while still stuck in her chair.

The other writers trickled out and Sophie dawdled gathering her things. The Writing Girls chattered about society gossip and the latest Paris fashions and other things Annabelle was only paying half a mind to.

In the distance thunder rumbled again. It would rain. Perhaps that would cool her heated skin. But even the thought of cool raindrops tumbling on her scorching skin made her breath hitch. She had become far too sensitive lately.

And then Knightly returned.

"I forgot my jacket," he drawled, leaning in the doorway. She fought hard for a gulp of air. God, she loved it when he leaned like that. Her mouth went dry. Words eluded her.

"Oh, goodness, is that the time!" Sophie said. "I have an appointment with the modiste." Annabelle was too tongue-tied to point out that she hadn't even looked at a timepiece.

"Yes, I promised Roxbury . . ." Julianna said, hot on Sophie's heels as they pushed past Knightly.

"Wycliff is expecting me . . ." Eliza said, and she too followed the others out of the room, leaving Annabelle and Knightly alone. Quite alone.

"Hello, Annabelle." His voice was low, and it sent shivers up and down her spine. Goodness, she had better steel herself if he only had to say *Hello, Annabelle* and she nearly went to pieces. She'd do well to remember that he was probably going to marry lady Lydia to save his newspapers.

But she had to reply to his hello; it would be rude not to. Annabelle, both Old and New, was nothing if not polite.

"Hello." Her voice had never sounded so breathless, as if she had dashed through Hyde Park with a vile seducer and nefarious murderer in hot pursuit.

"How are you?" he asked. The question was politeness itself, and yet he managed to imbue each word with a hint of wickedness.

"I'm fine, thank you. And yourself?" she replied politely. Young ladies were polite. Young ladies also did not imagine handsome partially clad men closing the door and ravishing them upon the tabletop. Oh very well, this one did. What had become of her?

"Oh, I'm good. Very good," he said, sounding wicked, very wicked. She longed to fan herself.

"Good," she echoed, as her brain was not up to the task of forming complex thoughts or sentences. It was still focused on him, leaning, against the doorway. She could see the muscles of his chest outlined through the thin fabric of his shirt. That vee of exposed skin taunted her, begged for her to touch. With her mouth.

"Might you need someone to escort you home?" he inquired.

The words were polite, but delivered in such a wicked way. And how torturous would it be to find herself in an enclosed carriage with him for the long ride to Bloomsbury whilst rain lashed at the windows, and the air was so electrified, and when he had mischief in his eyes?

Annabelle could not conceive of a greater torment. Other than his marriage to Lady Lydia. She ought to remember that. She ought not to think of all the privacy his carriage afforded, those plush velvet seats . . .

"I don't think so. Why?" she replied suspiciously.

"Because your fellow Writing Girls just left in quite a hurry," he said. "Which makes me think you may require alternate means of transport."

"I'll just walk," she replied, as if it were really no bother at all. As if Bloomsbury weren't on the far side of London. But really, how was she to restrain herself if she were alone with him and when he was looking especially sinful in a very seductive way, and when she knew how it felt to kiss him as if her soul's salvation depended upon it? Her soul suddenly felt in desperate need of salvation.

The thunder rumbled again. The wind rattled the windowpanes again, darkness drenched the city, and the rain now began in earnest, slapping against the windows.

"Really? You will walk from Fleet Street to Bloomsbury in the driving rain?" Knightly asked skeptically.

"Given the weather, I might hire a hack," she replied. "I am nothing if not sensible."

"Yes, hired hacks are a-plenty when it is raining," he said, which was of course utter nonsense. She thought he really ought to pick her up, sling her over his shoulder, and just be done with it, if he was so intent upon taking her home in his carriage. Her protest would be halfhearted, at best.

Clearly, she was doomed.

"I shall manage," she said, because that's what she did best: she managed to get by. Managed to restrain her passions. Managed to be polite when she wanted to act with outrageous impropriety. She excelled at managing.

"Come with me, Annabelle," he said in a low voice. He was leaning, and he smiled at her. He reached out, clasping her hand in his. The thunder rumbled and the rain picked up and, really, how could she say no?

# Chapter 45

### Love, Restrained. Alas.

**T**HE carriage ride with Knightly progressed exactly as she expected. It was a slow, sensual torture that tested her resolve. The velvet upholstery was soft under her bare fingertips. The rain lashed gently at the carriage windows, which became opaque with steam from the interior warmth of the carriage. The wheels clattered over the cobblestones, and the conveyance swayed in a gentle, rhythmic motion.

*Love under false pretenses was not love at all*, she reminded herself.

Even in the short jaunt from the door of *The Weekly* offices to the door of the carriage, Knightly managed to become drenched in the rain. With his jacket open, his white shirt now clung to his skin, revealing every outline of his sculpted muscles. Annabelle *managed* to steal only a few sly glances, which she prayed he didn't notice in the dim interior of the carriage.

Did other women lust after men like this? It wasn't exactly the conversation of polite or mixed company. Perhaps it would make a good topic for her column . . . if she was feeling wicked.

At this moment she was feeling wicked.

But determined to be good.

She did not want Knightly by hook or by crook.

*Keep telling yourself that, Annabelle,* a cruel voice in her head taunted.

Raindrops clung to his black eyelashes and then dropped off to roll down his impossibly high cheeks. She was struck by the strange desire to lick them . . . before she kissed him and tasted raindrops warmed from his lips.

Oh, for Lord's sake, Annabelle, she thought to herself.

She folded her hands primly on her lap, interweaving her fingers and clasping her palms together so she might not be tempted to touch anything. Be. Good. She would Be Good. She would make polite conversation so that she might be distracted from lusty thoughts of sitting on his lap rather than properly on the opposite seat.

"How goes the scandal with *The Weekly*?" she asked. Politely.

"We covered that in the meeting, Annabelle," he said, smirking, as if the blasted man knew she hadn't been paying the slightest attention all along. How mortifying.

"My apologies. I must have been woolgathering," she replied primly.

"I noticed," he said in a seductive tone that made

her heart skip a beat. "What was on your mind, Annabelle?"

*Licking you. Kissing you. The insane feeling of your hands on my skin. Every sensation from the one night we spent together.*

"Chores. For Blanche," Annabelle lied, shamelessly. Some things were just not said aloud, not even by Bold Annabelle.

"Why do you stay there?" Knightly asked. She wasn't surprised by the question. She could always tell it was on the verge of being voiced by her friends and those who were aware of how her family treated her.

"I have nowhere else to go," she answered with a shrug. It wasn't quite the truth, but she didn't know how to explain the real reason. Because they had almost committed her—a shy, gangly girl of just thirteen—to the workhouse or some other employment where she would have never survived. She worked for her own family instead, *grateful* to have been spared a worse fate.

"That's not true," he said softly. She winced, recalling his offer for her to reside with him—but as his mistress or his pet or his plaything. Not even Old Annabelle would sell herself so short. "I'm sure any one of your friends would and could take you in."

"I would hate to impose on them. Besides, I am needed there, which makes me feel useful. And they are my family. One ought to devote themselves to their family."

"All very good reasons," he said, then he leaned forward, looked deeply into her eyes. "They don't appreciate you, Annabelle."

"I know," she said, even adding a little shrug. Oh,

she knew. But having lost some family, she clung to those she had left. Even if it was Thomas, the most inattentive brother in Christendom, and his harridan of a wife. Annabelle couldn't say those words aloud, and it was bittersweet that she didn't have to with Knightly. He saw. He knew.

"Do you not feel the same way with your half brother?" she asked, turning the tables on him. "As much as he may scorn you, he is still your family. And people tend to stick with their families, for better or for worse."

"He doesn't," Knightly said flatly, and that was the end of that conversation. She refused to feel badly about introducing a sensitive topic, because after all, she had already lost him. She had nothing left to lose.

The silence, however, would not do.

"Well, how is the scandal?" she asked.

"There are rumors I may be arrested," Knightly said, uttering such devastating words as easily as one might say *There are rumors it is going to be cloudy tomorrow.*

"Arrested?" Annabelle gasped.

The carriage rolled to a stop in front of her home. What wretched timing.

She rubbed the steam away from the windows and peeked out. There was a rustle at the drapes in the drawing room window. Blanche was likely watching.

"Oh look, here we are," Knightly remarked lightly, as if he had not just mentioned such an awful fate looming. "Come, I shall walk you to your door."

They dashed madly through the downpour, arm in arm from the carriage to the front door. They stood under the porch, seeking its small refuge as rain tumbled down around them. His eyes were dark in the gray light, but they were locked upon hers.

It was a moment in which every breath, every gaze, was laden with depth and passion and vexing words unsaid. She recognized it from novels. She recognized it because she was living it in this real, heart-pounding moment.

Annabelle tilted her head up to his, and she knew her lips parted, practically begging for his kiss. To be fair, it seemed like he might kiss her. He brushed a wet strand of her hair away from her eyes, his knuckles gently grazing her cheek. His eyes never looked away from hers.

But he didn't kiss her. She'd have sworn that he wanted to. And yet—

"Goodbye, Annabelle," he said in his sultry voice. She stood there in the rain and watched him walk away. There was a swagger in his walk, and that, with the mischief she'd seen in his eyes, made her wonder just what Knightly was up to.

# Chapter 46

### The Arrest

*Dear Annabelle . . .*

**Unfinished letter on the desk of Derek Knightly**

*Knightly's Mayfair town house*

**I**T had been impossible to not touch her. He wouldn't allow himself, much as he wanted to, as part of the seduction. *Leave her wanting more.* Hadn't that been one of the schemes? Knightly knew now that however much he'd been tortured by her tricks, she must have suffered mightily in the execution. Seduction, and the willpower required for it, was no walk in the park.

Such were his thoughts as he wandered from one room to the next. He paused near the fire in the drawing room and leaned against the gray marble mantel. Annabelle, dear Annabelle. He craved her touch and ached to caress her so much that he feared his survival depended upon it. He wasn't sure he wanted to survive if he could not have her.

After that carriage ride in which they both suffered the torment of unrequited love, Knightly had allowed himself to brush one damp curl out of her eyes and indulged in the touch of her cheek, which set him afire. She had reduced him to that mere caress.

His desire for her had not been sated in the slightest by such a benign touch. In fact it only inflamed more, as he was reminded of the softness of her skin. Of how he had once touched her all over, and where no one had ever touched her. Not even Annabelle herself. That he knew of. God, that thought made him hard.

Nevertheless, he continued to stroll from the drawing room across the marble floor of the foyer, into the dining room with its mahogany dining table polished to a high shine. He stared at his brooding reflection in the extremely well-polished silver tureen. An oil painting over the mantel depicted a nude woman at her bath; he thought of Annabelle.

Usually, he felt pride in his home. It was the physical manifestation of his success—and of his bachelorhood. No womanly touches like a half-finished embroidery or fragile little knickknacks made the place seem welcoming.

The house felt downright cold. Yes, it was a rainy night. But fires were blazing in every fireplace in every room. The building seemed cold and empty because Annabelle wasn't here to fill it up with her sighs and laughter and kisses and death-defying escapades and just . . . her.

Annabelle, he wanted Annabelle. Needed her. Craved her.

He understood now why she had to say no to his lust-driven proposal that she move into this museum of a house and become his mistress at his convenience. He had asked her only to share his bed and be around for his comfort. She deserved so much more. She knew that, and he was glad of that.

He knew that now. He needed so much more of her now.

Loss will do that to a man; it'll make him realize what he's missing in a really damned painful way. Since he did not lose, he had embarked on that courtship to win her back.

But hell, it was slow going. He wondered how she had endured for all those years and months and weeks and days. He'd only been at this game of seduction and loving trickery for a fortnight and already his nerves were frayed, his desire overwhelming, his patience worn to a delicate thread. Yet she had steadfastly loved him and patiently waited for *years*.

What a nodcock he'd been. Perhaps he could even forgive her for that unfortunate name. Surely, he deserved worse, and he cursed himself. He definitely deserved this torture of wanting and waiting. Even worse, he knew exactly what he was missing. Intimately.

Knightly pressed his forehead against the cool glass windowpane of his second-story drawing room, overlooking the garden and the tree Annabelle had recklessly climbed.

A pounding at the front door echoed ominously through the house. He idly wondered who bothered to go out on such a god-forsaken night as this. Wilson, the butler, would see to it.

Annabelle? His heartbeat quickened.

No, those were not Annabelle's footsteps he heard

thudding in the marble-floored hall and pounding up the stairs. No, that was the sound of an army; of heavy boots; of men on a mission.

The door burst open, splintering the wood and slamming into the plaster wall. Knightly turned slowly to face the intruders. As if he had all the time in the world. As if he couldn't be bothered to hurry.

"You might have just tried the doorknob. Or knocked," he remarked dryly.

"That doesn't make quite the same impression, now does it?" Lord Marsden drawled. He stood in the doorway, legs apart and arms folded over his chest.

"I'm not intimidated, if that's the effect you sought," Knightly said. He took a small sip of brandy, savoring what would surely be his last taste of the stuff for some time.

"I'm only just beginning," Marsden remarked. And then without even looking, he barked out an order to the officers standing in formation behind him: "Arrest him."

"On what grounds?" Knightly inquired as his hands were shackled with cold metal cuffs behind his back. The glass of brandy had tumbled to the floor, staining the Aubusson carpet.

"Good old libel," Marsden said. "We're taking you to Newgate."

"Splendid. I've heard such great things," Knightly remarked.

"Now you can confirm the rumors," Marsden said, and he sounded happy, too damned happy, to have captured Knightly on such unimaginative charges and to have him carted off to Newgate like some common criminal. Knightly would take the arrest and the imprisonment, but he wouldn't let Marsden get the last word or fully enjoy the moment.

"Wilson," he called to his butler as they led him away, "see to the door and the carpet. Make sure that the invoice for repairs is sent to Lord Marsden, although I'm not sure that he can afford it."

# Chapter 47

## An Exclusive Report from the Confines of Newgate

LONDON WEEKLY OWNER ARRESTED!
Headline of *The London Weekly*, *The London Times*,
*The Morning Post*, and twelve other newspapers

*Newgate*

THE prison was as dank and disgusting as the stories led one to believe, including those *The London Weekly* had published. Eliza once spent two days in its confines, only to dramatically reenact Mad Jack's outrageous escape. The thought did cross Knightly's mind—he had *plenty* of time for thoughts to cross his mind—but while it would lead to an improvement in his lodgings, it would only delay the inevitable. Plus, given the schemes he had enacted, he might as well plan to stay awhile.

"You have to keep the paper going," he told Owens, who had come to visit as soon as word of the arrest and imprisonment reached him.

"I don't suppose we humbly offer apologies, etcetera, etcetera?" Owens dared to ask in a tone belying that he knew better.

"Have you suffered a head injury?" Knightly retorted.

"I'm just testing your sense of humor," Owens replied. "What's the story here? What's the angle?"

"I'm already in prison. I am already facing trial. We might as well go for broke," Knightly said frankly. "I need to see Lady Marsden. And then I'll need to see Lady Roxbury. We have some scandalous secrets to expose."

"As we at *The Weekly* are wont to do," Owens said cheerfully. "Scandal equals sales."

"And then you'll have to bring me writing things, or I will have to dictate to you. There will be a letter from me, from prison. Won't that be something? And then I'm going to take over Dear Annabelle."

"What?" Owens jerked his head up in shock.

"Is she still writing that rubbish about table manners and whatnot?" Knightly asked. After her absolutely inspired campaign to win his attentions, she was now writing about the proper way to grasp a teapot while pouring a cup of a tea, and a thorough examination of the merits of adding sugar versus milk in one's tea.

"The Nodcock story seems to have met an unfortunate end, and now we're stuck with boring articles on tea parties," Owens said, with one hell of a fiery and bloodthirsty glare aimed at Knightly.

Knightly had no choice but to face the facts: (1) everyone had known of Annabelle's love for him, (2) Annabelle had many champions, (3) he was indeed a nodcock, and (4) those champions were sure as hell going to make sure he remembered that, which would be fine because (5) he was going to win her, and love her.

"To the contrary, Owens. The Nodcock story is about to get interesting," Knightly said with a grin.

# Chapter 48

### The Newspaper Must Go On

*A rock was thrown through the drawing room window
of Lord Marsden's Berkeley Square residence. A note
was attached that read, "Free Knightly."*

    *The London Weekly*

*Offices of* The London Weekly

THE writers of *The London Weekly* were called to
order. From Grenville to the penny-a-liners, they all
crowded into the meeting room to hear what Owens
had to say.

"Knightly has been arrested on charges of libel.
He's in Newgate," he told the group. There were audible gasps and murmured questions and a stunning array of expletives. Annabelle's heart stopped,
which made breathing or thinking or moving or
feeling impossible. Knightly. Arrested.

"Newgate!" Julianna exclaimed above all in obvious shock. Newgate was a horrible, filthy place, and
Annabelle's beloved Knightly was there, locked up
like a common criminal when he was anything but.

"What did you expect, that they'd take 'em to Buckingham Palace?" Grenville retorted. Julianna silenced him with a withering look.

"What are we going to do?" she demanded. "Obviously we must do something."

"I can help him escape," Eliza offered. "I did a series of articles on how to get out of Newgate. Which couldn't happen fast enough. The place is just awful."

"We're definitely going to reprint those stories," Owens said with a grin. "And we're definitely going to keep the paper going. As Knightly said, he's already in prison. We might as well go for broke."

"You saw him?" Annabelle asked. The words were out of her mouth before she thought to censor them for the moment and inquire discreetly later. Everyone quieted and turned to look at her. Everyone knew that her concern went far deeper than anyone else's.

"Aye," Owens said in a low voice.

"How is he?" she asked softly. There was no need to raise her voice, for the room had remained silent. Everyone already knew she loved him. Even Knightly knew it now.

"He's spoiling for a fight," Owens answered, which was to say that Knightly was fine and in good spirits. "Penny-a-liners, you know the drill. Find as much dirt on Marsden as you can, get details from the prison. Lady Roxbury, Knightly asked to see you."

"Me?" Julianna gasped.

"Yes, something about Lady Lydia," Owens said briskly. And then he winced when he realized what he'd said and who had heard it. Annabelle was the recipient of more than a few worried glances.

"What about Lady Lydia?" Annabelle asked, because she was free to ask these things now. But she voiced the question in a small, hollow voice. When she had meant that Knightly ought to marry Lady Lydia it was some vague idea. Some noble sacrifice to save the paper. But now the hour was upon them in which Knightly faced prison or marriage to a highborn woman.

She was going to lose. She had already lost him.

"He asked to see her," Owens said, looking very pained to deliver such news, and she was sorry to have put him in such a position. She wanted to reassure him, *Oh, it's all right. My heart is already broken.*

Instead she said, "Did he ask to see . . . anyone else?" Her desperation to know if he cared for her at all overrode her fear of speaking before a group.

Owens shook his head no. He looked sorry, and she felt ashamed for making him feel that way. But she'd had to know that when Knightly was in jail, he did not ask for her. If there were any questions lingering about how he felt about her, she now had her answer.

She was right to refuse him. This was proof, but she was not consoled in the slightest.

"What does one wear when paying a call to Newgate?" Julianna asked, changing the subject. It wasn't the best most tactful question, Annabelle thought, given the fact that Knightly had not asked for her. But it was the least of her troubles.

"Definitely your worst dress," Sophie answered.

Annabelle's imagination starting spinning awful stories of Knightly's imprisonment. She envisioned rats and mice scurrying about, nibbling on toes of dead prisoners. She imagined the wretched specimens of humanity moaning and groaning (she didn't know why, it just seemed like the thing). All of this, of course, occurring in a relentless darkness, broken only by shafts of gray light from narrow slits placed high in stone walls that were moist from the dampness.

This vivid vision made her shudder with revulsion.

Poor Knightly! Her heart ached for what torments he must have to endure as a Newgate prisoner, keeping company with thieves and murderers.

Poor Knightly indeed, she grumbled silently, asking for Lady Lydia to visit him and not requesting the same of her. Obviously he was going to propose to Lady Lydia. Marsden couldn't very well lock up the betrothed of his dearest sister. Some things were just not done.

Clever, she gave him that, even as her heart positively throbbed in agony.

She had done the right thing, Annabelle reminded herself for the thousandth time. If he was going to marry a woman just to get out of prison, then he was not a man capable of love. And she wanted love, all-consuming, outrageously passionate, fiery, and not-even-death-do-us-part love.

If she wanted anything less, she would have married Mr. Nathan Smythe from the bakery up the road. Though it looked like she might after all.

THE Writing Girls gathered at Sophie's house at the conclusion of the meeting to wait whilst Julianna immediately went to visit Knightly at Newgate.

"Annabelle, are you all right?" Eliza asked. Worry

was etched in her features. She reached out to clasp her hand.

No, Annabelle thought. No, I'm not all right and I'll never be again because I have lost the love of my life. I had a chance and I threw it away and now I must live with this regret until my dying day . . . But she bit back those overdramatic sentiments and said, instead: "I was when I first heard the news. But since he requested Lady Lydia . . . it is clear where his attentions are fixed."

"I wonder what that is about," Sophie said. "It seems strange that he would call for her. Unless it is to plead his case with her brother."

"He must be planning to propose to her, of course," Annabelle said matter-of-factly. She wondered if he had a ring. Or if would be on bended knee when he asked. Probably not in Newgate.

"What an awful proposal. I would refuse," Sophie said with a shudder.

"What if Brandon proposed to you in a prison?" Annabelle asked, rephrasing the question to include her beloved husband.

"Brandon would never find himself in prison. Unless it was to rescue someone," Sophie replied.

"Well Knightly was bound to be arrested," Eliza said frankly, and to murmurs of agreement. "I'm only surprised it has not happened sooner."

Annabelle frowned, annoyed, because she found there was something wild and exciting about a man who might be imprisoned. It meant he was bold, daring, adventurous, as if he could be a hero or a villain in equal measure.

*Do not feel affection for him,* she commanded herself. *He is probably proposing to another woman this very minute.*

But then she thought of how it must feel to be locked up and away. He would feel so frustrated with the lack of liberty, and that must drive him mad. Would he go mad?

No, because he would escape first. He would find a way out. Knightly always found a way to get just what he wanted.

*If only he wanted her . . .*

*No, she was done with that line of thinking—done! Now she was going mad herself, oh blast.*

He was going to marry Lady Lydia. It was the sensible thing to do. Would she be invited to the wedding? Would she have to smile while he recited vows to love and cherish another woman?

"Annabelle, are you all right? You look close to tears," Sophie said, peering closely at her.

Her eyes did feel the hot sting of tears starting, but she would *not* let them fall.

"Or like you're about to cast up your accounts," Eliza added with a cringing expression. Indeed, her stomach was in knots.

"What if he does marry Lady Lydia? What do I do?" Annabelle asked, and she did not even try to disguise the anguish in her voice.

She had spent her whole life waiting for a Grand, True Love. And since she met Knightly three years, eight months, one week, and three days ago, she had been waiting for that Grand True Love to blossom between them.

She could never love another, she was sure of it.

She had always just assumed that he would marry her and love her . . . eventually. For the first time, Annabelle honestly confronted the prospect of a lifetime—a bloody lifetime, for she was only six and twenty—without love, without Knightly. The prospect was bleak indeed.

A lifetime of Blanche's barbs and orders and snide remarks. Forever living in a household where she was merely tolerated because she served so self-lessly.

A lifetime in which her brother—her own flesh and blood—ignored her and buried his face in *The London Times*—of all the newspapers in London, for Lord's sake.

A memory of one glorious night in which almost all of her secret wishes and dreams had come true ... One night in which she was not only wanted, but loved ...

After which followed a lifetime of remorse.

"You will be fine, Annabelle. You will be loved," Eliza said in a fierce whisper with an affectionate squeeze of her hand.

Annabelle didn't let go, even as Sophie and Eliza chattered on and she made an effort to follow their conversation about dresses and scandals and books they had read and Eliza's upcoming plans to travel to Timbuktu with her adventurous husband.

But Annabelle also watched the clock, await-ing Julianna's return. Watched it so intently that it seemed time would stop if she looked away. Finally, two hours, forty-nine minutes, and twenty-six sec-onds later, Julianna burst through the doors.

"You would not *believe* what I am now privy to," she exclaimed breathlessly. "Oh my Lord. Be still my throbbing heart. Fetch the smelling salts. Do you re-member when I found Drawling Rawlings in that unfathomably scandalous barnyard position with the most unlikely of characters?"

Sophie, her face an expression of awe, replied: "The scene you described as, and I quote, 'The single most scandalous compromising position of your career, second to Roxbury's.' That one?"

"This is better," Julianna said with a broad grin. "Better even than unmasking the Man About Town. This is the biggest story of my career."

Annabelle supposed Knightly's Newgate proposal to Lady Lydia might be classified as that interesting.

"I know what happened during Lady Lydia's missing season! She related it to me directly. And Knightly has given me *orders* to print every last salacious detail!"

# Chapter 49

## A Most Scandalous Edition of *The London Weekly*

LETTER FROM THE (IMPRISONED) EDITOR
*London, prepare to be scandalized.*
*The London Weekly*

*The Swift Residence*

**T**HIS particular issue of *The London Weekly* became the most widely read and discussed issue of a newspaper in years. Many would mention it in the same breath as Thomas Paine's *Rights of Man* or the *Declaration of Independence* from the Colonies.

A typical issue of the paper might sell twelve thousand copies, with each one read by a few, then read aloud to many more. The issues in which Eliza revealed the exotic secrets of the man known as the Tattooed Duke in a column set sales records, as did Julianna's very public battle of words and wits with the rival gossip columnist, the Man About Town and her now-husband Lord Roxbury. But neither of those topped this one.

From prison, Knightly authorized the purchase of a new printing press to keep up with the demand.

Even from behind bars, *The London Weekly* plainly belonged to him. His touch, his vision, and his love was apparent in every line of type on this, the most scandalous issue of a newspaper ever printed.

How scandalous was it?

Even the Swift household possessed a copy. It was the second one ever to cross the threshold. (The first was the issue featuring Annabelle's debut column. Only that page remained carefully folded and tucked into a copy of a Jane Austen novel.)

Annabelle wasn't even the one to buy this particular issue. Thomas, a lifelong loyal reader of *The London Times*, brought it home the previous evening, muttering something about everyone at his cloth company offices reading it. It was not until breakfast that Annabelle was able to read it privately, after finding it discarded in the bin.

On the front page was a defiant letter from the editor displaying Knightly's razor sharp wit, slicing and shaping the facts to tell the story he wanted. She could hear it—his voice, strong and commanding and so self-assured—as if he stood behind her and read the words aloud.

She loved him, of course, and admired him because when the world turned against him, he stood proud. Even from the dankest of prisons he possessed wit, intelligence, defiance, and grace. It made her love him all the more.

Annabelle poured a cup of tea and sat at the breakfast table, alone, and began to read *The Weekly*.

LETTER FROM THE (IMPRISONED) EDITOR
*I write this from Newgate, where I am imprisoned on*

*charges of libel. When has it become a crime to print the truth?*

*Taxes keep the prices of newspapers high, in a deliberate attempt to keep information out of the hands of the common man and woman. Yet the coffeehouse culture flourishes, and newspapers are shared, thus ensuring the printed word will be read and discussed.*

*It is foolish to try to put a stop to this. But fools will persist in their madness, will they not?*

*It is a well-known but oft unspoken fact that the government pays newspapers for favorable reports and portrayals.* The London Weekly *never took a farthing. This publication is beholden to no one but the reading public.*

The London Weekly *has long brought you "accounts of gallantry, pleasure, and entertainment." It has also brought a level of equality and truth to the press. which has resulted in great success—and my imprisonment. I stand by every word in this paper, especially in this particular edition. London, prepare to be scandalized.*

Annabelle caught herself with a wicked, delighted grin. Her heart was racing. Who knew so much adventure and anticipation could be contained in a newspaper? Knightly did. Like thousands of others all over London at that very moment, she turned the page, eager to delve into more.

But unlike the rest of London, Annabelle felt a glow of pride that she *belonged* to this paper and was a part of something so daring and great. She, little old Annabelle Swift, was a beloved member of an exclusive club: the writers of *The London Weekly*. If nothing else . . . she had this triumph in her life.

If nothing else, Knightly was and would always be the man who gave her a rare chance to be more than a Spinster Auntie from Bloomsbury. For that alone, she thanked him and loved him and granted him her undying devotion.

On the second page, she found Julianna's masterpiece. Even though Julianna had breathlessly confessed every last detail, Annabelle still read the printed version. She knew that Owens and Knightly had gone through it to ruthlessly remove anything that would not be supported by fact. The story, so detailed and salacious, occupied the entire second page.

FASHIONABLE INTELLIGENCE BY A LADY OF DISTINCTION

*The mystery of Lady Lydia Marsden's missing season has been solved, and was related to this author by the lady herself. It involves a lover, of course, as all great gossip does. Like the fairy tales, there are unfathomably cruel relatives; lovers, separated; innocence lost. But will there be a happy ending?*

*Lady Lydia took a lover, a man hired to teach her the fine art of dancing. It has often been noted that she moved across ballrooms with an unparalleled grace; that she could waltz better than any debutante, that she possessed such a poised and regal bearing and knew by heart the steps to every dance, even the most obscure country reels. We now know why. Hours spent in practice, in the arms of a man she had come to love.*

*For years their love was expressed only in the hearted gaze of illicit lovers, or hours spent in each*

*other's arms as they danced across the ballroom of
Marsden house. In time, that was not enough . . .*

*Rumors soon surfaced of Lady Lydia's condition
after a particular incident in which she was discovered casting up her accounts in a potted fern during
a breakfast party.*

*A remarkably intrepid reporter from* The London
Times *sought confirmation of the lady's condition by
impersonating a physician (he now languishes in Newgate, awaiting trial). The lady in question was discovered to have been in a delicate condition. Her lengthy
stint in the country—the infamous missing second
season—did nothing to stifle rumors to that effect.*

*As one would imagine, the lady's brother was livid
to discover that his sister was not only with child, but
that the father was a lowborn dance instructor. Even
more vexing, these lovers imagined a happy life together with their child. This was not to be, alas. She
found herself locked in the tower of the country house;
her lover was banished and threatened with deporta-
tion to Australia should he dare to see his beloved.*

*And what of the child? A boy was born and smug-
gled to its father. They live in squalor. 'Tis not merely
a tale of a young woman's missing season, but of love
thwarted. The lesson to be gleaned from this? Love
knows no rules or class or boundaries. And, we hope,
that only fools stand in the path of true love.*

To hear the story related by a breathless Julianna
was one thing; it was quite another to read it in black
and white. It quite explained Lady Lydia's letter to
Dear Annabelle, and she breathed a sigh of relief at
the personal note she had included in her previous
column. She had encouraged Scandalously in Love,

otherwise known as Lady Lydia, to await true love. It had been the right thing to do.

But what could Knightly be about, printing this? Marsden was livid already. What purpose could this serve other than to provoke the man further? Did Knightly *want* to spend the rest of his days in Newgate?

The line of questioning was disturbed when something else caught her eye . . .

On the rightmost column of the page . . .

The headline DEAR ANNABELLE . . .

Usually her column appeared on page sixteen or seventeen, tucked behind all the serious and important news, but today it was prominently featured on page three. This was odd, as she hadn't turned in a particularly interesting article. She had answered Mrs. Crowley from Margate's question about the proper way to hold a teapot, she advised Mr. Chapeau from Blackfriars on which feather to decorate his hat, and settled a dispute between neighbors on who ought to sweep the sidewalk. In other words, it might have been one of her dullest columns to date.

Certainly nothing worthy of page three. Certainly nothing worthy of her portrait. What was her portrait doing in the paper? Owens must have put that in . . .

Intrigued, Annabelle began to read.

### DEAR ANNABELLE: A DECLARATION OF LOVE
#### FROM THE NODCOCK

*Dear Annabelle,*
*You have succeeded in winning my attention. I can think of nothing but you, day or night—and*

*not because there is little else to do in prison, and not merely because of your low-cut bodices or other tricks to catch my eye. You are beautiful, Annabelle, inside and out. You intrigue me, Annabelle. I crave you, Annabelle. You have succeeded in winning my affections. Annabelle, I am in love with you.*

*Readers have marveled at the dim-witted and obtuse idiot you adored. I am a fool to have missed you for so long, and an even bigger one to have lost you once I found you. Dear Annabelle, please advise how I might win your favor, your affections, and your promise of a lifetime together.*

*Yours always,*

*D. Knightly, the Nodcock*

She couldn't quite believe the marvelous words just there, in black and white, making her heart beat hard and her breath catch in her throat. Hot, *happy* tears stung her eyes because once upon a time, on one otherwise unremarkable Saturday morning, her dearest wish came true.

He loved her.

Mr. Derek Knightly, man of her dreams, loved her.

Annabelle knew a Grand Declaration of True Love when it was printed in black and white. Her heart continued to pound hard and her breath hitched in her throat. Knightly loved her! And all of London knew it!

She had to go to him. Had to find him even if it meant storming into Newgate. She had to tell him YES.

# Chapter 50

## Newspaper Tycoon on Trial

### Town Talk

*The trial of newspaper tycoon Derek Knightly is such a crush, rivaling balls thrown at the palace. Everyone is eager to attend the most sensational trial of 1825. Especially as fears are high that one may not be able to read about it in the newspapers.*

The Morning Post

## The Trial

KNIGHTLY sat on a hard wooden chair before a plain wood table awaiting the start of his trial. All around him, people filed into the courtroom finding seats and carrying on tense, hushed conversations. He scanned the courtroom, searching for a lovely woman with milky skin, eyes blue like the sky, golden curls, and a mouth made for sin yet smiled so sweetly.

Increasingly his glances grew frantic—though he disguised the growing fear gnawing at him. Annabelle was not here.

Depending upon the outcome of this trial, he

might be locked away for years. His fortune might suffer. The ton could have no use for him now. So much hinged on the outcome of this farce, in which he would defend himself. Everything depended upon his absolute focus, sharp wit, and keen observation.

Yet he thought only of Annabelle. Where was she? Had she seen *The London Weekly*? She must have. Owens assured him that every last person in London had read it, or had it read to them, or discussed it at great length. No one was oblivious to its contents.

Had she seen his version of Dear Annabelle? Was there anything more anguish-inducing than a public confession of love with naught but silence in response? He would testify under oath that it was more punishing than Newgate.

Again Knightly deeply, painfully, empathized with what Annabelle must have endured all those years . . . waiting patiently. Always wondering. What she must have endured, each week as she published her exploits and her daring attempts to snare his attentions, when he had been as obtuse as ever. It was, in his mind, the very definition of bravery. To push oneself to great heights, risking such a great fall, with all of London watching.

"Order in the court!" the judge called out. His gray powdered wig shook with the force of his declaration. The gavel knocked hard on the wooden desk and echoed around the room.

Knightly would defend himself. He would do so with the premise that it could not be libel if it was, in fact, the truth. With Owens's help he'd lined up witnesses, including the Lady Lydia Marsden, who might be called to testify against her own brother.

Did he buy her testimony? Perhaps. He preferred to thinking of it as investing in her freedom. In exchange for her story, Knightly settled a small fortune upon her, allowing her to marry and set up a dignified household with her lover and son, despite the wishes of her brother. They thought they might take an extended visit to Italy. They could go first class with the settlement he was providing. He thought it worth every penny, because he knew about love now.

On the other hand, Marsden was going to have a very bad day.

He saw the other *Weekly* writers file into the courtroom and take seats in the gallery. His mother joined them, and she beamed proudly at him from her seat in the gallery. Knightly watched the lot of them obviously peer around the courtroom, murmuring the same question. *Where is Annabelle?*

"We are here for the trial of Mr. Derek Knightly, editor and owner of *The London Weekly* on the charges of libel," the judge intoned. His voice carried across the crowded room and all conversations ceased.

Marsden sat on the opposite side of the courtroom with a smug smirk on his face. Obviously he did not know that his sister—his own flesh and blood—planned to provide the testimony that would devastate his case.

The premise was simple: it was said that *The London Weekly* regularly published false, inflammatory, and libelous statements. Knightly would offer proof of every statement in every issue of the newspaper.

The judge said that would not be necessary.

Marsden's solicitor pointed out that the recent issue provided the most relevant and libelous and false statements.

Knightly said he was glad they brought that up, at which point Lady Lydia Marsden took the stand at his invitation. The courtroom erupted in audible gasps followed by a general uproar.

"Order in this court!" the judge hollered. He pounded the gavel again. *Thwack. Thwack. Thwack.*

Lady Lydia looked to Knightly with trepidation in her eyes. She had already stood up for him, so the damage to her reputation was done. But he lifted his brow, asking the question: Did she wish to go?

Lydia nodded her head. Somewhere, in the midst of their arranged courtship, they had developed a truce, which had led to something like friendship. He had earned her favor when he inquired about her wishes—it was an unfortunate fact of her life that he was only the second man to have ever done so (second to her beloved). When she shared her wish for a love match, he didn't laugh or dismiss her. The question haunted him—until he fell in love himself. And then he knew that nothing was more important than being with the one you loved.

Through her story, Lydia provided him the means to defend his livelihood, and through his fortune she would have the means to live with her soon-to-be husband.

Thus, Lady Lydia took the stand, facing quite a few people who had whispered vicious rumors and snubbed her at every opportunity, so that she might take control of her own story and write the happy ending she so desired.

Knightly stood to address the room.

*Where is Annabelle?*

"Lady Marsden, it is said that *The London Weekly* takes liberties with its facts. Can you confirm that your story, as it appears in this last issue of *The London Weekly*, is the absolute truth?"

"It is the truth as I told it," she said.

The reaction of the courtroom was explosive. Marsden paled. Other men shouted, more than one woman shrieked. The gasps stole around the room like a strong wind.

The judge's face reddened as he called louder and louder for order once, twice, thrice.

"How can it be libel if it is the truth?" Knightly asked the courtroom, which had fallen silent when he began to speak. "By definition, it cannot be. If Lady Lydia's story, which happens to be one of the most scandalous collections of words printed by *The Weekly*, is the truth, what does that say for the rest of the newspaper? We can examine every line. Or we can conclude that occasionally it is not the portrayal that is unflattering, but the actions themselves."

The trial carried on for the rest of the day, reaching ever more sensational heights, in which Marsden alternated between glowering and gloating. Knightly fought the urge to pace, to drink. He scanned the crowds, ever looking for Annabelle. Where was she? Worry set in—not for his fate, but for her. In the end the jury deliberated and the judge pronounced Knightly's fate. Not guilty.

The judge pounded his gavel to restore order before his concluding remarks:

"Good day, Mr. Knightly. You don't belong here."

# Chapter 51

### Dear Annabelle's True Identity Discovered

**DEAR ANNABELLE**

*This author discourages standing in the path of true love.*

The London Weekly

*Earlier . . .*

**A**NNABELLE had grabbed her shawl and was reaching for her bonnet for her journey to Newgate, where she was going to tell Knightly YES. It didn't matter that it was Newgate, the least romantic location in Europe, possibly even the entire Northern Hemisphere.

He loved her. She loved him.

Nothing could stop them now.

An obstacle immediately presented itself: Blanche and her friend Mrs. Underwood, the witch. They entered through the front door, effectively blocking Annabelle's path.

"What horrible disaster is in the news that has you weeping, a fire in an orphanage?" Blanche asked as she absorbed the tears on Annabelle's face and the newspaper she clutched in her hands. Mrs. Underwood hovered just behind Blanche's shoulder with an evil gleam in her eye.

"Nothing," Annabelle said stupidly. Then she cringed. It was tantamount to shouting *I'm not guilty!* or *Look at this!* or *Question me further!*

"Nothing? Nothing has you weeping like a schoolgirl at a rubbish novel? Let me see that!" Blanche said, snatching the newspaper from Annabelle's hands and quickly scanning the lines.

It was the picture that did her in. Owens must have found it and plunked it in to fill space, not knowing the damage it would do. Knightly wouldn't have exposed her thusly.

"You're Dear Annabelle?" Mrs. Underwood said incredulously from her position still behind Blanche's shoulder. She gave Annabelle a once-over and then pulled a face of utter disbelief. "I never would have thought you capable of that."

"What is that?" Blanche asked, frowning.

"Blanche, you are the only one who doesn't read *The London Weekly*. And it looks like you've been living with one of the Weekly Wenches," Mrs. Underwood said, her voice tinged with a cackle.

"I suppose this is the work of that gentleman caller you entertained," Blanche said icily.

"Has the Nodcock been here?" Mrs. Underwood asked, gasping with unabashed excitement. She was obviously going to dine out on this story of months, Annabelle could tell. And she didn't like it. She felt a flush of anger. "Blanche, have you met him? Oh goodness me. 'Entertained' is one way to put it. She had climbed into his bedroom window in the dead of the night!"

Amongst all the things Annabelle felt at the moment, she suffered a particular irritation that she would be so betrayed by a regular reader of the column. She had assumed, in her eternal good faith, that her readers were championing her. Perhaps the rest of them were. Just not Mrs. Underwood. She tried to inch toward the door. To freedom. To true love.

"Allow me to summarize the facts," Blanche said in a voice that allowed no contradiction. "You have been dallying with a man."

"Don't deny it," Mrs. Underwood said, wagging her finger. "All of London knows you did."

Of course they did. Because she thought to pen her most intimate thoughts and actions in the most widely read newspaper in London. Widely read, that is, save for her own household. A fire started to burn in her belly at the unjust treatment of her. So what if she dallied with a man she loved, who loved her back? She was a free, consenting adult in the eyes of the law and everyone else, save for Blanche and her horrid friend.

"You have been writing for this news rag," Blanche gasped with the same degree of horror had, say, Annabelle been caught digging up dead bodies in the cemetery and selling them to science. Not only was the act itself repugnant, but she didn't believe Annabelle possessed the strength.

Maybe I do, Annabelle thought. The fire in her belly grew hotter.

"I suppose all that charity work was a lie," Blanche carried on, her eyes narrowed. Annabelle could see the machinery churning in her brain as she stitched all the pieces together. One could practically see the steam rising from her ears and hear the roar of the engine.

"She's been writing for years," Mrs. Underwood said. "This column started four years ago, I think it was?" she asked, damning her even more. Annabelle decided her next column would be about minding one's own business.

Blanche drew a deep breath and squared her shoulders; the effect made her appear larger and more formidable. Her eyes narrowed and her mouth pinched into a mean line.

Annabelle knew she was meant to be intimated, or feel guilt or shame for her secret. However, instead of cowering as she tended to do, inspired by the brilliant and courageous man who loved her, she drew up to her full height—which was considerably taller than Blanche, she noted. She lifted her head high. She was a writer at the best newspaper in the world and she had the love of a good man. A man who was defiant and proud, and would want her to be defiant and proud, too.

"Three years, eight months, two weeks, and six days," Annabelle said, looking Blanche in the eye. Without blinking. Or blushing. The fire in her belly raged.

"And in that time I have given you room and board out of our own pockets when you have had an income of your own," Blanche said, absolutely aghast.

"Yes, and I did the work of a housemaid and a governess in exchange," Annabelle said. She could feel Knightly cheering her on and the thrill of his pride. Oh, she was so excited to tell him YES and to tell him about this scene in which Dear Annabelle stood up for herself.

He would be so proud of her. But it wouldn't compare to the pride she felt for herself.

Blanche's explosion started with a huff. And then a *harrumph*. And then a wail. She grabbed a fistful of Annabelle's hair, now an option thanks to Owens's coiffure suggestions, and yanked hard. Annabelle flailed, trying to stop Blanche without loosing a significant portion of her hair and scalp.

Mrs. Underwood hovered and cackled.

With a firm grasp on Annabelle's hair, her fingernails digging her scalp, and a wicked twist of her wrist, Blanche pulled Annabelle to the stairs.

Annabelle tripped halfway up and was dragged the rest of the way. She was kicked and shoved and ruthlessly forced up the creaky flight of stairs leading to her attic bedroom.

It was only there that Blanche released her, and she did so with a forceful thrust that sent Annabelle tumbling to the floor, landing with a thud on the hardwood.

"I'd set you out on the doorstep now were it not for Thomas. You just wait here until he comes home," Blanche hissed, eyes blazing with fury. Thomas was on a business trip. It was not certain when he would return.

With that, Blanche slammed the door behind her, and locked it.

# Chapter 52

### True Love Stops at Nothing

MISS HARLOW'S MARRIAGE IN HIGH LIFE
*This author suspects a highly anticipated wedding
will occur—soon. Three years, eight months, two
weeks, and one day after love at first sight.*

The London Weekly

*The tree conveniently growing outside
of Annabelle's attic bedroom
Midnight*

BEING a born and bred city boy, Knightly did not
have much practice climbing trees. Logic dictated
that Annabelle didn't have much experience with
it either, and yet she had managed it, therefore he
should be able to as well.

"Here goes," he muttered, grabbing onto the
lowest branch and pulling himself up. He thought
about taking care not to wake Annabelle's awful relatives and then decided he cared more about getting
to Annabelle alive and unbroken than he did about
the quality of their sleep.

If this went according to plan, it would be a loud

night indeed with his and Annabelle's cries of pleasure. He loved her. He needed to tell her, and to show her. Anticipation spurred him on as he grabbed one branch then another and pulled himself up. More than once he uttered a prayer of thanks for Annabelle's column in which she shared tips for midnight tree climbing.

Of course her bedroom had to be in the attic, three stories off the ground. Her fellow Writing Girls gleefully offered this information to him—after he was acquitted on all charges and ordered to find Annabelle and provide a satisfying resolution to her quest to secure the attentions and affections of the Nodcock. The Judge also let it be known he expected to read about a happy ending in the next issue of *The London Weekly.*

That would all have to wait. Some things were more important.

He could have called upon her tomorrow, with an entire hothouse worth of pink roses and sapphires to match her blue eyes. There was time for flowers and roses. But he could not wait any longer to tell her that he loved her or to show her that he would do anything to be with her, including climbing an old tree on a moonless night all the way up to her third-story bedroom.

Knightly finally hauled himself onto her window ledge. Fortunately it was a warm summer night and she kept the window open just a few inches. After all, why would she suspect that anyone would climb three stories into her bedroom? It was the act of a desperate man.

Finally he tumbled into her bedroom. Somewhere, a clock chimed midnight.

ANNABELLE awoke immediately, hearing someone thudding into her bedroom from the window. *The third-story window.* She lay still, her heart pounding and breath held, while considering her options.

She could feign sleep, or death.

She could discreetly reach for the pewter candle-holder on her bedside table and wield it as a weapon.

Or she could assume that it would be useless to fight whomever had gone to all the bother of climbing into her third-story bedroom window in the dead of the night. Obviously, the person was determined.

Or insane. She reached for the candleholder and clutched it tightly against her chest. She recalled that the door to the rest of the house was locked. Thus, she would have to fight or climb out the window and shimmy down the tree in her nightgown.

She was about to sigh and curse her luck when a voice spoke in the darkness.

"Annabelle, it's me."

She knew that voice. Her heart pounded hard, but no longer from fear. She sat up in bed, blankets pooling around her waist, her hair a tumbling mess around her shoulders. Of course he climbed into her window on the night she wore some plain, drab, spinsterish nightgown. She thought of all the silky underthings in her armoire and considered asking him to wait whilst she changed.

She sighed and cursed her luck.

"Derek? What are you doing here?" she asked. She set down the candlestick and fumbled to light it. With the candle lit, she blinked, not quite believing the sight of her beloved Knightly in her attic bedroom.

"Well I couldn't very well faint into your arms, now could I?" Knightly replied, grinning. She wondered if this was a dream.

"What are you talking about?" she asked. Men didn't faint and they certainly didn't do so into a woman's arms. It would be impractical. And embarrassing. Injurious. This must be a dream.

"Oh, Annabelle," he said, and she heard warmth and laughter in his voice.

"It's the middle of the night and you have tumbled into my bedroom. I'm not sure if I'm awake or dreaming. Don't 'oh Annabelle' me. What is going on?" she asked, utterly perplexed and not quite her cheerful self until at least a quarter hour after waking. "I thought you were in prison."

"I was. But the courts have found me not guilty," he told her. She released a breath she didn't know she had been holding.

"And so you have come here. At midnight," Annabelle said. He loved her, he had declared so in the newspaper. But it was the middle of the night and she possessed a fantastic imagination, which made her fear she was imagining this entire encounter.

But no, Knightly crossed the room and sat beside her on the bed. He brushed a lock of hair away from her face and brushed his lips across hers. There was no mistaking his touch.

"It so happens that I fell in love with an amazing woman and wanted to capture her attention," he told her. "Being a nodcock, I didn't know what to do other than rely on the experiences of a certain popular advice columnist."

In the dark, Annabelle smiled. A warmth started

in the pool of her belly, radiating through every inch of her. It was the pleasure of being loved, of being wooed. Of being a woman Knightly climbed a tree at midnight for.

"Well that all makes sense now. The lack of cravat—" she said, a laugh bubbling up.

"The male equivalent of a lowered bodice," he replied with a grin, kissing her softly where her neck curved into her shoulder.

"And the day you left your jacket behind?" she asked, tilting her head to encourage him.

"I don't have a shawl," Knightly said, and she laughed loudly and didn't care who heard her.

"And you have climbed into my bedroom. At midnight. You love me," she said. Merely stating the facts. Wonderful, delightful facts.

"I do, Annabelle. I love you," Knightly said, his voice husky. He took her hand in his and squeezed it tight. His mouth found hers for another kiss.

"I love you," Annabelle told him, with happy tears in her eyes and giddiness in her voice. "I love you. I've thought those words so much but I've never said them aloud. I can finally tell you, and it was worth the wait. I love you."

His mouth claimed hers for a kiss, and there wasn't much talking for the rest of the night.

*The following morning*

"ARE you ready, Annabelle?" Knightly asked with a spark in his eye, his mouth in a wicked grin. He carried her in his arms, like a princess, like a bride, like a woman he wanted to hold and cherish for a lifetime.

"Yes, oh yes," she replied, clasping her hands tighter around his shoulders.

He stood before the cursed locked door at the top of the attic stairs. They both eyed the obstacle warily. On the other side lay freedom. And happily-ever-after.

"On the count of three," he said. She nodded.

Knightly never got to three. With a deep breath and a quick, forceful kick on *two*, the door splintered on its hinges. One more deftly executed kick sent the wooden door clattering down the stairs and skidding across the second-floor landing before tumbling straight down the main flight of stairs, into the foyer.

The whole family gathered around the door, looking at it curiously before turning their heads up the stairs to see Knightly descending with Annabelle in his arms.

Watson and Mason watched wide-eyed with awe at this tower of masculine strength. Annabelle saw the delight in Fleur's eyes at the magical sight of a fairy tale come to life in her very own house.

Blanche appeared as always: immensely peevish, appalled, and enraged. Her mouth gaped open, rather like the fish Annabelle used to buy at the market, and no sound emerged. It seemed she had been struck dumb by the site of Annabelle, adored.

Even Thomas had emerged from his chair in the library to see what the noise was about. He carried a newspaper in his hand, and Annabelle's smile broadened because it was *The London Weekly*.

"Thomas!" Blanche shrieked, finally recovering her voice. "Thomas, do something!"

"I think we've done enough," he replied, nodding

to Annabelle before shuffling off to his armchair to resume his reading. The children tugged at their mother's skirt, pulling her out of the path of true love.

Knightly carried Annabelle across the threshold, carrying her from the shadows to the bright light of a beautiful new day and the start of the happily-ever-after she had hoped for, fought for, and won.

## Happily-ever-after

*Two years later*

**I**T began with a letter, and that letter commenced with the shocking words: *Dear Lord Harrowby.*

It had taken hours for those words to emerge from a pen Knightly commanded. He did not write *To the New Earl* or even *Dear New Earl* or avoid a salutation altogether. That he even sat down to compose this letter was a lifetime in the making.

But Annabelle had persuaded him to make this overture.

"You can spend your whole life waiting for someone to notice you or you can do something about it," she urged, idly rubbing her growing belly. She was right, of course. He was surrounded by proof: every morning he woke beside his beloved wife in a home filled with happiness and laughter. All because one day she had dared to ask for what she wanted. It had started with the simple act of pen to paper, with a letter . . .

He was thankful each day for his daring, darling Dear Annabelle.

Soon they would have a baby, and hopefully the

child would be blessed with brothers and sisters. Knightly never wanted them to know the estrangement he had suffered. He wanted them to always feel they belonged, together.

So he wrote the damn letter.

*Dear Lord Harrowby.*

Knightly wrote of never having his father's full time and attention—and how they both must have felt the same. He wrote of feeling competition with an adversary he only wanted to befriend. He wrote of his hopes that blood was stronger than slights or regrets. He thought perhaps their father would have liked his sons to be able to lean on each other.

He signed it simply *D. Knightly.* And he enclosed it with an invitation to a ball celebrating his elevation to the peerage. The title Lord Northbourne had been granted to him by the King in acknowledgment of his service to the burgeoning newspaper industry. "The first of the press barons," the newspapers had proclaimed.

Knightly sent the letter. Then he left his office at 57 Fleet Street and strode determinedly through the city streets at dusk, eager to be where he belonged: home with his beloved wife, Dear Annabelle.